Advance Pra...
Game Changers

"Women, soccer, romance, and the reality of living with major setbacks all coalesce in this new romance. *Game Changers* is a raw and real look at life, love, and how to survive it all in an engaging story that runs the gamut of emotions. If you love women and enjoy women's soccer, do yourself a favor and dive into Jane Cuthbertson's debut romance. You won't regret it."

~Judy M. Kerr, author of the debut mystery novel *Black Friday*

"*Game Changers* is a sweet and sensual debut novel from a talented new author. The romance carries the rare quality of being both wonderfully aspirational and intimately relatable. Cuthbertson's skill in balancing serious subjects with a lightness of heart leaves readers feeling hopeful, not only for the main characters but for themselves as well. Rachel and Jaye are each strong, sensitively drawn characters in their own right, but when pulled together, they make for the kind of match so many readers long to find, both in their books and in their own lives."

~Rachel Spangler, award-winning author of 14 romance novels

"*Game Changers* kept me on the edge of my seat as I wondered how the characters would manage to resolve the complications they faced. Jaye and Rachel are root-worthy in the best possible way, and their story is unforgettable. Highly recommended."

~Patty Schramm, award-winning editor and author of The Romance in the Yukon Series

Game Changers

Jane Cuthbertson

Launch Point Press
Portland, Oregon

ISBN: 978-1-63304-210-0
E-Book: 978-1-63304-212-4

FIRST EDITION

Editing: Judy Kerr, Luca Hart

Cover: Lorelei

Published by:
Launch Point Press
Portland, Oregon
www.LaunchPointPress.com

For Jill, who kept me here

Chapter One

Wow.

Am I really seeing this?

I park my car and turn off the engine so I don't plow into something, like the Subaru Outback with Kansas plates that is the only other car here. Then I take a moment to admire the most unexpected sight before me. It's a woman, oh my, a woman of considerable attractiveness: nice athletic build encased in blue jeans and polo shirt, blonde hair pulled back in a ponytail. She throws a quick glance toward my car, and I see she has open, even features and (I think) blue eyes.

What is she doing in a rural cemetery in sparsely populated West Texas in February?

What I'm doing in a rural cemetery in sparsely populated West Texas in February is a much easier question to answer. I grew up here, down the road a bit in Snyder, and my grandparents are buried in this little graveyard in Dunn, a hamlet so small that "wide spot in the road" is too grandiose a description. I live in Colorado now, thank goodness, but on my rare trips back to Texas I always try to come here to pay my respects.

This particular rare trip has had some complications. I'm in Snyder for my favorite aunt and uncle's sixtieth wedding anniversary, which the family is celebrating with a Mass, big party, and family reunion. The anniversary coincides with the Kathleen Nickerson Soccer Camp, which is a big deal as Nickerson is one of the best women soccer players in the world, and maybe the best goalkeeper ever. Girls and boys from all over West Texas have signed up to participate, and they have filled all the local hotels, so there's no room for me at the Hampton Inn this weekend.

I am bunking instead with my cousin Maggie. I love Maggie, but between her two kids, husband, and three or four dogs, their house is never, ever quiet. I suffer for this, as I'm definitely the withdrawn, reclusive type who values my solitude above all else.

This morning I awoke with the onset of depression, from which I have suffered all my adult life. Today's version is like a low-grade fever nagging at me from the back of my head, insidiously affecting my every move until I just want to pack up my luggage, leave Snyder, and disappear from civilization for a month.

I couldn't do that, though. I'm a mature adult, so when thoughts of the cemetery cut through the static of noise and melancholy, I jumped all over the idea, grabbed my keys, and drove off to this temporary distraction.

And now the temporary distraction has a temporary distraction. At first I'm a little annoyed I don't have the cemetery to myself. In my infrequent visits over the years I have never encountered another soul here, living or otherwise. Then I realize I've been given an opportunity. I'm alone in the middle of nowhere with a frickin' gorgeous woman whom I'll never see again after today. It's the perfect social situation for me. Why not enjoy it?

I get out of the car and shut the door. Opportunity has not just knocked, it's thrown a brick through the window, as Gorgeous Blonde is standing right in front of my grandparents' graves.

Chess Johnston and his wife, Rachel, died long before I was born. In fact, they died so long ago that my father, their son, barely remembered them. He loved them as much as any orphaned child could, though, made sure they had a fine granite marker as their tombstone, and named his only daughter Rachel in honor of his mother.

My father was an only child, too. I have tons of family, but it's all on my mother's side. So why is this woman here?

Only one way to find out. I pause for a second, then walk quietly toward her, watching the view get better and better as I draw near. The day is blustery, but even though it's February, the weather is pleasantly warm, and the woman's short-sleeve polo shirt shows off well-defined arms and shoulders. The jeans aren't skin-tight, but whatever this woman does to keep in shape seriously develops her upper legs. And her behind. This athletic build is Olympic quality.

She's seriously the type I'd go for, if I weren't a solitary recluse who suffers from chronic depression and awesomely awful luck in the romance department. The writer in me (and the writer in me has published three lesbian romance novels so far, with a fourth nearly finished) starts vetting her for inclusion as a character in a future work, notes how fantastic she look in her clothes—and bets she would look equally fantastic out of them.

I take another moment to admire this gift from the universe as my irritation fades, and the low-grade depression retreats to a dark corner. She is intently typing into an iPad. I'm not sure she's noticed me draw near. I decide to fix that.

"Long lost relatives?" I ask.

Bad move. Gorgeous Blonde is so startled the iPad goes flying out of her hands. Fortunately for all concerned, the tablet flies right at me, and though I'm kind of a klutz athletically, I manage to catch it before it hits the ground.

Proud of myself for coming through in this small moment, I present the saved technology back to its owner. "Sorry. I thought you heard me coming."

She takes the tablet back with a little uncertainty. We're about the same height, and as my brown eyes meet her—ah ha—gray ones, and get acquainted, I see she's a lot younger than I am, late twenties probably. After a moment she smiles. The gorgeous factor multiplies by ten.

Wow.

"Chess Johnston was my great-great-great grandfather's nephew," she says. "His father and my great-great-great were on different sides of the Civil War and stopped talking to each other when the South seceded. I've been trying to trace this part of the family for a long time."

I take this in. OMG, as they say nowadays. We're actually related. I can't believe it.

"So you're one of those genealogy people?" In addition to being a fabulously fit paragon of womanhood.

Again, a nod and a gush of information. "My mother got me interested in family history. I've done lots of online research, but I travel a lot, too, so when I get to a place I know relatives have been, I always try to find them." She pauses. "Or their graves. I've traced both sides of my family back almost three hundred years."

"I'm impressed," I say sincerely.

"Do you do genealogy?"

I have the sense I'd make her day if I say yes, but my inherent honesty wins out. I shake my head. "No. I grew up down the road, in Snyder, but I have family buried here, and whenever I'm in the area I pay my respects."

"So who are your long-lost relatives?"

My eagerness to chat up this woman now butts right up against my need for privacy. I take a moment to weigh the potential consequences, then choose the truth. I mean, I'm never going to see her again. Right?

"Hi, cousin," I say wryly.

Those gray eyes go wide. "What??"

I can't help it, I have to laugh. "Chess and Rachel Johnston are my grandparents."

This is, I realize suddenly, a "meet cute." I'd learned the term at last year's Golden Crown Literary convention, and though as a writer I'd used "meet cutes" before, I never knew they actually had a name.

"Meet cute" in romance novels occurs in a scene where the two protagonists first encounter each other, usually a situation of some awkwardness or oddity; for example, they are riding bikes on a secluded forest trail and crash into each other. Or they find out they are working the same job in Antarctica.

Or they are at a graveyard, talking in the middle of nowhere.

If this were a book, the wind would turn to rain, Gorgeous Blonde and I would take cover in one of our cars, exchange names and numbers, meet up later for dinner and long conversation, and quickly realize we're somehow meant to be.

But this isn't a book. And it never rains in West Texas.

My goddess-knows-how-distant cousin shifts her glance to the marker, then at me, as if she's not quite believing the "grandparents" revelation. I know she's checking out the dates.

<table>
<tr><td>**Chess Johnston**</td><td>**Rachel E. Johnston**</td></tr>
<tr><td>December 3, 1876 ~ July 10, 1922</td><td>May 11, 1895 ~ September 14, 1927</td></tr>
</table>

"My grandfather Chess was forty-five when his son was born," I explain. "That son, William, was forty when I was born. I'm fifty-two. We stretched the generations to the limit."

"Amazing. We *are* cousins!"

"Of some sort."

Gorgeous Blonde Thinking is every bit as alluring as Gorgeous Blonde Smiling. "Third cousins," she says after a second. "Twice removed."

I'll take her word for it. "So, do you actually have business around here?"

"A soccer camp in Snyder. My best friend runs them in the off-season, and I always help." At last one of us thinks to do introductions. "I'm Jaye Stokes," she says, offering her hand.

As we shake, I do a mental double take. I recall this morning's joking words to my cousin Maggie about Kathleen Nickerson, the tall, dark, handsome-but-moody Women's National Team goalkeeper, Olympic Gold Medalist, infamous bearer of Nickerson's Hair, being by far the biggest celebrity ever to visit Snyder.

"Kathleen Nickerson is your best friend?" And once upon a time my most secret ultimate object of lust, a secret I think prudent to keep.

Stokes' face lights up with delight. "You're a soccer fan!"

Little does she know. "I keep up with the Women's National Team. And the National Women's Soccer League, a little bit." Stokes' name, in fact, is familiar. I realize we're still gently shaking hands, and I loosen my grip. "You play for FC Kansas City." As does Nickerson.

"Yes. The Blues." She lets my hand go, but I see she's pleased I recognize her name. Her smile fades a bit as she adds, "But not the National Team."

This bothers her, I can tell. I'm struck with the desire to fix it somehow. Why? I must be overdosing on the beauty in my presence. Sheesh.

"Never say never," I say quietly.

I'm rewarded with a return of the smile. "You didn't tell me your name."

I didn't. I nod my head toward the gravestone. "Rachel Johnston."

"Seriously? Is that why you come out here?"

I had never thought so, but, well—"Maybe." Food for my thoughts, later.

I hear the distinct sound of an iPhone alert tone. Stokes jumps and reaches into her pocket to reveal the culprit.

"Oops!" she says after checking the display. "I didn't know it was so late. I'm supposed to be meeting Nickory in Snyder."

Disappointment scrimmages with relief that I'm about to get the graveyard to myself. Relief wins by a nose and a breath of inner confusion.

"It's only twenty minutes away," I say.

Stokes punches in a text, then puts the phone away. "It was cool to meet you. Are you coming to the camp?"

I laugh and avoid a straight answer. "I don't live here anymore. I'm visiting for a family thing."

Those eyes light up again. "More cousins?"

"Yes, but on my mother's side. No one you're related to." As we turn back toward the cars, my imagination creates an instant vision of me inviting Jaye Stokes to the anniversary party and the fun I'd have showing up with a beautiful woman at my side—then I shut it down abruptly. She's related to me, not my mother's family, and I'm not worth getting to know better.

"In fact," I continue talking, if only to clear my head of the fantasy, "I'm the last of the Johnston line out here."

"You're sure?"

I nod. "I'm the only child of an only child. I don't remember anyone talking about Chess having brothers or sisters. Rachel, yes, but not Chess."

Stokes stops and consults the iPad. "He had a brother and a sister. But both died young. I remember now. That's why I wanted to find him."

"Fills in a branch of the family tree?"

She grins. "It will if you give me your dad's information. Is he still alive?"

"No. He died in 1989." Twenty-two years ago now. "And there's no grave. He and my mother both chose cremation."

We reach the cars as I give Jaye Stokes both my parents' birth dates and death dates. She gets my birthday, too, to help complete a little piece of her genealogical mosaic. Then she hands me her phone, offering me a perfect opportunity to see her again.

"Can I get your number and email?"

I take the phone, hesitate, then hand it back. "Please don't take offense," I say gently, "but I'm a very private person."

"Even with family?"

"Sometimes especially with family. I have, like, fifty million cousins on my mother's side."

"I promise to respect your privacy and never sell or distribute your information for commercial purposes."

The tone is solemn, but I see the sparkle in her eyes, and it makes me laugh, conflicting directly with my now thoroughly cowed depression. A hint of it must show up as something, though, because she flashes me another beautiful but slightly sad smile and gives up.

She reaches out to shake my hand again. "If you ever come to Kansas City, try to get to a Blues' game."

"I will."

She gets in the Subaru, takes a moment to tap one last something into her iPad, then starts the car and drives off. I watch it disappear down the road, then slowly meander back to my grandparents' resting place, thinking about smiling gray eyes, thinking maybe I made a mistake when I didn't give up my number.

But I am a solitary woman, after all. Even if I do go to a KC soccer game, I'm sure I will never speak again to Jaye Stokes, third cousin twice removed.

"On Being Single"

I am a solitary woman. I always have been, though I did not intend or foresee it. Events this week (a visit to my hometown, a little too much time with my married cousins) have compelled me to this attempt to convey why being solitary doesn't bother me. In a world that insists on everyone being partnered up or looking to be partnered up, I choose a different path. There are reasons for it, both nature and nurture reasons.

Nature: I was an only child. Nurture: My parents, while good people, were not exactly geared for children. I know they loved me, but it was a love best expressed by distance. I got used to distance, thought it was the way everyone did everything.

Nature: I am an introvert. I am not big on crowds, I am not big on parties. Give me a quiet lakeshore or empty beach and the peace and stillness energizes my soul like nothing else ever has. Nurture: While not shy, I never quite fit in with the kids at school or the adults I later worked with. My awkward social skills made for some excruciating faux pas while growing up, and I now do my best to avoid people situations as much as I can.

Nature: I am a lesbian. Nurture: A lesbian growing up in a conservative, mostly-Catholic-but-also-a-little-bit-Baptist family in 1970s Texas is not going to find a lot of people like her to hang out with. I didn't find them. Terrified of my sexuality, especially since I took the Catholicism thing seriously through my teen years, I kept to myself rather than risk revealing my true nature and getting laughed at, excommunicated, disowned, and/or shot.

Nature: I was severely, chronically depressed for more than thirty years. Depression does not encourage one to run into the arms of people. It encourages one, at best, to find a nice cave or basement to hide in. Nurture: I was severely, chronically depressed for more than thirty years. It guided, if not controlled, every interaction I had with anyone, from family to schoolmates to teachers to coworkers.

None of the above sets up well for partnership, and, lo and behold, I am not partnered.

I never met that one special woman. Nothing ever came of the one-night stands of my twenties and thirties except the ability to claim I am not a virgin. I kept hoping, kept thinking someone would come along, but—no.

Fate? Karma? Bad choices? Bad luck? I don't know. At this point, my life simply is what it is, and I can, simply, live with it. Honest! If true love hasn't happened yet, there's no reason to think it should. Let's be logical here: I am an introvert who dislikes crowds, and I'm fifty-two years old. I don't put myself in situations where that special woman might be found. Ergo, I won't find her.

This is not as bad, to me, as it may sound to others. I'm not morose about it. I have a good life. I am a content, solitary woman.

When I return to Snyder I find, to my astonishment, no one home at Maggie's. Even the dogs are asleep in the back yard. Opportunity has thrown two bricks this day, and I take advantage of the peace to write my latest blog.

I blog because, duh, I'm a published author and I want to keep myself in readers' minds. This is especially important in my case since my literary output averages one book every three years. I don't usually blog about literary stuff, unless I'm promoting my latest book, and today is no exception. I take advantage of the format to work through the deep thinking I did on the drive back from the cemetery, to puzzle out the emotional confusion meeting Jaye Stokes seems to have roiled up in me.

I review the finished product. It's true, and fairly succinct, and it grounds me back into my normal existence. Pleased, I post the essay and fix myself a glass of iced tea, then settle in with an old Lori Lake classic, hoping to get a chapter or two read before the dogs wake up and start barking.

Six pages in I'm interrupted not by the dogs, but my iPhone. I glance at the caller ID, grimace a little, and hit the 'accept' button. "Hey."

"Rachel."

"Toni."

"You're in one of your moods, aren't you?"

"What do you mean?"

Antoinette Albaladejo is my closest friend. She's my publisher as well. She is also no fool. "One, you're in Texas," she says. "Two, that's the most personal blog you've written in three years."

I'm not ready to talk to anyone about what happened at the graveyard today, so I avoid a direct answer. "Are you saying I write too much?"

Toni is also a master of the silent sigh, but I spent twenty-five years as an air traffic controller and still have Vulcan-quality hearing. I sense the slight change in her breathing, the exaggerated patience.

"No, Rachel, you do not write too much. Nobody who's good ever writes too much."

"Thank you."

"It's got you, doesn't it?"

She doesn't have to specify what "it" is. I've come a long way in dealing with my depression, but, like the ghost of a bad marriage, it's never going to leave me. Toni knows this, and is ever-alert to nip my down times in the bud, before they can bloom into full flowers of suicidal devastation.

Today, though, "it" is not really the issue. "Actually, no. I was just pondering my life."

"Why?"

I scramble to come up with an answer that will throw her off the scent. "Like you said, I'm in Texas, spending a few days with my close-knit and noisy family. Perhaps I needed to remind myself how good I have it."

"Wouldn't it be better if you were not in Snyder at all?"

"Aunt Theresa and Uncle Joe are having their sixtieth wedding anniversary celebration. I actually want to be here for them."

"You're skipping the Mass, aren't you?"

"Yes."

"Thank goodness for small favors." Neither Toni or I had good experiences with "the faith" growing up. "Family stuff doesn't usually set you off. Why now?"

"I'm staying at Maggie's."

"Why?"

"There's a soccer camp here this weekend, and the hotels are full."

Oops—tactical error. Toni knows how much I like the Beautiful Game. "Women's soccer?"

Drat. "Yep."

"Are you going to that, too?"

"No." Probably not. "It's for kids. Twelve and under or something."

"Geez, Rachel," Toni says, exasperation clear in her voice. "Maybe you do spend too much time writing."

"What?"

"You should get out more into real life. You love watching soccer. Go to the damn camp and spend two hours lusting after a hot coach."

At least she knows better than to suggest I lust after some teenage girl. "You can't have it both ways, O Publisher of Mine. I can write books for you, or I can get out into the world. Pick a side and stick to it."

"I wish you could pick a good woman and stick to her."

"You know how I feel about inflicting my depression on someone else."

"The right woman wouldn't give a shit about your depression. She'd go after it with a blowtorch."

Okay, I'm done. "Not gonna happen, Toni." Which is why I wrote the bloody blog—to remind me this is true.

"Because you're a stubborn fool." Now she sounds like my mother, West Texas drawl and all. Maybe she thought to be funny, but the words hit the limit of my irritation meter.

"No, because I am a sensible woman who knows her past and her limitations. I gotta go now."

"Rachel, don't go away mad."

"I'm not mad. But I am going away. Catch you later."

The next morning, the day of the big anniversary party, Maggie informs me she has to go help prepare the food, and would I take her girls, Jean and Becca, to soccer camp?

"Please?" she begs. "You'll get to meet that Nickerson woman!"

At this point, I swear, I hear a sort of karmic giggle. Of course Maggie's daughters would be signed up for this camp. They've been playing soccer since they were barely out of diapers. But since the alternative is me going to help prepare the food—perish the thought, and perish half my cousins if they're exposed to my cooking—I agree.

"Take the mini-van," my cousin says, tossing me the keys. "Later you can tell me what she's like in person."

Right. I pack my MacBook, camp chair, a cooler of sodas and snacks, then load Jean and Becca and all their gear into the family's Honda Odyssey. We drive to the soccer field at Western Junior College. I get the girls signed in, they run off, and I set myself up far away from stray soccer balls, chatty parents and Gorgeous Blondes, to try and get some writing done.

The weather is, like yesterday, pleasantly warm. Less windy, but that makes it more perfect for soccer. Also, I discover, for musing idly about things which have nothing to do with my latest novel. I make an honest effort for the first half hour, but the writing just won't flow, so eventually I give in, sit back in the camp chair, and let my mind wander where it will.

I remember the day, September 14, but not the year my father first took me to the cemetery in Dunn. It was the early 1970s for sure; I was right around ten years old, a quiet, tremendously insecure little girl who preferred reading books to almost everything else, including being with other children. My father, an only child himself, could relate. My mother, born in the middle of a passel of kids in a huge Catholic family, never got it.

We went to Dunn that day to commemorate the placing of a new head-stone over the graves of my father's parents. Me, Mother and Father, and a grim-faced Baptist preacher made the trip, stood over the newly-planted granite, and the three of us listened in silence while the preacher spoke some fire-and-brimstone words about eternal life and heaven and how to get there by forsaking all of life's pleasures, simple and complicated.

Even at ten years old, or thereabouts, I was learning to tune out these kind of harangues, and soon I had stopped listening, and focused instead on the name of my grandmother.

Rachel E. Johnston. It was the first time I realized I had been named for her, and it shocked me. She had been born Rachel Elizabeth Lee in 1895. Yes, R.E. Lee. My family had strong Confederate roots and probably would have named her Roberta had that been in the Bible. She married Chess Johnston in 1919, bore my father William in 1921, and died in 1927 when she was thirty-two. For a long time afterwards, I thought I too would die at thirty-two (I was a weird kid), but as you can see I was wrong.

As the preacher droned on I shifted, eventually, from Grandmother's name to her husband's.

Chess Johnston was forty-two when he married Rachel. That's old for a first marriage, which it was, in his case. But my own parents married in their mid-thirties, and what I wondered about instead was why a young woman like Rachel would marry someone so much older. I asked my father about it later, but all he ever said was "It was pretty common back then," and I had to let it go.

I drift out of reverie long enough to ensure the day is still sunny and the soccer camp is in full swing. I rise from my chair and stretch, then stroll over to the stands and find the restroom. Back at my little out of the way spot, I pull a Diet Cherry Dr. Pepper out of my cooler, pop it open, and fall right back into the past.

This time I reflect on my father, William Stuart Johnston. If I was ten that long ago day in the 1970s, he would have been in his fifties, around the same age I am now.

Whoa.

Same age, but very different life paths. William, an orphan at six, was raised by Grandmother Rachel's brother, Jefferson, a hardscrabble farmer who had no money in the heart of the Depression but somehow managed to feed his family and make sure his kids, including William, learned to read and write. My father worked the farm as hard as anyone, but he also loved the world books opened up to him. After Pearl Harbor, he jumped at the chance to go out and see some of it. His view, though, whatever wonder he may have anticipated, was skewed by trips to islands with strange names: Guadalcanal, Tarawa, Iwo Jima. While growing up I often wished William had never returned to Scurry County, but the older I got, the more I thought I understood why he did. My father came back to the comfort of the familiar. Here the dirt was red because of geology, not because of blood. He earned a degree at Texas Tech, became a teacher at Western Junior College, and never left again.

He found a contentment, I believe, a way to detach from what he'd seen. Like his father, he married late, like his parents had only one child. Unlike them, he lived to see her grow to adulthood and leave West Texas herself. I never told my parents I was a lesbian, the driving force behind my exit. I learned very young they preferred silence to detail, and if he imagined I was getting out into the world the way he had once wanted to, that worked for us both.

I raise my head at the all-too-familiar shouts of both Jean and Becca.

"Rachel! Rachel! Jaye says she knows you!"

The munchkins are bouncing along with a tall, smiling blonde between them. She does not bounce, but moves with a grace I could watch for hours. Could have been watching for hours. Ah, opportunity lost.

"Hi, cousin," Jaye Stokes says cheerfully. "I thought you weren't coming."

I unfold myself from the camp chair, stand, and shrug. "I didn't know they'd need a ride. Have they driven you crazy yet?"

"Is she our cousin, too?" Becca cries excitedly.

"Becca," I say, "we're right here. You don't have to shout."

Jean stage whispers, "Is she our cousin, too?"

I shake my head. "Nope. She's from my father's side of the family. She's mine all mine."

"I think I like that," Jaye says.

Her sincerity brings back the same hint of confusion I felt yesterday, but I cover it up by turning back to the kids. "Why aren't you guys out there? Did Nickerson kick you off?"

"It's lunch time." Becca announces. If not quite a shout, town criers would still be proud. "Come on. You have to eat with us!"

Lunch time? I check my watch. Sure enough, high noon has arrived.

"Parents and kids are supposed to eat together," Jaye explains. "This is when Nickory will answer any questions."

"But not about the hair," the girls say in unison.

"Questions about soccer only," Jaye says.

"Okay, got it." The girls turn and sprint back toward the pitch. Jaye and I head back more slowly, walking side by side.

"Do you answer questions, too?" I ask her.

"If I'm asked. Nickory's the star, though."

I nod. This is certainly true. "I looked you up on Wikipedia last night."

Jaye Stokes' career pales compared to her friend's. She and Nickerson are both thirty-one, but she grew up in Iowa, while Nickerson hails from New Hampshire. Jaye had been a regular on U.S. Soccer's Youth National Teams, the Under-17, Under-18, and Under-20 squads and had attended soccer powerhouse North Carolina on scholarship. Respectable, for sure. But, while always in the pool of players from which the main National Team is chosen, she's never been named to the big squad itself.

She also appears to be single, but that's neither here nor there.

Jaye lets out a kind of half-laugh. "Checking me out? Why?"

Deciding "Because I'm trying to figure out if you're a lesbian" is not a viable reply, I improvise. "Family matters."

This rates a sideways glance. "Does this mean I can find out all about you?"

"Not on Wikipedia." This is strictly true. The Fyrequeene, lesbian novelist, has a Wikipedia entry. Rachel Johnston, semi-recluse, does not.

"So I'll have to ask you directly."

She doesn't get the chance, though, because we have reached the lunch grouping.

Or rather, the lunch horde. One hundred camp participants, plus at least one parent or guardian for each, plus the players and coaches running things, makes for a crowd I'm not prepared for.

I stop short. My demon depression roars out of its dark corner in the form of sudden panic (a favorite tactic). I have never liked too many people around me at once, and despite years of therapy, deep breaths, and forced trips to sporting events, my loathing of crowds has gradually shifted to fear.

I tighten my jaw, take some slow deep breaths, and mentally remind myself that it's only lunch. A simple, perfectly innocuous, noisy lunch with a lot of other people.

I feel a gentle touch on my arm. "You okay?" Jaye asks.

I smile at her, because it builds up my confidence, and because I'm determined to win this inner battle. "I'm not much of a crowd person."

She seems to gauge my concern. "How about we sit on the edges somewhere, then?"

We? "Uh, sure."

"Okay. Wait here."

Four long rows of picnic tables, ends pushed together, have been set up to handle the lunch offerings, while a fifth set of tables nearby holds massive quantities of Texas barbecue, with all the fixings. The dishes are laid out buffet style, every one to serve herself. How the kids will be able to move after this meal is beyond me but hey, I'm not playing soccer and don't have to worry about it. I watch Jaye wade into the crowd, find Nickerson, who's about the tallest person here today, talk and gesture for a moment, then wade back out. Along the way she spots and snags Becca and Jean.

"Last row, far end," she announces, and off we go to the designated spot. Jaye settles me and Jean in to hold our places, then takes Becca with her to get food for us four. When they get back, she makes sure I'm at the very end of the row, then anchors herself in the middle while several girls and their adults gather around us.

This works for me. I can jump up and run off screaming if I have to. Having the escape option allows me to sit and eat in relative comfort while getting caught up in observing Jaye, sitting there like she's the head of her own little picnic island. She happily takes questions from the kids sitting around her, compliments them on how they've done so far, asks them and their parents stuff about their own lives.

She's good at this. Every girl gets a little attention, and the parents can chat, too, but Jaye subtly keeps things focused on the children and soccer. She parries questions about her friend "Nickory" by saying the woman herself will be over in a minute, and soon I see that yes, indeed, the goalkeeper is working her way through the horde, spending a few minutes with each "island," then moving on to the next.

I know a fair amount about Nickerson. She's been a mainstay on the Women's National Team since 2002 and the best goalkeeper in the world since 2008. She and super striker Wendy Allerton are a big part of the reason why the U.S. Women are top-ranked internationally and always World Cup favorites. Because they are both six feet tall, reporters call them "The Twin Towers." They have anchored the U.S. Team for almost ten years.

Allerton is an extroverted chatterbox, bouncing from party to party and lover to lover (both sexes included) with gleeful abandon. Nickerson has been linked to the same woman since college, never talks to reporters except to say "no comment," and would be a complete dud media-wise except for the legend of "Nickerson's Hair."

Some people have tattoos, some have a posse, others have crazy jewelry. Nickerson has her hair. Since her first practice with the U.S. Under-17 team—when she showed up sporting an electric blue ponytail—up to and including the present day, Kathleen Nickerson has dyed her hair every color of the rainbow and beyond. Mostly she prefers solid colors. But sometimes she'll have stripes. The world has yet to see her attempt polka dots, but who knows? Soccer paparazzi eat it up, kids with indulgent parents copy her color of the season, and rumor has it the hair has both a Facebook account and Twitter feed.

I have the sense her hair has kept her more in the public eye than she would like, but she's been doing it so long she now cannot escape the monster created in her teens. Also, after she and Allerton led the US to Olympic Gold in 2008, Nike made a series of brilliant commercials with the pair. The ads played off Allerton's ebullience, Nickerson's reticence, and, of course, the hair, and were a huge success for all involved. Kathleen Nickerson took the money, lived with the fame, and made sure the hair continued to change shades and be a source of conversation. She also continues to be the best goalkeeper in the world, no argument. She once went an entire YEAR without allowing an opposing goal, and I swear half her popularity is because of, not in spite of, her endless capacity to say "no comment" to any and all media.

She is, in fact, responsible for hooking me on women's soccer. After the 2008 Olympics gold-medal match NBC corralled players for post-game comments. Nickerson, who'd shut out Germany, and Allerton, who'd scored both U.S. goals, were standing next to each other with microphones in their faces. Allerton was her usual effusive self, waxing enthusiastically about the game. Nickerson simply stood there, silent as always, arm around her teammate's shoulders, her hair sporting equal amounts of red-, white-, and blue-colored locks. The smile on her face was full of happiness, accomplishment, and deep-rooted satisfaction, and it pulled me right in.

That was it. I was in lust with not-afraid-to-be-herself Kathleen Nickerson, and in love with the Beautiful Game.

The lust for Nickerson faded over the years, a combination of her persistent silence and persistent girlfriend. My interest in soccer, though, still burns strong.

Today is the first time I get a glimpse of the real woman behind the hair. As Nickerson reaches our little group she stands behind Jaye, smiles at the kids, and gets them talking. Turns out "cold and forbidding" is an exaggeration. She genuinely likes the youngsters and is good with the crowd. She doesn't talk much herself, naturally, but is skilled at asking leading questions which let the kids chatter away. Interesting.

I also confirm that she is indeed the picture next to the word "Amazon" in the dictionary: tall, strong, handsome but not beautiful. She has broad shoulders, small breasts, a narrow waist, and legs perfectly proportioned for . . . for whatever you care to fill in.

And maybe her ego is not too monstrous after all. She doesn't freak out when someone breaks the rules and asks a question about her hair.

"What color is your head today?"

This comes from a girl, not a parent, and I think the odd phrasing catches Nickerson off guard, or maybe she's in a particularly good mood. She gazes upwards, making a funny face as she tries to see her hair (which she's wearing short this year), then turns back to the inquirer.

"It's called 'Desert Dust.' Now you have to ask a question about soccer."

Whether she made up the color name or not, it fits. Nickerson's hair is the exact shade of the soil at the graveyard in Dunn, a light orange-red ubiquitous to West Texas. I'm sure she did it on purpose, but it doesn't suit her (honestly, not many of her color choices do). My eyes fall to Jaye, whose natural blonde tresses I find much more appealing.

She catches my eye and winks. I surprise myself and wink back, realize I have a new secret ultimate object of lust.

I follow it up immediately with the thought that Jaye Stokes deserves better.

The camp's afternoon activities are more subdued than the morning's scrimmages, no doubt in deference to the copious amounts of food consumed by the children. The instructors divide the kids into small groups and do what essentially comes down to classroom teaching, talking and demonstrating different lessons while the students sit around and watch.

I watch, too, though there's only so many times one can observe a lesson in footwork. The instructors know this, and eventually they get everyone up, give them a ball, and have them practice what they've just seen.

The day's activities end when the camp leaders treat the kids (and their adults, too) to a half-field, five-on-five scrimmage. In addition to Jaye, Nickerson has brought several of her Kansas City teammates along, and they split up with players from the junior college also recruited to help with the camp. The short field makes for a very entertaining, fast-paced mini-game. The college kids are not bad, but it's clear Stokes and Nickerson are, by far, the best players out here today, more talented than even their fellow pros. Jaye doesn't score on her friend, no one does, but she makes "Nickory" show the campers why she's the best goalkeeper in the women's game and wins over a few fans herself.

And then camp is done. The goal nets come down, autographs are signed, and pretty much everyone gets their picture taken with Nickerson. Now I can think about, ugh, getting ready for this evening's party. At least I'll know everyone in that horde.

"Rachel! Rachel!" A munchkin blur comes running up. Becca again.

"Yes, O Noisy One?"

She laughs. "I need your phone!"

"Why?"

"I just do! Please?"

With a suspicious glare, which Becca stands up to admirably, I hand over the object requested.

"Be right back!!" she says and runs off.

"Hey!"

Becca makes a beeline right to Jaye, who separates herself from a small group of families who haven't left yet. She grins at me and takes the phone. By the time I've walked over, she's punched in whatever she set out to punch in and gives the phone back to me.

"Now you won't have an excuse to avoid me when you're in Kansas City," she says.

"There's a password on this phone."

"Becca knows it."

I shake my head. The kid is loud but observant. I make a mental note to change both my phone and laptop passwords. Meanwhile, I open up my contacts list and sure enough, there is Jaye's name and number.

"And I guess I have to go to Kansas City now?"

Her grin is definitely of the shit-eating variety. "Season opener is April sixteenth."

"What if I'm busy?"

"Becca says you're retired. So your schedule is flexible."

Becca is going to get thrown into the swimming pool at the party house tonight. Fully dressed. "Cripes! Do I have any secrets left?"

Jaye takes this more seriously than she should. "Don't be mad at Becca, I sorta put her up to it."

"Why?"

She opens her mouth to answer, hesitates, and her expression shifts from amusement to uncertainty to something I can't quite decipher. "Because we need all the fans we can get?"

It was definitely not what she was going to say originally. But it breaks the mild tension of my irritation and makes me laugh. "Okay," I say. "I'll be there."

The brief hitch in her confidence disappears. "Cool. Oh, don't be mad, but I sent me a text from your phone, so I'll remind you to buy tickets when the time comes. See you in April!"

With those last words Jaye Stokes turns and walks off, leaving me speechless, but also intrigued by her audacity.

Kansas City here I come.

Chapter Two

Friday night, before the season opener, I call Jaye. She has texted me a couple of times since garnering my number at the soccer camp, and I had always returned the text with a brief call. This is the first time I've initiated contact without hearing from her first.

"I wanted to wish you good luck tomorrow," I say after her pleased hello.

"You're gonna be there, right?"

"Yes."

"Great. I can get a field pass if you want one."

"Thanks, but I'm okay in the stands. I don't want to be any trouble."

"You're not trouble. You're my cousin!"

I laugh and think she cannot possibly be that nice. But maybe she is.

I enjoy the game so much I decide to blog about it when I get back home. I was going to say hi to Jaye afterwards, but she was busy signing autographs so I let it go. I have business in Denver on Monday so my trip to Kansas City is a quick one.

I get a text while driving home on Sunday: "Are you still in town? Let's get together!"

I have an iPhone5, currently meshed to my car stereo Bluetooth. "Siri, call Jaye Stokes."

In a moment my "Road Songs" playlist is replaced by one intriguing and (for me) persistent distant relative.

"Hi, Rachel. Are you still in town?"

"Hi. I'm headed home, just passed Salina."

"Bummer." I swear I can hear disappointment in stereo. "Why didn't you say hi last night?"

"You were busy with your fans."

"You're a fan, too. Are you coming next week?"

I hadn't planned on it, but the odd compulsion to please Jaye pops up again. "I think I might, yeah."

"Good. This time I'll give you a field pass."

"No, don't do that. I like watching the game from up high."

"You sure?"

"I'm sure."

"Promise you'll come talk to me afterwards. Don't run away."

"I will. Unless you score five goals and ESPN gets to you first."

Jaye's laugh sounds good in stereo, too. "Even then," she says. "Promise me."

I'm mystified at this attention, but agreeable. "I promise."

"So you live in Colorado?"

"Yeah. North Denver."

"Long drive."

"About nine hours."

"Gosh. Thanks for being a fan!"

I laugh. "The trip was worth it. You guys played a great game."

"And the crowd didn't bother you?"

"You remember that."

"Of course. But you were okay?"

"Yeah. It was fine." And it was, since I was sitting in one of the sparsely occupied upper rows.

Then Jaye surprises me. "Until the end, maybe. That's why you didn't stick around to say hi afterwards."

I take my time answering. "You're a smart woman."

"Hey, I went to college." Jaye laughs. "You should let me get you a field pass. There are a lot fewer people by the bench."

"We'll see."

We've reached the length of our previous conversations, so I expect Jaye to make her goodbyes, but instead she launches into another subject. "What job did you retire from?"

"I was an air traffic controller. They let you retire after twenty five years of service, so I did. Last year."

"Wow. Lucky you. Was it as stressful as they say?"

"Sometimes." I am a master of understatement.

"What do you do now?"

I don't know why I keep "writer" to myself. But I do, because I'd have to own up to being a lesbian writer, and that amps up my residual fear of being rejected because I'm a lesbian. No matter how the world changes, no matter how old I get and how little I've ever been rejected or discriminated against, the fear never goes away.

"Travel a little," I say. "Swim to keep in shape. Read a lot."

I hear her smile. In stereo. "I read a lot, too. Who are your favorite authors?"

I answer honestly, but again omit the lesbians. Mea culpa.

We end up talking for quite a while, bouncing over a range of stuff, never running out of words. My interaction with Jaye feels easy and unforced, like I'm making a new friend. I end up telling her a lot more about myself than I usually tell anyone. But I still keep mum about my sexuality and the writing.

I've gone almost a hundred miles before Jaye hangs up, her phone battery low. I put my music back on and spend the rest of the drive in a kind of blissful fog. I get home in the early evening, wish my house a happy hello, then type and post the blog about going to KC's first game.

I have no clue this is going to change my life.

Fyrequeene's Blog: April 17

"In Praise of Strong Women, and the Soccer Fans Who Love Them"

Those of you who read this thing know by now that I follow two sports, baseball and women's soccer. You know attending baseball games and soccer matches are the only time I willingly put up with crowds. Given that the National Women's Soccer League, or NWSL, is still trying to establish itself, I have a much better time at their games than at Rockies' games because the crowds are always smaller.

I do hope this changes. I'd like nothing better than to see the NWSL grow to the success now enjoyed by men's Major League Soccer. But until that happens, I am content to be part of a small, dedicated core of fans who follow the most gracious group of athletes I've ever seen.

Saturday I wrestled my crowd phobia into submission and attended the season opener between the Kansas City Blues and the Boston Breakers. It's a nine-hour drive from my home in Colorado to KC, but it was worth it. From a seat up high in the stands, I got to watch a tight, competitive match, admired Olympians on both sides making great plays and saw the "regular" pros make some outstanding plays as well. These women take their sport and their craft every bit as seriously as any baseball or football player, and if you like soccer, then you will like watching these games.

A lot.

Afterwards, the members of both teams lined up along one side of the stands to sign autographs for their fans. The players signed programs, shoes, shirts, and the occasional stuffed animal. They did it with smiles and a patience that belied the end of a long night. KC's Kath Nickerson and Becky Kaisershot were the big draws, of course, being Olympic standouts, but the fans made sure all of their players got some love and gave the Boston side affection as well. It probably didn't hurt that Kansas City won.

Every fan who wanted an autograph got one. In a world where many elite athletes can be outright disdainful of their supporters, these professionals truly appreciate the fans who watch them, the ones who pay for tickets and provide them the opportunity to do something they love.

I may be a reclusive curmudgeon, but I enjoyed the whole night: great weather, great game, great camaraderie afterwards, sportswomanship at its best. If you live anywhere near one of the nine NWSL cities, find time to go to a game this season. You won't be disappointed.

Game two for the Kansas City Blues is much tougher than the opener against Boston. Once again, the weather is fine and the competition sublime, but the opponent is Western New York, the Flash, and they have Wendy Allerton on their side.

I get to the field early, pick up a hot dog and Coke, and settle into my top row seat. Jaye had texted me on Thursday with another field pass offer, and I'd called her back, got her voicemail, and politely declined. By buying a ticket, I tell myself, I'm supporting the league.

Which is true. I've always wanted to support women's sports. Nothing against men, but they so dominate everything athletic that, frankly, they don't need my patronage (poor choice of words, but it proves my point). Women do.

Besides, I think as I chomp down on the hot dog, I see the game better from this vantage point.

The game starts, and I quickly observe that the teams are evenly matched. I suspect the deciding factor will be the battle between Nickerson and Allerton, the great stopper versus the great scorer. And I'm right.

Western New York's strategy basically has Allerton patrolling the area in front of KC's goal and waiting for opportunities. Even from my vantage point I can hear Nickerson as she works with teammate Becky Kaisershot to thwart their fellow Olympian. She shouts directions, sets up defenders, tries to make sure someone's always defending, or "marking," the Flash striker.

Despite all this effort, Wendy Allerton ultimately prevails. She uses her experience, skill, and height to turn two "opportunities" into goals. She's not the fastest player, not the youngest player—she's simply the best. She knows how to be in the right place at the right time, and despite my bias toward Kansas City, she's a joy to watch.

Nickerson, for the most part, reins her frustration in and never gives up. Early in the second half she makes a spectacular dive to keep Allerton from a third goal and a hat trick. This brings the crowd to its feet, and the Blues feed off the energy.

On the ensuing corner kick, Jaye Stokes heads the ball clear and over to a teammate. She follows the action up the field. The KC players work the ball beautifully, and Jaye is there to take the ball on the sideline as forward Kirstie Longstreet moves in front of the goal. Jaye floats a gorgeous centering pass. With a fast-as-lightning kick, Longstreet redirects the ball right into the net. I stand and cheer with the rest of the fans as KC makes the score 2-1.

Sadly for KC, the score holds right 'til the end. The locals are disappointed, but most in the crowd realize everyone played well. Allerton was simply too good on this night. The buzz of energy in the little stadium is still positive as people make their way to the autograph line. I'm drawn there, too, and take a seat close enough to observe the player/fan interaction.

And yeah, okay, to get a close-up glimpse of Allerton, one of the true legends of her sport. I'm pleased to see her engaging the fans with graciousness (honestly, how many great male athletes can you say that about?), paying particular attention to the youngsters. She signs the usual papers, shirts, and a poster or two. She also poses for a few pictures with Nickerson, who softens her grim-in-defeat expression enough to keep cameras and cell phones from shattering. The pair even do some quick riffs reminiscent of the Nike ads, and the crowd eats it up.

Someone official eventually pulls Allerton away, but the local heroines stick around until everyone gets an autograph. I see Jaye at the far end of the railing, figure she'll get to me when she's ready, and as the crowd gradually disperses, my gaze drifts upward to the night sky, where the beginning of a quarter moon becomes visible in the dusk. I watch it brighten, take a moment to appreciate this clear April night. I'm as close to happy as I ever get, and I let the universe know I'm grateful.

When I refocus on planet Earth, only a couple of players are left by the stands. One of them is Jaye, and she's staring at me with an expression of strange intensity. And maybe a little anger? This puzzles me, even threatens to wipe out the peace I'm feeling, but I'm still brave enough to break the silence.

"Hi," I say.

She startles me by climbing up and over the railing to take a seat next to me. "I'm either going to make a complete fool of myself," Jaye says, "or you are."

I'm so surprised I sputter out some old air traffic phraseology. "Say again?"

"Are you The Fyrequeene?"

I sit there in complete shock. It has never, ever occurred to me that Jaye Stokes would have any clue about The Fyrequeene. And I don't have to answer: I know my expression says it all. Jaye falls back into the seat and turns her head to the sky.

"I can't believe it," she says helplessly, then fires a glare at me again. "Why didn't you tell me you were a writer?"

"B-Because it's not what I do?"

"What?"

"I don't tell anyone I write."

"Why not? I *love* your books. I can't be the only one."

I'm flattered. I'm also completely at sea. "I really am a private person, Jaye."

She's not buying it. "Didn't you blog about going to a convention? The one for writers? Did you go as the Invisible Woman or something?"

"No. I went as The Fyrequeene. I never told anyone my real name."

I also hid behind Toni's (totally) metaphorical skirts the whole time. The conference was a good experience, but I'm ambivalent about going again.

"You've read my blog?" I ask this softly, almost like a little kid would, and something in my tone of voice melts away Jaye's anger.

"I've read everything I can find. The books, the short stories, the Xena stuff"— here the glare returns— "and last week's blog about our game." She rolls her eyes. "I couldn't believe it! Here's The Fyrequeene writing about a nine-hour drive, about sitting up high in the stands, about hating crowds, and it sounds exactly like what you'd said when we talked on the phone. But I asked you what you did, and you never said you wrote."

Jaye pauses, frowns at me, shakes her head. "I went back through your other blogs. You mention growing up in Texas and being an only child, and I knew. I've not only met The Fyrequeene, she's my cousin!"

Depression senses a real opportunity for dominance here and lets me know it. I can panic and withdraw—or try to salvage things. I opt for the latter and attempt a joke. "Don't worry. It's not the end of the world. No one has to know."

Jaye stares at me blankly, sees my tentative smile, and bursts out laughing. I give her a smile, pleased and relieved.

"It explains some other things, too," she says, but we're interrupted before I can find out what.

"Jaye! We gotta go!"

We both turn toward the voice. It's Nickerson. Even in defeat she projects the sturdy strength of an old growth tree, right up to the deep forest green color of her hair.

"The team's waiting, babe," she says to Jaye, the endearment startling me until I remember they are BFFs.

"Nickory, do you know who this is?" Jaye asks with enthusiasm.

Nickerson turns her gaze to me, and I have a sudden vision of the goalkeeper as a warrior queen, fiercely protective of those she loves. "Your cousin from Texas," she says.

I'm impressed. Jaye had introduced us briefly at the soccer camp, and I honestly didn't think she'd remember.

"Yeah, but she's also The Fyrequeene!"

The warrior eyes narrow. "The writer?"

"Yeah!"

Jaye is only the third person, other than Toni and her partner Paula, to know Rachel Johnston and The Fyrequeene are one and the same. Nickerson makes four. An exponential increase, and a cause for inner terror on my part. I swallow and try to remain calm.

Nickerson, meanwhile, is underwhelmed. "You're older than I thought."

Jaye glares at her. I see this, draw strength from it, then fire my own little salvo. "And I didn't think you'd let Allerton score two goals on you tonight. Great save to keep her from the hat trick, though."

Nickerson grimaces and dismisses me. But I'm definitely ahead on points. "Jaye," she says, "we really do have to go."

Jaye turns to me. "The team's going downtown for barbecue. Come with us?"

Barbecue is one of my favorite things. But my crowd tolerance has reached its limit, and my inner recluse is stronger than my inner foodie.

"I appreciate the invite," I reply sincerely, "But no."

Jaye puts a hand on my arm. "Come. It'll be fun."

I feel the warmth in her touch, and a certain electricity. Her expression is both parts eager and hopeful, with true invitation in her gorgeous gray eyes. But I don't give in.

"Jaye," I say with sincere regret, "I can't do a noisy restaurant on a Saturday night."

Her smiles fades. I literally see her remembering my thing about crowds. Then she rallies. "I'm not letting you get away again. Let's get takeout and go back to my place. I promise it'll be quiet there."

Nickerson makes a movement, a subtle shift of discomfort. Jaye ignores her, but I remember Jaye telling me she shares a house, or something, with her best friend, and offer a different option.

"Tell you what," I say. "I've got a huge room at the Hampton Inn down the road. How about we get takeout and go there?"

"Perfect," she says. I startle myself by falling into her smile a little. It's not flirtatious exactly, but I'm struck by the odd sense that it wants to be.

Jaye stands up before I can process my reaction. "I'll meet you by the players' entrance in twenty." She hops back over the railing and walks off with Nickerson. I stand slowly, wondering where the players' entrance is and sense something new inside of me. A tiny little change, a subtle vibration.

Like a small leak springing through a dam.

After a few minutes of playing lost wanderer, I successfully locate the locker room doors and park myself on a nearby bench next to an attractive African American woman who seems vaguely familiar.

She's more extroverted than I, so the mystery is solved quickly. "Hi," she says, holding out her hand. "I'm Bree Thompson. Who are you waiting for?"

I shake her hand. "Jaye Stokes. I'm Rachel Johnston, her very distant cousin. And you're waiting for Kath Nickerson."

I'm sure of my words. Bree Thompson is "the woman" in Nickerson's life, according to the Internet gossip on TMZ and such. Questions about their relationship tend to elicit the firmest of Nickerson's "no comments." Thompson has been in lots of pictures with her, though, and with Jaye Stokes, too. That's why she looks familiar.

"Yes," Thompson answers me, offering nothing more. "Wait, are you the one from the cemetery?"

"Yep."

"Jaye talked you into coming to a game."

"I've been a soccer fan for a while. Since the Clean Sheet Olympics."

When a baseball pitcher goes nine innings without allowing a run, it's called a shutout. When soccer goalkeepers allow no goals during a game, it's called a "clean sheet." In the six matches of the 2008 Games, Nickerson held every opponent scoreless. Thus, "Clean Sheet Olympics." In fact, Nickerson didn't just have a Clean Sheet Olympics, she had a clean sheet *year*, a feat no other goalie, male or female, has even remotely approached.

Thompson brightens. "Cool. I was there in Beijing. It was great."

I sigh with envy, but before I can say anything the locker room doors open to reveal Stokes and Nickerson. Jaye sees me and waltzes right up.

"Bree," she says with enthusiasm, "this is The Fyrequeene! Can you believe it?"

Bree raises an eyebrow. "You said you were her cousin."

"I am," I say, stifling another sigh. "But I'm also The Fyrequeene." Now five people know about Rachel Johnston and The Fyrequeene. Grrrr.

"What're the odds?" Jaye says, putting a friendly hand on my shoulder. "I'm related to my favorite writer!"

What? Favorite writer? Me? "Distantly related."

"Third cousins, twice removed," Jaye says promptly.

Bree laughs. "Will you be going to dinner with us?"

"Uh, no, I'm not a crowd person."

"I'm taking her to dinner," Jaye says. "We've never really had a chance to talk."

Bree nods, taking in Jaye, me, then Jaye looking at me. She turns to meet my eyes, her expression abruptly serious, and says a curious thing. "Jaye's the best. Be good to her."

As a frequent guest of Hampton Inn, I occasionally get free room upgrades. I have scored one this week, a mini-suite with a wet bar, sofa, and coffee table in addition to the king-size bed. Jaye and I pile into the room after picking up takeout barbecue at a place near the stadium. When I tell her I have only Diet Cherry Dr. Pepper her face lights up.

"I love Diet Cherry Dr. Pepper!"

Must be a family thing.

While Jaye lays the feast out on the coffee table I go get ice, laughing at myself. Charming a beautiful woman with soda pop? I have no idea where this is going, and as the ice bucket fills, I realize it doesn't matter. Jaye will like me or not, and I truly have nothing to lose. Life will either go on like it has, or I will have a new friend. Nothing but positives here.

I smile. Here's hoping for the "new friend" option.

I get back to the room and pour our drinks. Jaye is starving after running up and down a soccer field for two hours, so we park ourselves on the sofa, and don't talk much until she's inhaled a quarter of a chicken and half the coleslaw.

She comes up for air prior to attacking the potato salad. "Can I ask you something?"

"Of course."

"Why are you so secretive?"

"I'm not," I protest mildly, taking my chance to grab the coleslaw. "I'm private."

"Okay. Why are you so private?"

"I always have been."

"Are you out at work? Oh, wait. You're retired. Were you out at work?"

I shrug. "More or less. I kept a low profile, but people knew, and I never denied it if asked."

Jaye eyes me over a full fork. "Can I ask you another question?"

I eye her right back. "Quid pro quo, but yes."

My comment stops her for a second. But only a second. "Okay, fair enough. I've never slept with Nickory."

Thank goodness my mouth isn't full. "What?"

Her turn to shrug. "That's what everybody asks."

"Because you're friends?"

"And because I live with her and Bree."

"I'm not everybody."

Her eyes spark. Am I hallucinating flirtation in them? "I know."

"Besides, the real question is, did you *ever want* to sleep with her?"

Jaye freezes for a second and gives herself away. Puts the napkin down. "I see why you're such a good writer. You come at things from different directions."

"It is the more interesting question. But, it's also none of my business. Now what do you want to know about me?"

Jaye nods, grateful, I think, and maybe a little intrigued that I let the subject go. Do others keep pushing, I wonder? "Where did you get the idea for *Empress?*"

Ah, safer ground. Sort of. My books are ostensibly historical romances, but the history part always centers around some sort of catastrophe. Book one was set in Galveston, site of the hurricane of 1900. Book two was about Halifax, Nova Scotia, and the munitions ship which exploded in the harbor in 1917, devastating the city. For book three I kept both the nautical and Canadian themes, writing about *The Empress of Ireland,* an ocean liner whose sinking in the Saint Lawrence River in 1914 took almost as many lives as the *Titanic.* My romance involved two survivors who have to come to terms both with outliving a thousand other people and with their attraction to each other.

"I like to take stories off the beaten path. I've been interested in history forever, and if I can teach readers something they didn't know before, then it's worth it."

"And you have a thing for disasters," she says, taking back the coleslaw.

I start to object, then remember the subject of my upcoming novel—the Triangle Fire of 1911. "Disasters, and the early Twentieth Century," I say wryly.

I will admit to some vague prejudices about "jock-head" athletes, Jaye is tearing many of them to shreds. The conversation flows easily, like it did when we talked on the phone last Sunday. I'm happy to listen to Jaye, but I'm pleased to learn she's happy to listen to me, too. A lot of people spend their conversations waiting for the other person to shut up so they can talk again. Jaye seems genuinely interested in what I have to say.

She's not surprised to find out I was a history major, but is astonished to learn I never took a writing course after high school.

"Wow."

"Yeah. I'm kind of an idiot savant when it comes to writing."

"Why did you wait until your forties, though?"

"Actually, I've been writing since my teens. I just never finished anything until my forties. I was an air traffic controller for twenty-five years, and it kept getting in the way of my creativity."

"It really is stressful?"

"Absolutely. Combine it with depression and the job could be downright lethal sometimes." I hadn't intended to bring up the subject, but it slips out.

Jaye says, "That's why you write about disasters. About women who overcome the impossible."

I stop eating, struck by the interesting observation. I almost own up to never overcoming my own impossible, but back off. "I suppose you could be right. But if I think about it too much I can't write. So, I don't think about it."

Jaye's expression is bemused for a moment, like she knows there's something I'm not saying. Then she grins and lets me off the hook. "I understand. I play my best soccer when I let it happen, when I just take the ball and run."

Whew. "Have you always played soccer?"

"Of course. My parents signed me up when I was five, and from my first game all I wanted to do was play. Are you going to finish that?"

I surrender the last of the potato salad. "You're lucky to be so good at something you love."

Jaye takes a bite, swallows, and surprises me. "Yes and no. I know I'm good, but I've never gotten to the top. I've never been elite."

"You look pretty elite to me." Full double entendre intended.

"Did you know I was on the same Under-17 team with Wendy Allerton, Nickory, and Becky Kaisershot?"

No acknowledgment of my cleverness.

"I thought I'd take the next steps right along with them. The World Cup, the Olympics." She pauses. "And I didn't get there. I never made the final cuts."

Jaye puts the food container down on the coffee table. "One day you're right there in the hunt, the next day you're not. You're a little bit slower than the other players. Not a step, not even half a step. An eighth of a step slower. Subtle, barely noticeable. But all the difference between a decent pro and a gold medalist."

I think back to KC's only goal tonight, which Jaye started with a header to a teammate. She'd cleared the ball, raced up the pitch, ready to take the ball back and make the perfect pass to Longstreet. I saw no lack of speed there. Why would she think she's too slow?

I find the brownies we'd bought for dessert and hand her one. "But you're still doing something you love. You listened to your heart. I spent half my life working for other people and never did listen to mine."

"But you've published three books!"

"Yes. In my forties. But how many might I have written if I'd listened to *my* heart? You found out for sure how good you are." I laugh. "I never knew how much I loved writing until I got old."

"You're not old," Jaye says firmly.

I throw out my best maternal tone. "I'm old enough to be your mother."

"But you're not my mother." Jaye's eyes bore into mine as she says this, and now the flirtatious smile I've sensed all evening blooms in full.

Suddenly we aren't two distant relatives chatting. We're two women, two lesbians, exploring possibility.

The shift in tone flusters me. I cover my confusion by taking our cups and getting up from the sofa. I walk over to the wet bar and refresh our drinks, trying to rebalance my equilibrium, which tilted completely sideways when her last smile hit me. I don't succeed, and now know it's time to worry about how attractive I find this young woman.

Before I can finish pouring the soda, Jaye comes up close and slides her arms around my waist. She presses herself gently against my back.

"You're not my mother," she whispers in my ear.

Oh. My. I put down the can of Diet Cherry Dr. Pepper. Jaye's hold is loose enough for me to turn around and face her, and I feel a shiver of excitement at having those gorgeous eyes inches from my own. My ability to speak abandons me. I swallow hard and find it again. "But I'm your cousin."

She totally brushes that off. "Distant cousin."

"Distant enough?"

Her expression starts to smolder. "My dad's parents are second cousins. Queen Elizabeth and Prince Phillip are second cousins, through both sets of parents, and it's no big deal. Third cousins? Definitely distant enough."

Point made, she leans in, touches her lips to mine, and my world explodes.

Jaye's kiss is soft, a simple, lingering touch. But the sensations radiate through my body like a lightning storm, simultaneously waking up every single nerve ending and shocking me into stillness. I'm pretty sure my lips return the kiss. But the rest of me is more or less paralyzed, in the most amazingly good way.

Jaye stops before I hit total meltdown. I'm not moving, and she notices. "That was okay?" she says, a little uncertainly.

I swallow, head still reeling. My heart rate has tripled. But I manage to stutter "Uh, uh-huh."

Her uncertainty vanishes. "Then I can kiss you again?"

I literally cannot form a coherent reply. "Uh-huh," I squeak out.

This time my nerve endings overrule the shock enough to let me be a more fully involved participant. The next few minutes evolve into a long, slow, deliberate exploration of incredible intensity. I've never gotten enough kisses in my life (does anyone?), and I savor this one like a rare and exquisite sunset. Sunrise. Day at the beach. Night on the mountains. All of the above, all at once.

We don't go crazy, we never quite ratchet things up to wildly passionate, but the heat steadily increases. Jaye and I are completely into each other. I know I've never kissed or been kissed like this, and I don't want to stop anytime soon.

But I'm the one who pulls back, finally. I get a glimpse of Jaye's face, lost in the moment, and it's the most beautiful thing I've seen in my life. Then she opens her eyes and comes back to planet Earth.

"Wow," she says.

"Yeah." My tone is a mere echo of hers.

She leans in again, this time to nuzzle my ear. "I've wanted to do that since we met."

"You have?"

"Mm-hmm. I'd like to keep doing it." She trails a series of soft kisses down my neck, and I fight to keep my knees from buckling, which means I hold Jaye more tightly, which plays right into her plans. Her mouth finds mine again, and its touch is pure fire.

"Can I stay?" she asks.

The words, and the implication, finally wake up something practical in my brain. I feel Jaye's arms around me, feel the firm, muscular lines of her body where it presses against mine. To take this further, to have sex with this woman, would be nirvana. Touching her already is. But, brain says to heart, how much will this mess us up?

Is there something to mess up? "If I say yes, is that it? Is one night all you want?"

Jaye doesn't let me go, but her body tenses, and her up-til-now confident expression falters. I have no idea if the time she takes to answer me is a good or bad thing.

Finally, she asks "What do *you* want?"

"I don't know." She looks crushed. Quickly I elaborate. "I mean, I write romances. I don't live them. I'm not used to this."

Jaye envelops me in a close but gentle hug. I rest my head on her shoulder, let her presence encompass my body, my aura, my entire being. I feel protected, and safe, and the feelings are utterly wonderful. Suddenly I'm fighting back tears. If anyone has ever held me like this before, I don't remember it.

She tightens the hold a little. "I know I surprised you." Understatement of the month. "But I've been thinking about touching you since February."

"You never said anything."

"This is the first time I've had you alone. You can't text a kiss."

I file the line away to use in a book someday, assuming I ever set something in the 21st Century, and gently caress Jaye's cheek. "Thank you. You've made an old recluse's night."

"You're not old," she says promptly.

"But I'm definitely a recluse."

"Because you want to be?"

"Sometimes."

We both pick that as the signal to step back, and we end up with Jaye's hands on my hips, my hands on her shoulders.

"Can I see you tomorrow and try this again?" Jaye asks.

"I leave for Denver in the morning. I have business back home." This is actually true, though now I'm wishing it wasn't because I sense something inside her backing off.

"You're not trying to let me down gently, are you?"

"Are you kidding? I'm giving you the chance to let me down gently."

"Why?"

God, am I fucking this up or what? "Remember what I said about my depression? You need to know that story. I can come back next weekend."

"We're in Portland next week. And Washington the week after."

Ouch. I rest my forehead against Jaye's chest. The comfort of the contact almost negates the disappointment of not seeing her for three weeks. Wait—what am I thinking?

I lift my head, raising my eyes to hers. "We can talk on the phone if you want."

Her expression brightens. "Do you Skype?"

"No. But I think my computer has FaceTime or something."

"Perfect. Are you sure you have to leave town?"

I sense I'm making a mistake again, but stand my ground. "I think we both need to think about this. I want you to be sure you know what you're getting into."

And I, too, want to figure out what I'm getting into.

Chapter Three

Monday morning I'm back in Denver, standing in front of my mirror, post-shower, verifying that I have not turned into a runway model. Eyes, still light brown. Hair, still beauty-salon brunette with the gray roots starting to show (hmm, time to make an appointment with Krystal, my stylist). Face, still fairly wrinkle-free, but some definite age lines around my mouth and eyes. Body, decent shape thanks to a nearly-obsessive swimming routine (I have in fact already hit the pool this morning, up at dawn for an hour's worth of laps), but gravity has taken its toll, and I'm certainly nothing to call Playboy and rave about. I've always considered my features pleasant—and unremarkable. Definitely fifty-two years old. Definitely not a runway model.

What on Earth does Jaye Stokes see in me?

I beat myself up for half of my drive home Sunday: I should have stayed, I should have slept with Jaye, I should have stayed, I should have slept with Jaye, etc., etc., ad nauseam. Those kisses on Saturday night were amazing, but we'd parted awkwardly and I felt like it was my fault.

Jaye, though, said all the right things to make me feel better when I called her Sunday evening. She insisted I let her know when I arrived home safely, and I obeyed. She understood she'd rushed a little. She wanted to talk to me every day. She wanted to know my story. And she wants more than a one-night stand.

And by the gods, I think, as I dry my hair and get dressed, I want more, too. A sweet, intelligent, sexy curveball has been thrown into the carefully constructed compromise of my life, and I don't know whether to succumb to delicious temptation, or duck out of the batter's box.

Surely this can't come to anything. Maybe Jaye is simply satisfying a curiosity she's yet to articulate, something quickly answered and left behind. After all, there's the age difference, my hermit tendencies, the fact we live in different states. I can probably hope, at best, for a lovely spring-to-autumn affair, something I'll treasure and from which I may get a few immortal lines.

I roll my eyes at this thought and smirk at my reflection in the mirror. "Yeah. Right," I say out loud.

My ringtone of the month is Kelly Clarkson singing about getting stronger, and it sounds loud and clear as my phone goes off. I consider there are no coincidences, check the Caller ID, and feel mild disappointment that it's not Jaye.

"Toni."

"Rachel." Toni, like me, is Texan. Like a lot of Texans, she does not waste words. "Please tell me you have yet again revised your Wikipedia page?"

The Fyrequeene's Wikipedia entry is a running joke. Literally. Toni had someone at her company make up an article with the usual Born There, Lives Here, Did This, Did That, and now Writes Books, etc. Dull. Also, far too revealing since it mentions my real name. I read the article once and immediately decided to see if it was true that anyone could revise a Wikipedia page (it is). I took my name out and remade my bio into a "raised by this cute family of feral cats" and "lives in a small cabin on a crystal mining claim west of the Moon" sort of thing. The page now accurately lists my writing credits. Everything else is fantasy. Toni is not amused, but there's nothing she can do because each time she has the entry "fixed," I change it again.

Not helping Wikipedia's credibility, I know. But life's too short to pass up a chance to maintain my privacy and have fun at my own expense.

"I did some work on it last night, yes," I tell her. I'd been too restless to sleep after the long drive and my spirits-lifting phone call with Jaye.

Toni quotes: " 'Shadow Woman for the NWSL'?"

"It's a soccer thing."

"Are you saying you finally slept with Nickerson?"

"You know me better than that."

"Sadly, yes. Change your mind about the book's ending yet?"

"Maybe."

As a rule, lesbian publishers want happy endings. My latest effort centers around the Triangle Fire of 1911, which killed eighty-three people, mostly young immigrant women (early Twentieth Century disasters for four hundred dollars, Alex!). The first unhappy ending I've ever written in my life kills off the lovers. Toni is not pleased, and we've been arguing over me changing it since January.

"You yourself said you write books because—wait. What?"

"I said maybe. I'm thinking about rewriting it."

"Are you serious?"

"Yes. I could even be working right now except I'm talking to you."

A suspicious puzzlement comes wafting over the cell signal. "Are you sure you didn't sleep with Nickerson?"

"Positive. In fact, I turned down the chance to have mad passionate sex with a bright and sexy soccer player *not* named Nickerson."

Silence. I press my ear to the phone, hoping not to hear the sound of a fainting body hitting a floor. But Toni is made of stronger stuff.

"What the hell happened in Kansas City this weekend?"

I laugh. "I think I entered an alternate universe."

"Right. You're coming over for dinner tonight, and you're going to explain everything."

"Is Paula cooking?" Paula is Toni's long-time partner. She was my air traffic supervisor for a while and the reason Toni and I met in the first place. She's also a goddess in the kitchen.

"No. She's in San Diego on business."

Bummer. "Then why don't you come over here. I've got spaghetti. But come tomorrow. The sexy soccer player is calling tonight."

"Aren't the painters coming today?"

Oh, yeah. Any minute, as a matter of fact. "Yep."

"I'm not having dinner in a disaster area. My place. Tuesday at seven. I'll have something delivered. Bring wine."

I had not lied to Jaye when I said I needed to be at home today. I was coming to the long-awaited end of several remodeling projects to make the house in Denver my home. I'd had the basement finished, bought some new furniture, replaced the carpet in my loft, and installed a large bay window and window seat there to take advantage of its view of the mountains. New paint, inside and out, was the last step, and this job had been scheduled two months ago with a woman-owned company of fabulous reputation. Sexy soccer player or no, I wasn't going to put it off.

The painting crew arrives at ten a.m., right on schedule, and they get right on taping off trim and prepping wall surfaces. I spend the next hour talking to Teri, the company owner, going over the colors and plans we'd discussed previously.

"Should be less than ten days if the weather is good," she tells me. "Most of the work is prep. Painting will be a snap. Have you got a place to stay? We get kind of noisy."

"Bose headphones and the basement," I tell her. The basement has already been painted. "I promise to keep out of your way."

She nods. "We should be painting by tomorrow. We'll do the interior first, which will take a couple of days. You probably don't want to be here then. Paint fumes are powerful. Stay with friends, or treat yourself to a hotel or something."

Hotel? The tiniest spark of an idea flares in my head. "Good idea."

After we're done talking, I watch as she efficiently coordinates with her two workers before she departs for another job. I go down to my basement hideout to work on the revised ending to my book. The day passes quickly. I emerge only for lunch, buying pizza for the crew and myself. When they knock off for the evening, I come up to find an alien terrain of ladders, tarps, covered furniture and edging tape all over the place. It's a mess, but a mess with purpose, and I smile, anticipating the end result.

I nuke the last two slices of pizza for dinner, then go back to the ladder-free, tarp-free comfort of the basement and settle in to call Jaye. She'd sent me an email with detailed instructions on using FaceTime, so I'm able to get her gorgeous face up on my computer almost right away.

"Hi, Jaye."

"Hi, Rachel."

"You look great."

"You look better."

I shake my head to clear the sappiness. "Haven't changed your mind yet?"

"I'm not going to."

We spend a couple of minutes talking about how our days went before Jaye gets serious. "Please tell me about the depression."

I'd planned on doing exactly that, but Jaye getting right to the point still startles me. "You don't waste any time, do you?"

She shrugs. "I'm going to tell you it doesn't matter, so we may as well get it out of the way now."

I zone out for a moment, take a deep breath, and come back to the computer screen. "Have you ever been depressed?"

"Yes," she says immediately.

"Have you ever been depressed for more than a week at a time?"

"Yes."

I believe her, and wonder briefly what *her* story is, but I'm not done yet. "How about for thirty-five years?"

Now she blinks. "I'm only thirty-one."

I nod my head slowly. "I've suffered from depression since I was seventeen. Since before you were born. I don't come with baggage, Jaye. I come with a big fat steamer trunk, and it goes with me everywhere."

Jaye's turn to take a deep breath. "I'm listening."

Okay.

Depression, for some, is a chronic illness. I'm one of those unlucky ones. I can still remember waking up every morning of my junior year in high school, getting out of bed, and feeling misery descend on me like a thick black blanket. I was enveloped in a shroud of darkness and insecurity, filled with shame about my sexuality, guilt that I couldn't "get over" being sad all the time, and battling constant thoughts of suicide. A voice from within this shadow regularly told me I was worthless and hopeless and perverted, so it would be a big favor to everyone if I found a gun and blew myself away.

I didn't grow up in a state or a family where I could talk about this, so I dealt with it alone. Somehow I survived high school and escaped to Lubbock and college where no one knew me, and things eased up. On the surface, I did okay. I got a bachelor's degree, earned and held a responsible job, even ventured out to a few gay bars once I moved to Colorado. I was functioning, I was fooling people, but even at my best the darkness hovered over everything I did.

I kept hoping to find a lover, a woman who could help me banish the hell I was living in, but of course, I didn't. Either my own social ineptness or the depression managed to sabotage every attempt I made at building my sexual encounters beyond brief affairs. By my mid-thirties, the misery was so awful I was thinking about suicide all the time, though I never actually attempted it. Still, the darkness combined with the stresses of being an air traffic controller finally became too much, and something inside of me snapped. The resulting nervous breakdown cost me a year of my life and very nearly my job. But it also forced me into therapy, forced me to find better ways to cope.

When I came out the other side I was eating better, exercising more (this is where swimming became an essential part of my existence), sold on the benefits of having a therapist, and recovered enough to work again. But the depression, while better controlled, wasn't gone, and I knew it never would be. I could still hear that shadowy voice telling me I was worthless, so I made a conscious decision to stay single. Inflicting this pain on anyone else didn't feel fair.

"After the breakdown," I say in conclusion, "I managed to make an okay life for myself. I got serious about my writing and found it a good counterbalance to the depression. If I could bring characters together and have them fall in love, find happiness in their lives, then what my own life lacked became easier to deal with."

I shut up, finally, and watch Jaye's image. The FaceTime connection is almost HD quality, which is great eye-candy wise but also shows me her very serious, sober expression. Well, I think silently, better to know now if she's going to run. I won't blame her one tiny little bit, and maybe we can stay friends.

"Nobody ever came along to challenge your solitude?"

"Not after my breakdown. I never gave anyone a chance."

"Until now."

"Until now, maybe. You kinda snuck in under my radar."

"Will you give me the chance to stay there?" Jaye asks. "Or do you really want to be single?"

"I never wanted to be single."

"Good," she says, her expression still dead serious. "Because I'm going to do my best to be there for you."

I give Jaye's image a wistful grin. "I won't make it easy."

"I'm up to the challenge." Jaye's face relaxes, transforms into its own beautiful smile. "Bob Marley said once that 'if she's worth it, she won't be easy.' You're worth it, Rachel. Trust me."

Tuesday morning I'm down in the basement as the painters do their work, and I'm toying with a radical idea. Jaye was so sincere last night, and it resonated with me so deeply, I don't want to wait almost two weeks to see her. What if I surprise her in Portland? Traveling there will get me out of the house for the actual painting part of this project and show her my sincerity about changing my solitary ways. I hope.

I spend the next hour plotting things out. The team will arrive Friday, one day ahead of Saturday's game, so I will arrive Friday, too. The flight will be pricy, but I can use my frequent stayer points for the hotel (which is also the team hotel for KC this trip, yay) and save some money there. Also, Portland's light rail system runs from airport to hotel to stadium and back, so I won't need a car.

Yes, it's possible. I don't pull the trigger, though. Not yet.

After a successful day of writing on my part and painting on the crew's part, I head out for Toni's. She's called and told me to plan on Italian, so after a quick stop at King Soopers I show up on her doorstep with some garlic bread and a very nice chianti.

"You're glowing," she says as I hand her the wine.

"Must be the radon in my basement."

"Rachel."

"That's a writer's crutch. People don't glow."

"Yes, they do. Who is she?"

I know I'm blushing because my cheeks are hot. Maybe I *am* glowing. "I told you. A soccer player."

"And there hasn't been sex yet?"

"No. But I'd lay odds there's going to be."

"And she's how old?"

"Thirty-one."

"And you're how old?"

"Younger than you." Though not by much.

"So is this a mid-life crisis fling?"

"Not for her." Toni rolls her eyes, and I get serious. "We talked about that last night, and no. It's not a fling."

Toni heaves a deep sigh as we get everything on the dinner table and settle in. "Okay. Start from square one."

I tell her about the cemetery, and the soccer camp, and Jaye finding out I was The Fyrequeene. "She's read all my books, she reads my blog. She said she felt a connection with me, the writer, and me, the person." I blush again. Okay, okay. I'm glowing. "We certainly had a connection Saturday night in KC"

"But no sex."

"No. We could have, but I wanted to give her a chance to back out."

"And she didn't?"

I tell Toni what Jaye said last night, over FaceTime. She takes it in. Toni is fully aware of my history with depression, and she's not afraid to cut right to the heart of things.

"What if all she wants is a conquest?"

"Why me? I'm no challenge."

"Maybe she collects celebrities."

"Toni, I'm not even a celebrity in my *own* mind. And haven't you been saying for years I should find a good woman?"

Toni can't deny this, and she knows it. "Yes."

"All my instincts are telling me Jaye's a good woman. Let's give her a chance."

My friend does not look convinced.

Dinner with Toni settles things for me, and Wednesday morning I go online to buy airline tickets, book the hotel room, and get a ticket to the Blues/Thorns soccer game. When this is all done, I sit back and take a deep breath. I've thrown caution to the winds, which, trust me, I never do, and I'm finding it a heady feeling. I hope Jaye will feel the same way.

I fill in the days to Friday with writing and evening talks with Jaye. I hear her voice, I see her on Face Time, but there's still a very unreal quality about the whole situation. Romance, real living breathing romance, doesn't happen to me. My lifelong insecurity rears its persistent, irritating little head, and I keep waiting for the darkness to join up with it and take me down.

But while I wait, I pack a weekend suitcase, print out tickets for the soccer game and airline flight, and get ready to brave the behemoth of Denver International Airport. Crowds again. I shudder and briefly wish I still had my ATC ID badge, which always let me breeze through security.

Thursday night's chat with Jaye is brief, but satisfying. So far, every moment involving her has been satisfying, even when we're talking about nothing much. She does want to know when I'm coming to Kansas City again.

"I'm not sure," I tell her, and it's the absolute truth. So is this: "But I'll see you before you go to Washington."

Friday dawns clear and gorgeous, and my trip to the Rose City, as the Portland chamber of commerce likes to call it, goes smoothly. I arrive at high noon, find the train to the hotel, and my luck holds when they let me check in early. The Blues won't get here until evening. I have a few hours to kill.

I attempt a nap and manage to doze off for about fifteen minutes. Then I try to read the latest Jane Fletcher novel, but I can't concentrate. I should be nervous, or worried, but as my iPhone strikes five o'clock (ha-ha, kidding), I'm not nervous at all. I'm excited and eager. Everything about this caper feels right.

I had told Jaye to call after she was free from team duties. "So we can talk for a while." I'm hoping it won't be too late, and we'll have the chance to actually see each other tonight. As long as she likes my surprise. The magic hour finally arrives a little after seven, and my stomach does a flip flop when I hear Jaye's voice.

"Hey, Rachel."

"Hi. No FaceTime?"

"Nah. I'm in the room with Nickory, and I didn't want to be making goofy faces while she's here."

"Goofy faces?"

"Yeah. Goofy 'I miss you' faces."

I try to keep my voice nonchalant. "I miss you, too."

"You're all I can think about."

"You still remember how to kick a soccer ball, I hope?"

She laughs. "That's like riding a bicycle. I'll always know how to play soccer." Jaye pauses, then says, "I wish you could be here at the game."

Here we go. "Yeah? And if I was?"

"I'd score a goal for you."

"On demand?"

Jaye's voice drops half an octave. "Wait until you see what I can do on demand."

My stomach does a three and a half somersault reverse inward twist. "I thought you said Nickerson was there."

"She is. She's rolling her eyes."

Lo, the perfect opening. I pop the lid on the jack-in-the-box. "Okay. Why don't you get away from her for a while?"

"Where would I go, the bathroom?"

"How about room 1722?"

"What?"

I smile and cross my fingers. "I said, how about room 1722?"

A solid five-second silence ensues, which doesn't seem like much unless you're hanging in suspense. Then Jaye says in a hushed voice, "Oh, my God" and hangs up.

I put the phone down and wait. Five seconds is child's play compared to the minute or so that passes before I hear a tentative knock. I get up, open the door, and there Jaye stands, the expression on her face encompassing surprise, wonder, and delight—with a little bit of irritation, for spice.

"Hi," I say far more casually than I thought I could. "Come on in."

She doesn't move. "You're really here."

"I really am. I hope it's okay."

Suddenly I'm wrapped up in a hug worthy of Hercules. I kick the door closed, hug Jaye right back, and get the same sense of comfort, trust and rightness I got last Saturday. It feels fantastic. Then we kiss, long and slow and tender. That feels fantastic, too.

Jaye comes up for air first and glances around. "This room is smaller than your other one," she says with a wicked grin. "We're going to have to use the bed."

Before I can do or say anything, Jaye tumbles us onto the mattress. She kisses me again, with enthusiasm, and we make out for a few minutes before I bring her back to Earth.

"You have a soccer game to play tomorrow, remember? Aren't you supposed to save your energy?"

She gives me a smirk, then rolls over onto her back, pulling me with her. She settles into place with her arms around me and goes perfectly still.

"Fine," she says. "I'll just lie here."

"Works for me." I snuggle in.

When I was younger I would have jumped (literally) at the chance to ravish a beautiful woman who has thrown me into bed, but now, knowing how rare and precious moments like this are, I am content to hold her close, feel her arms around me, feel my head on her shoulder, feel the connection of our bodies. I'm still turned on from the kisses, for sure, but despite the erotic charge, I'm not driven to rush down the path to orgasm.

We'll get there, have no fear. But not quite yet.

Jaye, for whatever reason, plays along. The tension in her body slowly eases. She relaxes into the bed, and into me, and I hope she feels as comfortable and unstressed as I do.

"This is nice," she says, many minutes later. Her voice sounds slightly surprised.

"This is wonderful."

"You're not going to let me stay, are you."

"Don't you have a curfew?"

"Nickory would cover for me."

With some reluctance I shift so I can lift my head and gaze into her eyes. "If we wait, we'll have the whole night tomorrow, right?" I give her a quick, soft kiss. "I want the whole night, without any worries about games, or curfews, or schedules."

"It's not because you still have doubts?"

I lay my head back down on her chest. "Of course, I have doubts."

Suddenly Jaye's body tenses again, and she starts to sit up. This means I have to move, too, and after a couple of awkward maneuvers and rearranging of pillows we are both upright, seated on the bed and mostly facing each other.

"Here's the thing," Jaye says. "I'm not playing you, Rachel. I don't lie, and I don't jump into bed with the nearest warm body. You've completely changed my life, and I want to completely change yours. Okay?"

The sincerity in her voice resonates through me like a sweet symphony. But I've not lived a life where I get this lucky.

"Okay," I say, but she hears my uncertainty and frowns.

"Tell me your doubts. Right now. I'll shoot them down, and we'll go from there."

Fair enough. "I truly have been single all of my life."

"Because you wanted to be?"

"Gods, no."

"Then I don't care."

"Even knowing the worst?"

"I want to know the best, too, and I'm sure the best is way, way better than any stupid depression."

Goal to the lower left corner of the net. 1-0, Jaye Stokes.

I try again. "I'm twenty years older than you are."

"I don't care."

"We hardly know each other."

"Isn't that why people get involved? To know each other?"

Good point. I realize I'm acting like a putz. "Goddess, you're too perfect."

"And you're too scared."

Penalty kick goal past a diving goalkeeper. 2-0, Jaye Stokes.

"Yes," I admit. "Terrified."

"Why?"

I take a deep breath. "Have you ever wanted something too much?"

"Yeah." A shadow crosses her face. "I didn't get it."

"I bet it hurt."

"Yes, it did." She caresses my cheek with her palm. "But I tried my hardest. I didn't give up before I got started."

The long kick from downfield rockets in under the crossbar. 3-0. Stokes caps the match with a hat trick.

"Next?" She says, ready for more.

"You win," I say quietly, and she slides forward to take me in her arms. We end up lying down again, my head on her chest, returning to comfortable.

"You win, too, Rachel."

Yes, if I can quell the terror and insecurity and have a little faith. "It won't be easy. I have no clue how to be with somebody."

"I'm not exactly an expert, either. We'll manage. You came up here because you want this, right?"

So true. "Have I really changed your life? I mean, we still hardly know each other."

"In the cemetery, when I saw you for the first time, I felt it. Something slid into place, like the last piece of a jigsaw puzzle."

Wow. How wonderful it must be to have such complete certainty. And why, if Jaye is right, don't I feel it? I want her, am thrilled with her attraction to me, but if she's the one I've always hoped for, why am I not as sure as she is?

Because it's too good to be true, my ever-pessimistic inner self tells me. Jaye shifts position, pulling me even closer to her. She wraps her arms around me. Strong arms that envelop my soul and calm my fears. Can I dare to depend on them staying there?

"You want to be sure?" she asks, like she's been reading my mind.

"Yes. But there's no way to be sure."

"I'll score a goal for you." Her lips touch my skin, a soft caress. "Then you'll be sure."

Portland is the one-hundred-carat diamond of the NWSL. There are at least fifteen thousand people in the stands for this Saturday evening contest. The fans know their soccer, they love their team, and they show their love with loud raucous cheers and singing, a veritable riot of enthusiasm.

The big crowd is distinctly unsettling to me, but I'm handling it okay because I have other things on my mind. Jaye held me last night until she had to make curfew, fortifying me against anxiety and depression. Tonight, if all goes well, she won't leave me until we have to get to the airport Sunday morning. Tonight, if all goes well, she will indeed change my life. I can only hope there will be something equally meaningful for her.

My seat is a little more than halfway up in the stands, right at midfield. I'm wearing a KC scarf, so my loyalties are obvious, but the Thorns' fans are still friendly, even after the game starts.

Websites devoted to women's soccer have rated Kansas City and Portland as the two best teams in the league this year. Tonight they prove it, feeding off the energy in the stadium and giving the crowd a crackerjack match. Though I never played soccer, I've watched enough that I see the flow and pace of the game. I usually figure out what a team is trying to do strategy-wise, and I can tell the Olympians from the seasoned pros from the fresh-out-of-college and still learning.

Tonight Jaye is above them all. KC's coach has put her up front and in the middle, more pivotal to the offensive efforts, and the position fits her like a glove. She glides across the pitch, making and taking passes to get her team close to the goal, setting up scoring chances for the wings and the forward. She plays as if seeing everything from a bird's eye view, and it's a beautiful thing.

I remember what she told me about being "an eighth of a step too slow," and shake my head. Other than Kirstie Longstreet, the Blues' striker, Jaye is easily the fastest player on the field, and she uses her speed to full advantage.

It's not her fault they don't score, and not her fault Portland gets an early goal when Sandra Conway, Canada's version of Wendy Allerton, beats Nickerson with a perfect shot from ten yards out. The crowd goes wild, but KC fights hard, hangs in there, and midway through the second half, Jaye feeds a short pass to Longstreet, who immediately kicks it back to a sprinting Jaye. The move is known as a give-and-go, and it fools two defenders, leaving Jaye with only the ball and grass between her and the goalkeeper. Jaye shoots, putting the ball in the net past the diving goalie to level things 1-1.

I jump up shouting, waving my scarf like mad as the crowd goes quiet. Jaye accepts the hugs of her teammates before looking up and throwing a quick salute in my direction. Even from here, I see her huge, radiant smile.

I sit slowly as the action resumes, and suddenly it hits me. *"I'll score a goal for you."*

Scoring is difficult in soccer. One can't do it on demand, particularly at this level, where even the best players, like Allerton and Conway, average less than a goal a game. But last night Jaye made a promise, and tonight she delivered, beating the odds for her team. And for me.

The last of my anxiety flees, inundated by the rush of happiness surging through my veins. We have something, Jaye and me. We have something special.

The game ends tied at one, an appropriate result for the two best teams in the league. If the season plays out as expected, the Blues and Thorns will eventually battle to determine a winner, but that's months in the future. My right now, Jaye's right now, is only minutes away.

I let the crowd thin out and give the players time to work the autograph line before making my way down to the field. I find the dressing room area, and when Jaye finally emerges, she spots me right away. I watch her approach, take in the happiness on her face and the piercing shine of her eyes as they meet mine—and I know I'm going to have the night of my life.

"The team's doing dinner, and you're coming with us," she insists, taking me by the hand. "I want to be with you for the rest of the night."

Portland. Saturday night. Any restaurant will certainly be noisy and crowded. I open my mouth to make my automatic objection to this idea, but Jaye kisses me in front of her teammates, the fans in the stadium, and all the stars above. Another rush of happiness washes my doubts away. For her, now, I will do anything.

Once we're seated at the restaurant, I sit quietly next to Jaye. I'm introduced as a "friend," but everyone who saw the kiss knows what's up. Still, they think it's cool I've come all the way from Colorado to see Jaye, and my KC scarf means I do support the team. They ignore me quickly in favor of giving Jaye her props and teasing Nickerson for giving up a goal. I'm surprised the warrior queen lets them get away with it.

Jaye holds her own in the banter department, but it's soon clear, to me at least, that she's got things other than soccer on her mind. Over the appetizers our eyes lock, and for a moment we are the only two people in the galaxy. I casually brush my hair back, making sure it's not caught fire.

Across the table Nickerson watches us with a stony expression. She knows what's going on, and apparently she's not happy about it. I suppose I can understand her point of view. She doesn't know me from Eve, and here's her best friend diving in head first. Perhaps she tried to get Jaye to slow things down. If so, the effort failed. Jaye wants me. Wants us. This thought warms my heart, and makes it easy to ignore Nickerson's glare.

Jaye and I both order salads for dinner as they don't take a lot of time to eat. She sets a speed record for consuming lettuce and salmon. I make it through about half of my Greek vegetarian when I feel a hand run along my thigh.

"We're skipping dessert," Jaye informs me. Her eyes smolder, and her skin is flushed, as if hiding an inner fire.

"No," I counter, giving her the flames right back, "We're having dessert somewhere else."

Definitely the right thing to say. Jaye takes my hand, interlocks our fingers, and stands up. "Let's go."

I stop her long enough to pull out my wallet and hand some money to Kirstie Longstreet. "Please give the waitress the change."

"In a hurry?" She asks with a knowing smile and a killer Georgia twang.

"Train to catch," Jaye says, and pulls me gently out of the restaurant. I imagine—I hope—wolf whistles coming from behind us as we leave.

We do have a train to catch—the light rail will take us right back to the hotel. As we wait at the stop, Jaye gives me a sexy grin. "Did you like the goal?"

"I can't believe you did it. You were amazing out there tonight."

Jaye leans up close and puts her lips to my ear. "I plan to be even more amazing when we get back to your room."

I mentally cross my fingers and think, *"So do I."*

By the time we reach the hotel I'm energized, wild with anticipation, and utterly turned on. As we enter the elevator I'm tempted to steal a kiss, but we aren't alone, so I squeeze Jaye's hand and catch her eye. Her fingers tremble as they interlock with mine. She smiles at me, and the air hums with tension.

She wants this, too.

The elevator finally opens to the seventeenth floor. We step out into the hall. As the elevator doors close, Jaye takes me in her arms and gives me a kiss full of pent-up energy. My legs threaten to give out for a second. I rally to keep me standing, and she lets me kiss her back with equal intensity.

"I couldn't wait," she says when we at last break off the kiss.

"Come on," I say, fighting off the urge to run full speed to the room.

I let Jaye enter first, then follow her in and slam the door shut. Even as I throw the deadbolt on the door, she is turning me around, sliding her hands in my hair, pulling my face to hers. I've always thought moving across a room while being lip-locked to someone else was romance fantasy stuff, but we do it, working our way to the bed in a tangle of arms and feet and what has to be gracefulness, since we neither stumble nor fall nor bump into anything—

—until we tumble onto the mattress as one, still kissing, lips and tongues competing to see who can learn each other's face first. Eventually we expand the contest. Jaye pulls my shirt loose from my jeans. I get my hands under the tail of her shirt to touch the skin of her back, all the way up to her neck, then all the way down to the band of her pants, and below. Jaye moans as I cup her ass. She returns the favor by getting my zipper down and her own hands inside my clothing.

Jeans, though, are harder to work under than sweats, and this necessitates a frustrating pause in the action. No matter how writers and movie directors make it seem, clothes don't magically melt away. Jaye sits us up, pulls me onto her lap, and grips the fabric of my top in both hands.

"Wait!" I say. "I like this shirt."

She stops moving and gives me a sheepish grin—yes, she was indeed about to rip the buttons off. After a deep breath, she gives me yet another searing kiss, and undoes my shirt buttons one . . . by one . . . by one . . .

by one . . . slowly, surely, carefully. She manages this while keeping our lips in contact the whole time. Job complete, Jaye pulls back, slides the shirt off my shoulders with exaggerated care, and tosses it across the room.

"Better?" she asks.

"Much. Your turn."

Jaye's shirt is a pullover. I get it over her head easily and fling it to keep mine company.

She's not wearing a bra. I'm struck still at my first view of her breasts. They are small, perfectly formed, the pink nipples already pert with arousal. I brush my thumb against one, and Jaye closes her eyes and gasps. I like that and get my other thumb in on the act. She lets me explore her until both nipples are rock-hard. I'm about to kiss the delicious, smooth flesh of her when she stops me.

"No fair," she says. "I want to play, too."

Jaye reaches around to undo the hooks of my bra. In a second my last piece of protection is gone, and all my aged glory is there for her to see. I know I'm in good shape for my age. But gravity has also taken its inevitable toll. Will the plain-sight evidence of my older years wake her up and send her running?

Jaye takes her time staring at my chest, then cups one of my breasts in her hand and slowly massages my nipple with her tongue. The sensation is a jolt of lightning, enough so that I very nearly come, right then and there.

She seems to sense this and backs off. "Lie down now." I slide off her legs to comply and she shifts position, sets herself up to get the rest of my clothes off.

"You, too," I say, reaching for her pants, but she takes my arms and puts them above my head.

"In a minute."

Jaye hovers above me, pauses for a moment. Our breasts are almost touching, her gray eyes are shaded now with dark smoke. I've written plenty about lovers' eyes "darkening with desire," but this is the first time I've ever seen it in person.

"We've found each other, Rachel," she whispers, and kisses me again, hard, pulling all the passion in the room into one little spot of contact. Whatever I have left of coherent thought shatters and blows away.

We don't so much fall asleep as end up unconscious from our pleasures and exertions. When I come to again, it's dark outside and in (when did we turn the lights off?). Jaye's body half covers mine, her head rests on my shoulder. Softly, oh so softly, I brush my fingers along her back, a gentle touch of appreciation and wonder.

"I like that," comes a murmur against my collarbone.

"Good. I'll keep doing it."

The murmur morphs into a laugh. "You're not tired?"

"I can sleep when I'm alone again in Denver. This is special."

Jaye shifts a little, as if settling deeper into me. My hand keeps moving, giving her the barest touch of my fingertips to her skin, like I'm trying to leave a thin layer of air between us. Her breath quickens.

"That's amazing."

"I'm glad." I laugh softly. "There's something so magical about the feel of a woman's skin, yes?"

I get no vocal answer to this. Instead Jaye takes her free hand and starts her own slow exploration, her fingers making soft circles as they caress my hip, my thigh, then come up to the edge of my breast. Now it's my breath quickening, and it's all I can do to keep touching her like she's touching me. Something will have to give soon.

"God," I mutter breathlessly, "this is incredible."

Jaye raises herself up, making lovely use of all her athletic strength to suspend herself slightly above me. I do my fingertip thing on her shoulders, tracing the firm line of muscle all the way down her biceps, then over to her breasts. She lowers her head, touches her lips to mine, and blows my conscious mind to smithereens.

We kiss for a long time, and somewhere amidst this heaven Jaye slips to the side, shifting enough to get her left leg in between my thighs. I feel her wetness against my skin, and I'm sure she feels mine. As she begins a slow thrust against me, I sense we are crossing the line between hot sex and making love. Awareness of the difference sends a shiver through me, a shiver of delight, anticipation—and the faintest, guess-who's-still-here touch of apprehension, too.

But Jaye kisses one of my nipples, which shoots down the apprehension, lets the delight take over.

If depression insists upon visiting, it can wait until I'm alone again in Denver.

Chapter Four

Fyrequeene's Blog: May 3

"Playlist"

On a flight home from magical Portland I listen to Pandora and hear a new song. I like it, get caught up in it, wonder who the artist is and if I can find it later. I love that music can do this, take you to another place and mood and completely away from where you are, especially when "where you are" is a crowded metal tube 35,000 feet off the ground.

But when the song ends, a new one begins, shifts me away from the mood and the place I was in, shifts me before I was ready to leave.

So much of life is like that, I realize. We talk about "being in the moment," then make sure our moments run together so we can't stay in them at all. Adding in noise, chatter, appointments, and video streams dilutes the moments even more, so their true nature is lost.

With this in mind, I switch from Pandora to iTunes and bring up an old playlist of mine, try to have a little more control over this particular slice of place and time.

"Queer Sensibilities" is a mélange of songs whose subject should be obvious. I put it together a long time ago (the original compilation was a cassette tape) when I wanted a background to contemplate sexuality, to lose myself in the romance of two women kissing, touching, exploring each other. When I wanted to imagine such things for myself, let it light me up and bring me to life like nothing else. Like literally nothing else.

I always had to imagine. Love and intimate connection could never be real for me. Back then I thought of my lesbianism as a gauntlet thrown in the face of the world, a challenge to everyone who would condemn me for my desires, for my love of women.

And make no mistake, I love women. I wanted to shout it from the rooftops. I wanted it to be taken as a matter of course. But I also wanted to be different, wanted to feel like I was privy to something rare and wonderful, something most of the world didn't get. Because this love is so special to me.

I was angry then, and it may well have affected what chances I had for actual romance. I couldn't balance my incredible attraction for women with the fury that much of the world did not accept it. I couldn't simply love and flaunt it in conservative faces because I was too afraid those conservative faces would kill me. And so I hid, I kept myself apart, I stayed alone.

A lot of the songs on the playlist reflect this: "Angels Never Call" by Til Tuesday; "Tony" by Patty Griffin; Bronski Beat's "Smalltown Boy."

But my anger has faded now, with age and therapy, and thanks to the beauty of iTunes, I've added songs to the list to remind me how the specialness of who I love, who I desire, burns as strong as ever.

"Crimson and Clover" by Joan Jett; "Harmony" by Heather Peace; "Damn I Wish I Was Your Lover" by Sophie B. Hawkins; "Hang Out in Your Heart" by Chely Wright.

To name a few.

As the metal tube shoots through the sky, I listen to each song with a long pause in between tracks. I savor the thoughts and feelings each recalls, good and bad, and ultimately appreciate where I am now, even reveling in the strength of the desire I hope never goes away.

I am a lesbian. It is not the entirety of me. But it may be the biggest component part.

Monday morning, 6:06 a.m., my eyes pop open. I'm back home in Denver. For most of my adult life getting me up voluntarily before nine a.m. took an act of military planning, like with D-Day. Since my late forties and the joys of pre/peri/post-menopause, however, I come alert, like clockwork, between six and seven a.m. every day. The adjustment period for me, a confirmed night owl, was long and challenging.

But I learned to embrace mornings, and today I wake up raring to go. Time to swim, yay. But when I try to get out of bed, every bone in my body creaks, and every muscle screams in protest.

At first I'm mystified, wondering if I've got the flu or light-speed-onset arthritis. Then my brain engages. Wow. Now I know why writers so seldom have fifty-two-year-old women as romantic leads.

"We can have the hot sex," I say out loud, "but we can't move for days afterwards." This strikes me funny, and soon I'm laughing so hard I lose the seated position I'd struggled to and fall right back onto the mattress, everything creaking as I go down.

I've laughed a lot in the past twenty-four hours. Jaye and I woke up with smiles on Sunday morning, laughed our way through first-morning pillow talk, into some fantastic morning sex (no laughing there, just more amazing sensual connection), and laughed in panic as we barely got dressed in time to catch our respective flights.

This morning's amusement fades as I remember one particular moment:

I had come out of the shower and Jaye greeted me with a long-stemmed rose.

"I took a chance," she said. "Went to the lobby and the gift shop was open." She brushed the petals down my cheek, and she was glowing, absolutely radiant. I got lost in the soft sensation of the rose and the beauty of Jaye, my lover (lover!), standing before me.

Oh, please don't come to your senses anytime soon, I thought, managing to swallow the words in my throat. "Thank you," I said instead, with as much feeling as I could put into it. "Thank you for last night."

Her smile rivaled the early morning sun shining through the window. "You're going to let me do this again, right?"

"Buy me roses? Sure." I gave Jaye a wink, then took her in my arms. "And the sex? We can do that again, too."

"Good." Jaye's eyes drew me right in, and only the threat of exorbitant airline change fees ended the passionate kiss that followed.

We did get to the airport on time, barely. I spent the flight home listening to music, writing up a new blog entry on my laptop, and eagerly, almost painfully, anticipating the next time I could see Jaye.

Now, sitting in my bedroom on a bright Monday morning, I remember the feeling I'd had after her game last week, the leak springing through the dam. Something long repressed, long dammed, has been freed. Emotions I didn't know I had gush forth from me. I have given myself to a woman completely. I'm not the same person I was two days ago.

"We've found each other, Rachel."

Could this be true?

I rise, get my swimsuit on, and head out to the pool. I do a series of long, slow freestyle laps, stretching my body out in the buoyancy of the water. The smooth motions soothe my muscles. I hardly creak at all when I'm done. In the afternoon, on FaceTime from my basement, I relate the story of my oh-so-slow exit from bed and how I still find it funny.

"It's not because you're old," Jaye says, her lips twitching with amusement.

"Hey, we both know—"

"Rachel, I couldn't get out of bed either." Her face goes pink. "I found out there are some muscles you don't use to play soccer. But I used them Saturday night."

"You're blushing!"

The pink suffuses with pleasure. "I'm so glad you came to Portland."

"Me, too."

"Any chance I'll see you in Washington?"

"Nope. I don't have enough money in the budget. But Kansas City, as soon as the painters finish."

On cue, the sound of a ladder being moved across the room clatters above me.

"You could come stay in KC," she says, "and get away from the noise."

There's a loud *clunk!* as something lands hard on the floor. Not heavy enough to be a body. I hope it wasn't an open can of paint.

I roll my eyes up at the ceiling. "I think I need to be here to make sure the house survives."

The line isn't that funny, but soon we're both laughing fit to save the world. Laughing with joy.

"Why do you always call me?" Jaye asks on Thursday. We're talking every day and have yet to run out of things to say.

"As opposed to beaming over to Kansas City and meeting you in person?"

"No, silly. As opposed to texting. I send you a text, and you call me back. Why?"

"I don't text."

"Why not?"

I shrug, shake my head. "It's too easy to send five words to somebody and think you've communicated with them. I want to do better with you. Call me. Leave a voice mail. I'd rather hear your voice than read a text any day."

"I don't see why you're so stubborn," Jaye says, and honestly, coming from someone who grew up in the texting generation, she's being reasonable.

"We're going to have one chance to do this right. 'Right' is not tapping out letters on a phone. 'Right' is talking to you as often as I can. And if it means I don't hear from you every hour, then fine. That will make hearing from you all the sweeter."

I've discovered a slightly ghostly quality to my iPhone's FaceTime. The voice and the image don't quite sync, and the movements have a half-second delay. When one is absolutely still, though, and quiet, it conveys detail very well.

Jaye is still right now, and quiet. I take in those captivating gray eyes, the planes of her cheekbones, what I'm coming to see as the perfection of her face. She, meanwhile, is coming right to the heart of something.

"You're a writer," she says. "Texting should be right up your alley."

I beg to differ. "Texting is like popcorn for dinner instead of a good healthy meal. It's temporary and unsatisfying."

"I think you had a bad texting experience and are afraid to admit it."

The perception shuts me up. I forget about FaceTime for a second, forget Jaye can see me grimacing in acknowledgment. Forget right up until she laughs.

"Please say you don't play poker."

"I don't."

"Good. Because you'd be broke." Jaye sobers up again. "What happened?"

My turn to go still, while I order my thoughts. "A text is instantaneous. It goes out, it gets there. And one comes to expect an instantaneous reply. I always replied right away to texts, or at least as soon as I saw them. I was friends with someone who didn't, and I let it drive me nuts. Unreasonably so. I don't want it to happen again. Especially with you."

"This 'someone' was only a friend?"

"Yes. But it's a long, complicated story."

I can tell Jaye is curious, but she lets it go. For now. "Voicemail works the same way," she says.

"No. Not the same. Voicemail implies whoever you're calling is too busy to talk. So you leave a message and you're okay waiting. Texting, you expect a reply."

Jaye frowns. "I suppose."

"Hey—consider it one of my charming little quirks."

"You'll tell me if I ask, won't you—what happened with this friend?"

"Yeah. But I'd rather tell you in person."

The frown disappears. "You know, I like that you want to do so much in person."

"Yes . . . you may have created a monster."

"Come to Kansas City as soon as you can."

Late Friday evening, after her team has arrived in Washington, I call to wish Jaye luck for the game. I forget to use the FaceTime app, but before I can cancel and try again, there's a click like someone's answered. I wait for Jaye's greeting, but get only silence.

"Jaye? You there?"

A voice, definitely not Jaye's, says "Just a minute."

I hear murmurs as the phone changes hands, followed by the pleasing tones of my lover's voice. "Hi, Rachel."

"Hey. Who was that?"

"Nickory. She was closer to the phone than me."

A tiny little alarm goes off in the back of my mind. "Closer to your phone."

"Yeah. You know how hotel rooms are."

I suppose. I turn the little alarm off with a joke. "I guess we're not on for phone sex then?"

There's a short pause. "Maybe later, after she's asleep?"

"She's listening, isn't she?"

"Of course!"

We both laugh, Jaye more comfortably than I. The rest of our conversation is full of affection and "I miss you's," plus my update on the painting situation, and it almost makes me forget the little incident with Nickory. Almost.

The Blues' match against Washington goes well. I connect computer to TV and watch the live stream on a big screen, jumping up and down when Jaye scores her second goal of the season. She also gets an assist on a subsequent goal, while Nickory shuts out the home side. KC wins 2-0. The team is firing on all cylinders, which bodes well for the rest of the season.

I'm happy for Jaye and the Blues and even happier to go see the next game live and in person.

Saturday morning at three a.m. I'm on the road. The painters are at last done, the house is finished and fabulous, the furniture is back in place, and my irritation at the minor glitches along the way is gone. I have a cooler full of snacks and Diet Cherry Dr. Pepper, a trunk full of luggage, and a heart full of motivation. I had asked Jaye if she thought it was okay for me to stay a few days, and she enthusiastically endorsed the idea.

"You can stay with us," she says, referring to her, Nickerson and Bree Thompson.

"Not the first night, though. I want you all to myself."

My face breaks into a smile as I remember her acknowledging the wisdom of this idea. I take full advantage of a near empty freeway and generous speed limit to bring the plan closer to fruition, arriving at the Hampton Inn in plenty of time to check in and drive to the stadium for the Blues' afternoon game.

I watch the team warming up as I head toward my seat, my eyes zooming right to number 22. I don't have to search, I just know where she is. Jaye is doing passing drills with a couple of teammates, and when she sees me, she kicks the ball deliberately in my direction, then takes off after it, watching me all the way. As she gets closer, a line of energy, of connection, streaks out and reels us toward each other.

I stand against the railing, riveted, as Jaye approaches. I can't take my eyes off of her.

"Hi, Rachel," she says, the most seductive syllables I've ever heard.

"Hi."

Our smiles outshine the sun. Jaye comes up to the railing, and I see she's planning to climb over, but a coach shouts at her, so she gives me a quick wave, picks up the ball, and runs off, taking a piece of my heart with her. My legs are shaking.

It's official. I've got it bad.

Today's opponent is Chicago, the weakest team in the league. Despite the NSWL's relative parity, someone has to be last, and this year it's the Red Stars. KC wins easily, 5-0. Jaye gets two assists, yet another goal, and now has a three-game scoring streak. I cheer for all this, of course, but I also listen to the fans talk around me during the game, and it's clear they think Jaye is doing something special.

"What's the difference?" I ask her after all the autographs are signed and pictures taken. "People say you're playing better than you ever have."

Jaye and I are headed back to my car hand in hand. I feel the energy between us, but I'm also aware of all the other people around. Portland is one thing, Kansas City and the conservative Midwest is another. I scan for disapproving stares.

Jaye is oblivious. "I'm playing a new position this year. In seasons past I played more on the defensive side, but the coach moved me up to attacking midfield after we traded a player. Attacking mid means exactly that—I have more chances to score or to help our forward score. It's been fun."

"I can tell. You were on fire out there tonight."

We're at the car now, and Jaye comes up close and wraps me in a hug. "It's also because of you," she says.

I like hearing her praise, but still shake my head. "I can't take credit for your brilliance."

"But I can give it to you," she murmurs in my ear. "There's an electricity in my body, like I'm stronger and faster and—better."

The touch of her, the feel of her breath against my skin, shoots a fair amount of electricity through me, too. Our eyes meet, and I see Jaye's go dark. She's going to kiss me right here and now, in broad daylight at a public parking lot.

"The world is watching," I say softly.

"Good. Then they'll know you're mine."

Before our lips meet, the toot of a car horn startles us both. We turn toward the sound and see Bree behind the wheel of a Volkswagen Bug, a big grin on her face. Nickory is sitting next to her, not smiling at all.

"Get a room, you guys!" Bree calls.

"We have one already!" Jaye laughs.

"But you can't go there yet," Bree says. "We're doing dinner, remember?"

Bree has insisted on a cookout this evening. Jaye and I, not thinking clearly, agreed. I wish now we had pushed the social time to Sunday.

Jaye drops her forehead to mine. "We could pretend she's not there."

"No, no. It'll be all right. Come on." I walk to the car, more or less dragging Jaye along with me.

"Jaye knows the way, right?" I ask Bree jokingly, knowing they share a place in Overland Park.

"Here." Bree hands me a piece of paper. "Put the address in your GPS so she doesn't have any excuses. We'll see you in thirty. And we'll call 9-1-1 if you don't show up on time!"

The Bug scrambles off. Nickory did not once glance our way, choosing instead to stare straight ahead. Something is definitely up with her.

Jaye doesn't notice. "Do we have to go?" she asks me, pleadingly.

"Yes," I say firmly. "But the sooner we get there, the sooner we can leave, or sneak off to your bedroom if you absolutely insist."

Now it's Jaye dragging me toward my Toyota. "I absolutely insist."

We clamber in, and as soon as the car doors slam shut, we turn to one another. Our kiss is long and passionate and full. I draw sustenance from it, bracing myself for who knows what may lie ahead with Kathleen Nickerson, the warrior queen.

Even with a brief detour to the liquor store for wine, we get to the townhome well before emergency services need to be alerted. I'm surprised to see Bree and Nickory are still outside, standing by Bree's car, like they've been waiting for us. Which turns out to be true.

"Jaye and I need to run to the store for salad stuff," Bree says after I've parked.

"Why me?" Jaye asks.

"Because you have an eye for vegetables." This is said perfectly seriously, but from the way Nickory is watching me, I know we've been set up. By her or by Bree? I guess it doesn't matter.

Jaye allows herself to be commandeered for duty, and as they go, Nickory lets me into the house. The three of them share a large, single-level townhome in an upscale complex with lots of trees, nice landscaping, and a decently sized pool. The front door opens into the living room, behind which is the kitchen/dining area. I see a patio and small yard out the kitchen's back door. A hallway to the left near the dining room table probably leads to the bedrooms. Nickory does not offer a tour but gestures me toward a sofa in the living room area.

"You want a beer?" she asks politely.

"No, thanks. But water is fine."

Nickory goes back to the kitchen, and I take a look around. Whoever did the decorating knows something about color and taste. I suspect Bree, but that could be my "jock-head" bias creeping in again. The townhome is comfortable and, despite Nickory's demeanor, welcoming. The place is also plenty big enough for four.

Good, I think, then briefly wonder where the hell my inner recluse has gone.

When Nickory returns with a tall glass of ice water for me and a Stone IPA for herself, I've settled in a standing spot by the fireplace. I don't get into a lot of psychological dominance stuff, but I'm fully aware of our height difference. I suppose I want all the help I can get. Subconsciously or otherwise.

Nickory is oblivious as she sits down on the couch and pops open her beer. She's captained an Olympic team. She is the warrior queen. It's her house.

But I'm old enough to wear purple and say what I think. I decide to get right to the point.

"You're acting like you don't want me here. Why?"

The tall goalkeeper frowns. "Is it that obvious?"

At least we're not beating around the bush. "I was paid to be observant for twenty-five years. I did my job well." I'm looking at her, but she's not returning the favor. Fine.

"I like you," I continue, more or less truthfully. "I like Bree, I really like Jaye. What's wrong, and how can I fix it?"

Nickory takes a long swallow of beer, then deigns to give me a glance. "Is it true Jaye's your first girlfriend?"

Ah. "Basically, yes. She's certainly the first one I've ever felt this way about."

"That bothers me." Nickory hoards her words, as if, once spoken, they are gone forever.

"It doesn't bother Jaye. And she's old enough to make her own decisions."

"Not always good ones."

This ticks me off. "Spoken like a true friend."

That ticks her off. "I've known her for fifteen years. I don't know you at all."

"True." I finally stop hoarding my own words. "Short version? I'm a writer, an introvert, and honest to a fault. I try to be a decent human being, and I intend to be as good to Jaye as I can. I'm not an axe murderer, Nickory."

She glares at me. "You don't have to be to break her heart."

I glare right back. "Don't you think the odds are better she'll break mine? She's the gorgeous blonde athlete who, when she gets wise, can have anyone she wants."

"You don't think she's wise?"

My eyes narrow. "I'm not going to discuss that with you without discussing it with Jaye first."

The comment, for all its awkwardness, registers. Maybe in a good way. Nickory downs another swallow of beer. Releases another sentence. "She's not going to break your heart."

"I sincerely hope not. And I'll do my best not to hurt her."

Nickory's eyes threaten to pin me against the mantlepiece. "You'd better not." The anger is understated but clear.

"What makes you think I would? Like you said, you don't know me."

"She's been used before."

New information, but none of my business until Jaye chooses to make it so. I frown while the warrior queen sits there, the strong and silent type. Frustrating, too, because she clearly cares about her friend and refuses—or doesn't know how—to articulate it.

I forge ahead. "Nickory, listen. I don't want to take your relationship away. I respect your friendship with Jaye. I'm not out to replace you or push you aside. I'm out to make Jaye happy, for as long as she wants me around. This was Jaye's idea from minute one. Doesn't that count for something?"

The warrior queen sits glowering.

"Doesn't that count for something?" I ask again.

Nickory sets her jaw. "Yes," she admits.

The Bug pulls into the driveway before I can pursue my slim advantage. "Okay, then. Truce?" I ask instead.

Kathleen Nickerson, all six feet of her, stands and faces me. I know she means to intimidate, but there's steel in me, too, and I meet her eyes without flinching. Her shoulders relax, a little, and she nods.

"Truce." She offers her hand, and we shake on it. Something lingers, unfinished, but it's tabled for now, if only because we both want to keep Jaye happy.

Despite the prelude, dinner turns out to be a success. Bree grills New York strips to perfection. Jaye concocts an adventurous, tasty salad (guess she does have an eye for vegetables). The wine is my contribution, and it seems to relax everyone and ease the tension between Nickory and me.

There is comfortable conversation afterwards and the Royals' game on TV in the background. Nickory and Bree are parked on the sofa, I'm in the "comfy chair" opposite them with the coffee table between us. Jaye sits on the armrest next to me, fingers gently stroking the back of my neck.

We have not been able to sneak off to the bedroom, and the soft caresses are going right to my libido. But I'm determined to build on the truce thing, so we make nice and keep talking. I even get a little brave.

"So," I say to Nickory, "are you from, like Hickory, New Hampshire, or something?"

This gets puzzled reactions from all three women. I elaborate. "'Nickory from Hickory'?"

Nickory rolls her eyes and gestures to Jaye. "Her idea."

Jaye, grinning, takes the pass and heads up the field. "She needed a nickname. There are about a million "Kates" and "Katies" out there, almost as many Nickys, and nobody's going to call her Kathleen. So I'm watching her in training one day, with the Under-18s, blocking shot after shot after shot. Nothing was getting in." Jaye eyes her friend fondly. "And this old nursery rhyme popped into my head."

I'm quick on the uptake. "Hickory, Dickory, Dock."

"Yeah," Jaye says. "Only I started shouting "Kickory, Nickory, block!" Before long I had the whole team chanting it."

Is the tall quiet goalie actually blushing? If so, it blends well with her new hair color—KC Blues blue.

"Eventually I hear this," Nickory says, taking up the tale, "and while I'm standing there trying to figure it out, I get whacked in the head by a crossing pass."

We all laugh.

"But a nickname was born," Jaye finishes.

"Even the TV people tell the story now," Nickory says. "Though they usually claim somebody different came up with it."

"Wendy Allerton," says Bree.

"Becky Kaisershot," Jaye chimes in.

Nickory gets the last word. "But it's definitely Jaye's fault."

We laugh again, and I watch them interact, see the clear affection and love they have for each other. True best friends, I realize. I hope I can end up on Nickory's good side.

Bree sits next to her lover on the sofa, casually holding hands with her. She's part of this equation, too, and it strikes me, not for the first time, to wonder how long they've all been a kind of Three Musketeers.

"How long have you two been together?" I ask.

"Ten years," Bree says.

"Wow," I say, honestly. "I shouldn't be surprised, but I am. In a good way."

"We met in college," Bree says. "Nickory took a while to come around, but from the first time I saw her, I knew."

I feel a squeeze on my shoulder. "Me, too," Jaye says.

My eyes lock with Nickory's for a brief second. I put my hand over Jaye's, tilt my head, and catch her leaning down to kiss me. We time it perfectly, sweetly. Barely keep it decent.

Bree whistles in approval, and when I glance over, Nickory is more neutral than grim, but still not convinced.

Well, bummer for her. I have Jaye's approval, and Jaye's approval conquers all.

We prepare to drive back to the hotel after the Royals' game ends. I've only had a couple of glasses of wine over the course of the evening, but three times as much water. I'm sure of my sobriety. Bree questions the expense of a hotel room when Jaye has a perfectly good bedroom here at the town home, but I have a ready answer.

"If we stay here," I say, "you will not get any sleep tonight."

I may have sounded matter of fact at the time, but I know for sure I was blushing like crazy while Jaye held my hand and restrained herself from ravishing me right then and there.

Ravishing me. A fifty-two-year-old hermit, and somebody can't wait to get *me* into bed. I wonder, idly, if it's getting a little chilly in hell.

We don't attack each other at the hotel door this time but walk calmly into the room and all to the way to the foot of the bed. Then Jaye actually picks me up in a bear hug.

"God, I missed you." She puts me down so she can cup my face in her hands. She pulls me into a series of long, deep kisses which only nibble at the edges of a long separation. We help each other out of our clothes and take the bed by storm.

Confession (pun intended): I grew up Catholic and was flat out repressed in my younger days. The few times I had sex with someone else I tended to let my partner take the lead, tended to quietly defer to what they wanted. Even in Portland, with Jaye, I had held back a little. Tonight, though, I make up for lost years. Tonight the part of me craving, loving, adoring women and sex sets out to indulge herself, and make Jaye thoroughly happy.

I am awed to find out how erotic a lover's cries can be. To bring someone to such heights of pleasure, feel the thrill of connection as she calls my name—as well as a few god and goddess names—is almost enough to make me come myself.

Of course that happens, too, as Jaye more than returns the favor over the course of the night.

By morning every other guest on the hotel floor knows that "Rachel! Oh, God, Rachel!" and "Jaye! Yes, yes, Jaye!" are, shall we say, in the honeymoon stage, and a large part of me is glad to be making up for the times I traveled alone, kept awake by the sounds of others' lovemaking coming through thinly-insulated walls.

My eyes wait until almost seven-thirty a.m. before snapping open. Despite the long drive from Denver, despite the game and the dinner and the rattle-the-windows lovemaking, I'm wide awake, deliciously entangled with another. My head is pillowed on Jaye's chest, and I hear her heartbeat, feel her steady, even breathing. I lose myself in this chance to listen to the life coursing through her, as if given the keys to a secret treasure.

Whatever I've managed to convey of intimacy in my writing, I know now I was winging it. I had no real clue at all.

Jaye stirs and slowly comes conscious to the day. I greet her with a long, slow good-morning kiss.

"I don't think we should show our faces at the breakfast buffet," I say, the echoes and sounds of last night's pleasure still ringing in my ears.

Jaye giggles uncontrollably. Before I know it, we're both in a full-blown laughing fit, then we're kissing again. We collapse against each other, lying side by side on some very finely wrecked sheets.

"How did I get so lucky?" she asks me.

"I'm the lucky one."

"We keep saying that."

"Then it must be true."

Jaye gets serious suddenly. "I knew. I knew the first time I saw you, you were special."

I blink. Throw out my usual defensive joke. "Even though you didn't get my phone number?"

She caresses my cheek. "I got your license plate number. That day in the cemetery."

"You did?"

"I thought if I had a name and a plate number then I could get your address and figure out how to contact you without sounding like a stalker. But I didn't need to, did I?"

"Wow." My heart suddenly fills to bursting with affection and desire and, OMG, this big scary thing called love. Whoa. This is only the second time we've slept together. It's not supposed to happen this quickly, right?

I cover my emotions by rolling back on the bed and laughing. "You realize I met you two days after I wrote the 'On Being Single' blog?"

"You're kidding."

I shake my head. "Truth."

"Is that why you didn't call me for so long?"

"No. I took the encounter for what it was, something short and sweet."

"And full of potential."

I shake my head again. "Not for me."

"Why?"

"Exactly. Why would a woman twenty years my junior be interested in me?"

Jaye frowns. "You keep bringing up the age difference like it means we've got no chance."

She's irritated, and she has a right to be. I roll toward her again, give her a quick kiss. "After last night? I think we have a chance."

This does not mollify her. "But if we don't, it's because I'm younger than you?"

Yes, frankly. But I'm not about to say that. I frown, not quite certain how to proceed. "I don't know. I suppose we could be like Bogart and Bacall."

"Huh?"

Oh, please, please, please let her not be too young to know who Bogart was.

"Humphrey Bogart was twenty-five years older than Lauren Bacall. They married when he was forty-four, and she was nineteen. And they were happy for," I pause a second, "for the thirteen years they got before he died of cancer." I give Jaye a hug. "I don't intend to die of cancer any time soon."

"Good," Jaye says. Then, "Humphrey Bogart was the one in *Casablanca*, right?"

Thank you, Universe. "Yes. He and Bacall met on the set of *To Have and Have Not*. We'll have to watch it sometime."

"For sure. Especially if it helps you believe anything's possible."

"After last night, I think everything's possible."

Those must be the right words because Jaye rewards me with one of those deep searing kisses we're getting good at. Heavenly, wondrous. But even so, when it's done I'm still thinking seriously. "I've been alone all my life. It's hard for me to believe that can change."

Jaye holds me, silent for a long, long moment. "Okay, confession," she says finally. "You're the first person I've spent more than one night with since I was seventeen."

I am astonished. "You're kidding."

"I'm not proud of it, but yeah. So this is change for me, too." Something in her expression tells me there's more to learn here, but she continues before I can ask for details. "I know this is only our second time together, but I want a lot more." Jaye grins. "Bogart."

I grin back. "You can have all the days you want. Shweetheart."

We do not do the breakfast buffet. Bree calls to suggest brunch and we quickly agree. I send Jaye off to shower while I pack up my clothes.

When I come out of the bathroom after my own shower, I find Jaye staring at the luggage. "How long is 'a few days'?" She asks.

I come up next to her, put an arm around her waist. "Um, through next Saturday's game? If that's okay?"

Her expression is one hundred percent surprise and delight. "Totally!"

Worth the price of the trip right there, though the looming shadow of the warrior queen tempers my enthusiasm somewhat. Still, this is time with Jaye. This is why I'm here.

As we drop the key off at the front desk the clerk confirms the room number and the wisdom of our leaving the premises.

"342?" she says. I nod, and she gives us a long, knowing smile. Her expression reminds me of an "I'm-on-to-you" smirk I saw in a movie once.

"I hope you enjoyed your stay." Her tone is too perfect, too neutrally modulated.

I smile back, accepting my gotta-be-obvious blush with a zen calm. "It was great."

"Fantastic!" Jaye chimes in. I push her toward the door before the desk clerk verifies her statement, and we barely make it to the car before bursting into laughter. I have a sudden vision of sharing laughter with this woman for the next thirty years, and it makes my heart pound almost as hard as last night's orgasms did.

I give Jaye a quick but thorough kiss.

"Nice," she says, pleased. "Can I get more of those?"

"Whenever you want."

"We're going to have a great week."

Chapter Five

Fyrequeene's Blog: May 22

"Nickerson's Hair"

There have been many, many forms of self-expression in this world. One of the more unique ones: Kathleen Nickerson's hair.

Nickerson, for those of you who do not follow women's soccer, is the greatest goalkeeper of her generation. National Team stalwart, World Cup and Olympic veteran, she has accomplished things on the pitch others can only dream of. If she were a guy they'd have her right up there with Michael Jordan and Tom Brady.

Or maybe Dennis Rodman.

Nickerson's hair is discussed in soccer circles, lesbian circles, sports channels, and gossip magazines. Everyone, at one point or another, has talked about Nickerson's hair. Even my seventy-year-old therapist who hates sports knows about The Coif that Captured CONCACAF.

First photographic evidence of this futbol phenomenon appeared in the late 1990s, when a young New Hampshire goalkeeper made the national Under-17 team. The tall, gawky-but-graceful teenager wowed the coaches with her skill between the posts, her ability to anticipate the movement of a soccer ball—and her electric blue ponytail. Asked to tone down the display, Nickerson went "Mohawk," leaving a smaller but still vivid vision of blue atop her head. When she proceeded to allow zero goals in her first five international matches, the coaches left her alone.

The only person who doesn't talk about Nickerson's hair is Kathleen herself. A surprisingly reticent woman,

"No Comment" Nickerson simply changes hair color every couple months or so (and always right before big tournaments) and goes on with her life. If it isn't easy being green? A power red might do. In the mood for subtle? Navy blue almost looks natural after a few months of neon yellow.

Her stats reveal a woman dedicated to being the absolute best at her craft: 165 caps, three World Cup teams, two Olympic gold medals, and an astonishing 21-game international shutout streak, including every match of the 2008 Beijing Games. But they do nothing to explain why Kathleen Nickerson seems compelled to explore the limits of palette possibility.

I, however, have a guess or three.

One, if Nickerson has a tattoo, it's well hidden. I'm thinking she doesn't; she chooses to mark up her hair instead, thus making a variety of statements she can later eliminate when she tires of them.

Two, Nickerson is a stubborn woman. From those first U-17 coaches up to and including the infamous US National Team Coach who told her in 2007 she was off the squad if she didn't dye her hair a "normal" color, Nickerson's rebellion spawned a monster I suspect she no longer controls. She initially did as commanded, only she used all the "normal" colors, showing up with hair in locks of blonde, brown, black, silver, gray, white, auburn, and carrot-red. She was benched and watched the US get humiliated in the World Cup. The coach was fired shortly afterward. Nickerson is still with the team, and she's worn her hair her way ever since.

Three, Kathleen Nickerson has a long-time companion, a most attractive African American woman. Between the two of them, they have said "no comment" more often than both houses of Congress during budget battles. Nickerson does not deny their relationship, and by corollary does not deny her lesbianism. But she doesn't talk about it either. Yet even the most reticent of us need to talk sometimes, and Nickerson talks with her hair.

To which I raise a glass of blonde champagne and say, "Hair Hair!"

" 'The Coif that Captured CONCACAF'?" Jaye says with some incredulity. "Do your readers even know what CONCACAF means?"

"Hell, I don't know what CONCACAF means," I counter calmly. "It's a soccer group or something. It was alliterative. It worked for me."

Jaye wraps her arms around my waist. "Confederation of North, Central American, and Caribbean Association Football."

I wrap my arms around her waist. "Forgive me if I don't rush out and amend my original sentence."

Jaye laughs. "Nickory's going to kill you for that blog."

"Is any of it not true?"

"No. You've kind of nailed it."

"Then I can die with a clean conscience."

It is Wednesday afternoon. Bree is at work, Nickory is off doing goalkeeping drills, and Jaye has come in from doing midfielder drills. I've pulled her into the bedroom with the intention of completely unmaking the bed.

For the first time in my life, I'm spending a week under the same roof with three other women. Surprising, perhaps, but true. I always lived alone in college, could always afford my own place after I started working. I never played a team sport and never traveled or roomed with teammates. And does anyone ever count living with their parents?

Early reviews about my presence are mixed. Jaye and Nickory's schedules revolve around soccer: gym workouts, individual practice, team practice, men's soccer on TV at night. Bree is a nurse at one of the big hospitals on the Missouri side, and she's on day shifts this week, which means I usually have the townhome to myself late mornings and early afternoons, allowing me to get a great deal of writing done. Today's effort is my latest blog, which reflects the fraying of my wary truce with Nickory.

I'm getting along fine with Bree, and with Jaye, too, duh. But Nickory and I clash ever so subtly every time we're in the same room. I used my pen as a sword and a pressure release, and now, having heard what Jaye thinks, I'm ready to let it go and change the subject.

I smoothly pull Jaye's shirt over her head and off her body. I'm getting good at the clothes-removing thing. "I am so glad you like sex," I tell her.

Jaye pulls my shirt off of me, equally smoothly, and lets the blog go. "I wondered, you know," she says, going for the button on my jeans.

I put my hands on her shoulders for balance, and she slides the jeans off one leg at a time. "Wondered what?"

"When you surprised me in Portland, but wanted to wait until after the game, I wondered if—well, I guess it was the only time I thought about your age. That you thought you might be too old, um, for sex."

I laugh at the ridiculousness of this idea as I tug at the elastic of her sweatpants. "I've never thought that. In fact, I always worried if I ever met someone special they wouldn't want sex as much as I do, and then where would I be? All this pent-up libido and nowhere to express it."

Jaye has a smug expression as she unhooks my bra. "Not worried now, are you?"

"Not anymore. I'm glad you can keep up with me."

Our mutual laugh turns into a long, deep kiss. A slow heat builds up inside of me and starts radiating out. The fire emerges as a blush, I guess, but I feel its depth, how far it has to travel to surface. For me, a new and slightly scary phenomenon. I tremble a little, then slip my thumbs into Jaye's underwear and slide them down to her ankles. She falls onto the mattress, and I pull the bikini briefs free. "Come here," Jaye says, trying to pull me down on top of her.

I remain standing. "Indulge me for a minute." I spend that minute, and more, slowly and thoroughly perusing my lover's glorious nakedness from head to toe.

Jaye watches me, a little wide-eyed. "What are you doing?"

I pull my eyes away from this wondrous sight to meet hers. "Looking. Okay?"

Bemused, but game, she nods. "Sure."

"Good. Turn over."

Jaye complies, and I take in her sculpted shoulders and her back, admiring every inch of muscle and smooth, fair skin. Geez, even the minor bruises and scrapes that come from playing soccer for a living draw me in. I bend over, start at the back of her neck, and gently lay a trail of kisses down her spine. By the time I reach her hips she is breathing hard.

"Keep going, Bogart."

I laugh, shooting for low and sultry and probably failing. I stand up again and run my fingers along the backs of Jaye's thighs, then all the way down her calves to her feet.

"Okay," I say. "Turn over again."

And she does, the glint in her eyes now decidedly aroused. "If you're trying to torture me, it's working."

I put a finger to her lips. "Shh, almost done."

I go back to my perusal, moving toward the foot of the bed so I can run my hands along her calves again. They are sturdy and firm, rounded muscle set up tight against the bone, and I don't know why but I find them sexy as hell. I run a series of kisses along each one, from ankle to knee. Jaye opens her legs up, invites me inside.

"Keep, going, Bogart," she says, breathless now.

I climb onto the bed, kissing my way up her inner thigh, almost but not quite arriving where she most wants me to be, then shift slightly and come back down the other side, a slow, leisurely descent, my lips tasting her skin, savoring the feel of her. Adoring her.

Driving her crazy.

"Rachel, please!" Jaye's voice is a half-whisper, her tone is full need.

I raise my eyes to meet hers. "Don't worry," I say softly. "You're coming."

I settle myself between her legs and kiss her again, this time at the apex of leg and hip. One to the left, one to the right, then directly to the center of her. Jaye's sex is a wet, silky paradise, and I run my tongue along the length of it, exploring all of her with a thoroughness born of thirty years of pent-up libido.

Jaye's cries leave no doubt about what I accomplish. We may or may not find out later if she was loud enough to animate zombies. I stay with her, inside her, until the orgasm stills, then I kiss my way up her body and settle my head on her shoulder.

"I'll grant I don't have a lot of experience here," I say, "but you come like no one else."

She laughs, fully achieving low and sultry. "You make me come like no one else."

"I'm so glad you like sex."

Jaye keeps laughing, grins at me wickedly. "Turn over."

Before I can obey, we hear the boom of a door slamming, hard. The townhome's front door, I think. Jaye and I freeze for a second, startled, but hear nothing after but silence.

Jaye sits up. "Nickory?" she calls.

I lie back, mood broken. Our afternoon delight is over. "Maybe it's Bree."

"Bree's shift ends at four. It's Nickory."

We get up and dress, but when we leave the bedroom we find we're alone in the house. Jaye is mystified. I am not.

"She came in and heard us," I say, parking myself at the kitchen table. "And she got mad and left."

"But why?" Jaye's tone is skeptical. I watch her as she grabs a pitcher from the fridge and two glasses from a cabinet. She pours us cold water and joins me at the table. "It's not like there's never been sex here. I've heard them plenty of times."

I nod. "Have they ever heard you?"

A glare. "No! You're the first woman I've ever brought home." Her glare fades to thoughtfulness. "Do you suppose she was embarrassed?"

Kathleen Nickerson does not strike me as the type to be embarrassed. "Why slam the door?"

"To warn us we were bothering the neighbors?" Jaye's eyes twinkle, and I go with it, unable to dampen her infectious happiness.

"Damn," I say. "We might have to go back to the Hampton Inn."

Jaye shakes her head and finishes her water. She pours another glass and changes the subject. "Did you find what you were looking for?"

It takes me a moment to remember my "perusal" of her incredibly sexy body, but with remembrance comes a slow, satisfied smile. "No."

Jaye raises an eyebrow. "Explain."

"You don't have any tattoos."

Jaye raises her other eyebrow. "You did that whole crazy sexy thing to see if I had any tattoos? As if you haven't already seen enough of me?"

My smile goes nova. "It was a great excuse to check you out."

Jaye sits back. "Can I do the same thing?"

"No need. I promise I don't have any tattoos."

"Then why should I?"

I shrug. "It's a little unusual for your generation. To not have any."

"That's not true!"

"Name one person your age or thereabouts who does not have a tattoo."

Jaye grins at the sure winner. "Nickory."

Point number one in my blog is correct. Good job, Rachel. "But she has the hair."

"I guess. Do you want me to get a tattoo?"

I shake my head. "No. I like you exactly as you are."

"Actually, I was going to get one, once," she says thoughtfully. "But Mom and Dad always said to be sure that if I got a tattoo, I had to be ready to live with it." She raises her hands and "quotes" her next words for emphasis. "For. The. Rest. Of. My. Life. When I was seventeen and still knew everything, I decided when I made the Olympic team I'd get an Olympic tattoo. I knew I could live with that For. The. Rest. Of. My. Life."

As she sounds out the words a second time, her smile fades, and her tone drops into a rueful sadness. "But, as we know, I never made the Olympic team."

I gently squeeze her hand. "It's not too late."

"Yes, it is. I guarantee you there have never been any over-thirty Olympic rookie soccer players."

"You'll be the first, then."

Jaye smiles, but doesn't pursue it. "So what's your excuse?"

"On the tattoos? Same as you. There was never anything I wanted to commemorate that permanently."

"Will there ever be?"

I hear a semi-hopeful note, and it loads the question. I lean forward and give Jaye a gentle kiss. "I won't ever get a tattoo. But there are other ways
to commemorate things."

"Like how?"

I sit back and hold up both my hands. And load the answer. "No rings, see? I might, maybe, could be persuaded to wear a ring."

We both go still, aware I have put something out there, something profound, without ever addressing it directly.

Jaye stands up, comes around to my side of the table, and pulls me into her arms. "I'll keep that in mind."

The next morning my eyes pop open at five a.m. I get up to swim at the townhome's community pool, and, since I don't have a waterproof music player, my thoughts coalesce around Jaye's best friend and why she and I clash.

I remember one of my first impressions upon meeting Nickerson, the one about being fiercely protective of those she loves. Does she see me as a threat to Jaye? Or does she simply not like me?

We've put on a polite veneer, Nickory and me, but a couple of times I've noticed her question something I say in a snarky way, to make me seem stupid. She's good at it, so subtle that even now, four days into my stay, I can't prove she's zinging me on purpose.

But she is, I have no doubt. As I exit the pool and towel off, I wonder if Nickory might be jealous, then immediately laugh off the thought. Who could be jealous when they've got someone like Bree Thompson for a lover?

Bree is the glue holding the Three Musketeers together. In our brief acquaintance, I've watched her do most of the cooking, all of the mediating, and provide the nebulous-but-crucial core which keeps the arrangement sane and thriving. Our conversations reveal a bright, discerning woman who loves her partner deeply, and accepts her partner's best friend as a roommate. If I was Bree, I'd be jealous. But I don't see any hint of green-eyed monster in her at all.

When I get back to the townhome Bree, speak of the devil, is sitting in the kitchen, coffee in hand and iPad tuned to the virtual morning newspaper. She's in her scrubs.

"Working again?" I ask after we say hello.

"I need to leave in thirty minutes," She says as she gestures toward the countertop. "Bagels and cream cheese by the toaster."

Sounds good. I hit the bathroom, change out of my bathing suit, and return to the kitchen to load up on food and caffeine.

And a little chat. "Interesting blog you posted yesterday," Bree says casually.

I calmly add cream and honey to my hot tea. "I was blowing off some steam."

Bree peers at me over her coffee mug. "Because she walked in on you guys?"

"I'd already posted it by then. Besides, she didn't walk in on us."

"Kat may not have opened the bedroom door, but she knew what was going on."

Kat. Hmm. Bet Bree's the only one who gets away with that name. "Yeah, kind of hard to miss." I finish stirring my tea and take a tentative sip. "Am I the only one who feels like she and I are one wrong move from a major fight?"

Bree snorts. "You wouldn't have a chance."

"Depends on the terms. Fists? I'm toast. Words? She's buried before she starts. Pistols at ten paces? Probably even."

Bree bites back a laugh and nods, like I've confirmed something. "You're both alpha personalities. Nickory's not used to having someone like herself around."

The statement floors me. "I'm not an alpha personality!"

Bree shoots me a "honey, get a clue" laser, a glare which combines sarcasm and street smarts the likes of which only certain people can convey.

"Bullshit. You're both leaders, deep down. She's led the National Team. You could lead armies into battle if you had to. You've just never had to."

I open my mouth to protest again, but stop short. Think about my former occupation, where my fellow controllers and I were totally in charge of the skies around Denver. We were the generals, each plane and its pilots the soldiers, even if no one ever referred to it in those terms. I had the big picture, knew the strategy, issued the orders to make the whole game run smoothly. There was hell to pay if a pilot tried to do something I didn't want him doing in my sector. I excelled at commanding this battlefield, reveled in it sometimes, thrived, too, until the stress and responsibility of keeping so many people safe slowly ate away at my health and stamina.

Bree sees this all play across my face, raises an eyebrow, and smirks.

"Okay," I say. "Maybe. Is that why Nickory hates me?"

"She doesn't hate you."

My turn for a sarcastic glare. I'm not as good at it as Bree. "No, she ignores me or puts me down because it's fun."

"No, she doesn't."

"Yes, she does. And I don't know why. I'm not an enemy, am I?"

Bree takes a long sip of coffee, gives herself time to formulate a reply. "She's always been protective of Jaye."

"To the extent of driving girlfriends away? Is that why Jaye never brought anyone home before?"

"She told you that?"

"Yes. And I believe her."

"You should. Jaye's crazy about you."

"Is that what Nickory doesn't like?"

Bree frowns, and finishes her coffee. Something else is going on here, and I'm about to ask what when the sudden entrance of a third voice startles us both.

"There you are. I didn't like waking up alone."

Good thing Bree's coffee mug was empty, because it goes skittering across her iPad. As Bree makes a great catch to keep it from shattering on the floor, I turn to see a sleepy-eyed Jaye smiling at me. Wearing a rumpled t-shirt and shorts, blonde hair tousled, she's delightfully sexy.

"I got up early and went swimming," I tell her, feeling the mild tension of the last few minutes disappear.

Jaye puts her arms around my shoulders, hugs my neck. "Good. Now you're done, you can come back to bed with me. 'Morning, Bree."

Bree stands up and puts her coffee cup in the sink. "Hey, Jaye."

"Come on," Jaye says, tugging me out of the chair. "I want to wake up properly."

I get to my feet, roll my eyes at Bree as if to say "who's the alpha personality now?" and let myself be led away down the hall.

Jaye is subdued on Friday. I don't call her on it until we're doing the after-dinner dishes.

"You've been quiet all day. Is everything all right?"

"I don't want you to leave."

Yes, and I don't want to leave her. But it's still too soon for all of that, right?

"I wish I could stay. But I have another trip to prepare for."

"What trip?"

"I'm driving to Cape Cod next month." This is an annual thing for me, something my perennially single self always anticipates with pleasure.

"When exactly?"

I tell her, and watch as dismay spreads across her face. "But that's right after our next road trip. I won't see you for, for almost a month!"

"No. I'll drive through Kansas City on the way. I'll see you then. Plus, I bought a ticket to your game with the Breakers in Boston. And—" I hesitate.

"What?"

"I noticed you have ten days between the Boston game and your next game against Houston. I was hoping you could get a couple of days off and come to Provincetown with me."

Jaye dries the last of the glasses as she thinks about this. "That's possible. We usually have Mondays off, and with the long break, I might be able to get Tuesday, too."

"Try. I'd love to share P-Town with you."

Jaye smiles, but she's still not back up to cheerful. "Do you have to go back to Denver? I mean, couldn't you stay here until it's time, then leave? You said you had enough clothes for a week. Wouldn't that cover your trip, too?"

Hmm. I have to service the Toyota, but I could take it to a mechanic here. I have clothes, yes, plus my computer and ice cooler. Money is a matter of hitting an ATM. I pay my bills online. I *could* stay.

Except for one thing. I glance over toward the living room where Nickory and Bree are watching TV. Do I bring up the tension between me and Nickory? Between Jaye's lover and her best friend?

I decide not, opting for another reason which also happens to be true. "It could work. But I'll be honest, Jaye. I'm not used to sharing a house with three other people, and I'm starting to feel a little crowded."

I see her hurt expression and try to explain myself better. "If it was you and me alone I'd stay in a heartbeat." With a wet hand I playfully deposit soap on her nose. "I can't get enough of you. But for me, four's a crowd, and I think I need some down time."

A long silence passes while she thinks about it. Then a quiet sigh, and a surprise. "And you want to get away from Nickory."

Jaye's perceptiveness is one of the things I'm coming to love about her. So is the willingness to bring up a potential difficulty. She's braver than I am, I think to myself.

I put the last pot in the drain rack and pull the plug in the sink. "Yeah," I say. "I'm sorry we're not getting along better, and I don't want to do anything to mess up your friendship."

"Other than blog about it?"

"Maybe I don't want to risk doing anything worse."

Jaye finishes drying the pans before she speaks again. "I'll miss you."

"I'll miss you, too. But I planned this trip in January. I've made deposits and reservations."

She shushes me. "It's okay. I understand."

Kitchen chores done, I wrap my arms around Jaye and pull her close. "Come to Provincetown," I say.

Jaye rewards me with a soft kiss. "I'll try."

Saturday goes by way too fast. Bree is working, and the other two Musketeers both have errands to run, so I spend the day alone at the townhome, reluctantly packing for the drive home tomorrow.

I suppose my life in Denver needs some attention, but I acknowledge it's a life with no real ties. Sure, there's Toni and Paula, valued friends, but they'd value me, and I them, no matter where I lived. There's no job, no family, nothing to hold me to Colorado. Well, except the newly remodeled and painted house. The house I decided would be my home. A house plenty big enough for two.

I consider the ease with which I've slid into Jaye's life, the ease with which she's slipped into mine. Were she not living with Nickory, I probably would have stayed when she asked, stayed until my trip to Cape Cod. That would have been a good chance to find out if we can really be together, or if I'm too locked into my solitary ways.

But Jaye does live with Nickory, and it's far too early to ask her to change the arrangement. As wonderful as our relationship has been so far, we're still moving awfully fast. No need to ramp it up to light speed.

Yet.

Packing done, I take a nice afternoon catnap since Jaye is not likely to let me get much sleep tonight. When I get to the stadium, I at last make use of the field pass Jaye has gotten me. I walk down the sideline to join Bree, who has come directly from work.

"Bogey!" she shouts as I draw near. "Come on down!"

I half-glare at Bree as I sit beside her on the team bench. "Did you call me Bogey?"

"Yes," she says.

"Why?" As if I don't know the answer.

Bree tries hard not to laugh. "Jaye said you guys had a conversation where you compared yourselves to Bogart and Bacall."

"So now I have a nickname?"

"She does love a good nickname."

"Lovely."

"You don't like it?"

I sigh. "In my former job, "bogey" referred to an unknown or unidentified radar target, usually something expected to be a problem. Then there's Bogey Man—

Bree stops me. "I think you need to be telling Jaye this, not me."

"Yes. Agreed." I cast my gaze out on the field, spot Jaye, and see her let loose a kick sending the ball right toward us. Covering two-thirds of the pitch in full flight, the ball makes one bounce, and all I have to do is stand and raise my hands to catch it on the hop. Bree chuckles. Jaye makes her way over, and I wonder if it's possible to grow tired of someone who smiles every time she sees you.

I deeply hope not.

"Hey Bogey!" Jaye calls.

My heart leaps inside of me, but I don't smile. Time for the Bogart Discussion, Part Two.

"Jaye," I greet her neutrally. "Bogart."

"What?"

"You can call me Bogart. You cannot call me Bogey."

"But that's what they called him. I Googled it."

"Okay. Did you Google Bacall?"

"You're going to call me Bacall, right?" She's like a kid in a candy store. "That would be so cool."

Bree doesn't bother to hide her laughter this time. I manage to stay dead-pan. "I could call you Bacall. I could also call you Betty."

"Betty?" Apparently Jaye did not Google Bacall.

"Lauren Bacall's real name is Betty. She's Betty to all her friends."

"But I don't want you to call me Betty."

I raise my eyebrows. "Whyever not?"

The light comes on. "Oh. But Bogart's okay?"

"Bogart is fine."

I'm rewarded with her amazing smile. "Good."

I'm also rewarded with my first nickname. Ever.

Tonight's opponent is the Seattle Reign, who win the NWSL prize for clever team name, playing on the city's local climate and the team's implied dominance. Clever, though, is not enough to keep Kansas City from raining goals all over them. Jaye gets the first one, a right-place-at-the-right-time, easy put away off a rebound. Her scoring streak is now four games and counting. Nickerson is uncharacteristically porous, giving up
one goal in each half. Seattle's goalie surrenders more, though, and the final score is 4-2.

I watch the game from the field for the first time ever, standing next to Bree. The game plays out differently at field level. The viewpoint is limited, so it's harder to see the flow of play develop. This makes me even more appreciative of Jaye's abilities, how she leads the team and directs play amidst all the movement and controlled chaos. One can see the confidence she has in her game now and how her teammates feed off of it.

"You've seen her play before," I say to Bree after we high-five on the last goal, another Stokes-to-Longstreet special. "Is she always this good?"

"She's never been this good," Bree says. "Jaye's always been decent, but she's never been the playmaker. This year she's a playmaker."

I'm happy for Jaye. I'm proud, too. I don't think it's because of me, but if Jaye does and it works, why deny the beautiful result? "She's amazing," I say.

"She says the same thing about you."

"What?"

"Oh, honey, it's meant to be." Bree says sincerely. Fondly, even. "You two aren't fooling anybody."

"We're not trying to."

"Mm-hmm."

"I wish Nickory thought so."

Bree's tone does a complete one-eighty. Curtly, she says, "She'll come around."

Whoa. I want to pursue the subject, but the game has ended, and Jaye and Nickory are walking over.

"We have to do autographs," Jaye says to us, "but afterwards maybe we can take you up on dinner?"

"Sure," I say easily. I've been offering all week to treat the Musketeers to dinner out in exchange for my rooming with them. "As long as it's not five-hundred dollars a plate, anywhere's good."

"There's a great barbecue place near the townhome," Jaye says. "We'll go there."

"Are there any bad barbecue places here?"

"The Texas-style ones," Nickory says. I glare at her, but refuse to let myself get angry.

"Careful," I counter, "or it'll be Taco Bell."

"Aaugh!" Jaye grabs her friend's hand to pull her away and limit the damage. "Let's go."

"See?" Bree says after they've gone. "She'll come around."

I wish she sounded more sure.

Chapter Six

On Sunday morning I get a very pleasant surprise.

"Remember what you said about getting time off?" Jaye asks after we've kissed our way into wakefulness.

"Yes. Does that mean you can do Provincetown?"

"Probably. But I can also do today and tomorrow, if it's all right."

"What do you mean?"

"I have today and Monday off. If I catch an early flight on Tuesday, I'll be back in plenty of time for practice." Jaye's face is alight with eagerness. "I want to see your house. I want to see Colorado. I want to spend two more nights with you."

I want to make this wish come true. "Won't a plane ticket cost a fortune?"

"No more than what you spent going to Portland."

Fair enough. "Can you drive a stick shift?"

She can.

After a quick breakfast and some frantic packing by Jaye, we set off.

Never has the Kansas prairie passed as quickly as it does with Jaye keeping me company. We talk sports, play the alphabet game, listen to a writer's podcast, compare music, and misbehave a little, not quite to the point of running the Toyota off the interstate. Nine hours fly by, and we pull into my driveway Sunday evening happy to know road trips are another point of compatibility between us.

I live in the northern suburbs of Denver, a nothing-special, upper-middle-class subdivision, typical except for the view of the mountains.

Jaye gets out of the car and gazes west, staring. "Wow."

I stand next to her and we watch as the sun, hovering above the not-too-distant Flatirons, gradually stains the sky pink and orange.

"Yeah. You get used to it, but it's always beautiful."

She's impressed by the house, too. It's big for one person, two stories plus basement. An open floor plan gives one the impression of even more space, which, along with the view, is why I bought the place.

"Come upstairs," I say, taking her hand so she doesn't have a choice. We climb to the second floor, where the stairs open onto a loft area with a bay window. The original design had three small windows set into the bay, but as part of my remodeling frenzy I'd had the upper half of the wall redone into one big expanse of glass, added a window seat, and given myself a favorite room. I've kept the furnishings simple: overstuffed recliner chair, lamp, and a little table. I plan to spend lots of time here reading, writing, and admiring the spectacular mountain view.

We watch the sun some more, then Jaye says, "Can people see in through the window?"

"I had a reflective coating put on the outside glass, so no. Not unless I turn the light on."

Jaye takes me in her arms. She gives me a kiss which guarantees all my nerve endings quickly become fully alert and ready for action. "We're not going to turn the light on. Do you have some blankets?"

Quilts. I have quilts, and they do nicely for a first go 'round, but we discover floors are not conducive to the comfort of either a thirty-one or a fifty-two-year-old body, and before round two we move in the mattress, sheets, blankets, and all, from the master bedroom. We make love as the moon becomes visible in the great bay window, talk a little, then enjoy each other's closeness as we lie entangled in the sheets. Jaye, I'm sure, is about to fall asleep when I suddenly burst out laughing.

"What's so funny?"

"In the past week" I say, still giggling a little, "with your enthusiastic participation, I've scandalized the entire floor of a Hampton Inn, braved the knowing stares of your snickering roommates, and risked life and limb to have sex in a car going seventy-five miles an hour." I pause. "I am not living your grandmother's retirement!"

Jaye lies there, silent. I'm beginning to think I've screwed something up when she says, "Does this mean you want knitting needles for Christmas?"

My giggles blow back into laughter. I see the twinkle in her eyes by the light of the moon. Then she's laughing too, and tickling me, which of course I have to counter.

After some general messing around, we stop to catch our breath. Our faces are close, and the beauty in Jaye's nearly stops my heart. *I love you,* I think, then kiss her, soft and slow, so I don't say the words. But Jaye must feel it, because she pulls back from my kiss enough to meet my eyes.

"You're still scared, aren't you?"

How is it she gets me, so well and so quickly? I roll over onto my back, eyes aimed now at the white blankness of the ceiling. Easier to talk about difficult things, sometimes, when you're watching nothing.

"I've lived with depression for thirty-five years, Jaye. You're the first person who's wanted me like this, I've never lived a life where I could believe this was possible. It's wonderful, but it feels fragile, too. Like I'm holding it with a gossamer thread. If I say the wrong thing, or make a wrong move, the thread breaks and you'll float away."

Jaye's hand slides against mine, gently connecting me to her. Her to me. I finish up my little pity party. "There's been so much disappointment, and the depression caused so much pain." I pause and swallow. "Hard to overcome, even now."

With complete sincerity, Jaye says, "So I'm balancing it out."

Not at all what I expected. "What?"

"The first half of your life was dull and sad. The second half will be adventurous and happy." Jaye moves close and wraps me in her aura and her arms. "We'll bring each other joy, Rachel. We'll make each other whole."

I'm overwhelmed by her words and by the warmth and security of her arms around me. But I can't help the laugh that tumbles out.

"Oh, Jaye, you're a fucking lesbian wet dream. You're too perfect."

"No, I'm not." Jaye cuddles up against me. "Let's sleep now. Tomorrow I'll tell you the worst thing that ever happened to me."

"Worse than losing a close-held dream?"

"Shh," she says, kissing me good night. "Tomorrow."

We have one full day together in Colorado, and rather than spend it all in bed, tempting though the idea is, I get us up and dressed and out of the house by eight-thirty a.m.

"This had better be good," Jaye grumps as we set off in the car.

"Breakfast at the Walnut Cafe in Boulder," I say. "Then Estes Park and a day in the mountains."

She brightens. "Plan!"

"Then this evening we're having dinner with my friends Toni and Paula. They want to meet you."

"Is this like 'meet the parents'?"

"More like 'meet the mega-protective big sisters.' But don't worry, we'll have most of the day to ourselves."

Breakfast and coffee go a long way toward lifting Jaye's spirits. Rocky Mountain National Park completes the job. We are rewarded with abundant sunshine and, since it's a Monday during the school year, a day nicely bereft of tourists. I regale Jaye with a few of the more interesting facts about the park and Colorado as we drive toward Trail Ridge Road. We stop briefly at a huge open meadow and take in newly-blooming wildflowers and listen to the sounds of nature and birdsong, wonderful birdsong. I'm hoping to spot an elk, but it's the wrong time of year, and we don't get lucky.

Jaye enjoys herself thoroughly. I enjoy her delight and her presence, marveling at how comfortable it feels, being with her. I'm in entirely new territory here: spending time with a lover, taking her places I think she'll like, trying to please her, and liking the challenge.

We drive up Trail Ridge Road as far as it's been plowed this spring, about nine thousand feet in elevation. I am astonished when Jaye tells me it's the highest she's ever been.

"I grew up in Iowa," she reminds me. "And you don't need mountains to play soccer."

I stop at a pullout and motion her out of the car. "This is why I told you to bring a jacket." We stand at the rock wall dividing us from a thousand-foot drop and some spectacular mountain scenery. Even with the sun, the temperature hovers right around freezing.

Jaye stares out at the view, appropriately awed, her breathlessness more than the mile-plus altitude. "You're so lucky to live here!"

"I'm lucky to be here with you."

She turns to me, touches her forehead to mine, says softly, "Thank you."

We stand there, suspended in contentment, until a gust of wind comes up and threatens to freeze us in our tracks.

Jaye shivers. "Car now?"

I laugh through my chattering teeth, and we go back to my Toyota. I turn the ignition and crank up the heater, but before I can put the car into gear Jaye stops me.

"I haven't forgotten I owe you a story," she says.

I take my foot off the clutch, undo my seat belt and get comfortable. With the beauty of the mountains around us, Jaye has chosen a good place for what I'm guessing is a hard thing for her to talk about. Smart woman.

I reach across the console and take her hand. "Fire away."

"Remember when you asked if I'd ever been depressed?"

"Of course."

"I let you believe it had to do with me not making the National Team, but that's not true." Jaye takes a deep breath, then continues, her voice quiet but clear.

"When I was sixteen I fell in love. Up to then, soccer was all I thought about, and it was great. I played for an elite travel team, there were colleges all over the country scouting me, and I made the Under-17 squad, my first national team.

"The person who told me about the U-17's was the travel team's assistant coach. She'd always been there for me, pushed me hard, but told me when I did good, too. I wasn't exactly the teacher's pet, but I see now she favored me."

I can guess what's coming. I brush her fingers with my thumb and let Jaye tell it at her own pace.

"She told me I'd made the team when we were in the locker room, after practice. Everyone else had left. I was literally jumping up and down, I was so happy. I jumped right into her arms and hugged her, and she hugged me back. She told me how delighted she was for me, and I thanked her for helping me, yadda yadda yadda, but the whole time we're standing there with our arms around each other. After I said thank you for the fifth or sixth time, she stopped smiling and kissed me."

Jaye's face softens as she casts herself back through the far distance of memory, and I comprehend how even now, that moment of first love is still sweet.

"It was like something inside of me exploded. Like something woke up. All I wanted her to do was keep kissing me, and she did, for a long time. Then she took me back to the office, locked the door, and made me come."

An interesting choice of words, I think, but definitely don't say. Not "had sex with me." Not "made love to me." *Made me come.*

Her eyes focus again, turn to meet mine. "I was instantly in love. She was thirty-four, and I thought she was the end of my world."

"And you were sixteen?"

Jaye heaves a deep sigh. "Yeah. Total jailbait. But I was crazy for her, and I thought she was crazy for me. I knew we had to keep it secret, which wasn't hard after I made the national squad. We couldn't get together very often, although my dad was letting me borrow the car by then, and I used it to get to where she was a couple of times."

Another sigh. "I thought when I turned eighteen we'd go public and be together forever. I kept saying this, kept assuming it, and she let me believe it, right up until the day she dumped me. She just dumped me and left. Never talked to me again."

She speaks those last words with a finality leading me to believe I shouldn't ask for details. Hard as it is to resist, I don't ask. I let her tell me what she will.

"She did it the day before I left for a big tournament in Venezuela. I was completely shattered, but I used soccer as an escape and it worked. I had a great tournament, scored two goals and impressed everyone. But I wasn't talking off the field, not to anybody. Nickory was my roomie in Caracas, of course she noticed, and got me to pour my heart out one night. That's when we became good friends. She got me through it."

This time, without actually meaning to, I do voice my thoughts. "And she's been taking care of you ever since."

"Nickory?" Jaye's tone is fond. "Yeah, I guess she has. But I was depressed for a long time. I was almost out of college before I slept with anyone again."

"And even then, you said you focused on one-night stands."

"Yeah. Not too many of those." Jaye squeezes my hand. "Guess I've got some pent-up libido, too."

"And another older woman in your bed." Older even than the soccer coach bitch.

"You're not her, Rachel." Jaye's tone is sharp. "You're completely different. And completely wonderful."

I shake my head. "And you are *so* a fucking lesbian wet dream."

She doesn't laugh. "No. After the tournament, when I got back home, I was moping so much my parents got worried, and eventually I told them what had happened. They made sure the coach got fired. She never worked in soccer again, so far as I know. I ruined her career."

I beg to differ. "No, you didn't. She got what she deserved."

"She was a great soccer coach. She could have gotten a college job, easy. Maybe even a spot on the national team staff."

"So? It's not your fault she couldn't keep her libido in check. She took advantage of you, and it probably wasn't the first time."

Jaye winces. "My parents kept telling me the same thing. But some of my teammates, when they found out . . ." She trails off, but I can guess how those teammates might have reacted. "I mean, it wasn't like I was twelve. I was practically an adult. In some countries it all would have been perfectly legal."

"You weren't twelve—but what if one of her other victims was? Or what if some girl in the future would have been? Then you saved her, and maybe a few others, too."

Jaye stares at me, shocked. "I never thought of that."

I bring her hand up to my lips and gently kiss the back of it. "I'm sorry your first love was so traumatic. I'm glad you came through it. I barely survived being seventeen myself, and I wasn't in love with anyone."

"Can I ask you something?" Her tone is low and quiet, cueing me in to the fact that her question might be difficult.

"Anything."

"Did you ever think about suicide?"

As soon as the words are out, I know how Jaye would answer, and my heart aches for the teenager she was. "Yes. Pretty much my last two years of high school."

"But you never tried—?"

"No," I reply, shaking my head slowly. I came frighteningly close once, but I'll save that story for another time. Or another existence. I kiss her hand again, putting all the empathy I have into the gesture. "It's such a twisted space. Isn't it?"

She glances away, but not before blinking back tears. "Yeah. It was awful. I know now those feelings were mostly hormones and teenage angst. But it was still hard."

"You were strong enough to escape. You survived. And I'm so glad you're here."

Jaye puts her arm around my shoulders and pulls me close to her. It's an awkward hug, with the car's center console in the way, but her head ends up resting on my shoulder, my jacket absorbing her tears. The sun moves from my moonroof to the back window before Jaye speaks again.

"I'm not perfect, Rachel. I'm scared, too. I'm sure of us. But I was sure then, too."

"Hey—you keep doing what you're doing. I'm not going anywhere. I know we're not going to be all sunshine and wildflowers. We'll hit bumps in the road. But if you have questions, ask. If you have problems, say so." I laugh a little. "Like you said in Portland: We won't give up without trying our hardest. Okay?"

"Okay," she says, and we seal the intention with a kiss.

Jaye is not completely back to her usual bubbly self when we pull up the driveway to Toni and Paula's place. They live in a newer subdivision between Denver and the airport, on a three-acre lot with a rambling ranch house. Toni insisted on living out on the flatlands east of I-25 because it reminded her of the Texas prairie where she grew up. Paula, a military brat who's lived everywhere but Antarctica, didn't care. Their view of the mountains is good, but not as good as mine.

We exit the car and walk hand in hand to the front door, her grip threatening my circulation. "I think this is the first time I've ever seen you nervous."

"Meeting 'mega-protective big sisters' might have something to do with that."

I ring the doorbell. "Be yourself," I tell her, "and give as good as you get with Toni. You'll do fine."

" 'Give as good as I get?' What are you talking about?"

The front door opens before I can answer. Toni greets us. She's not tall, and she's a little on the chunky side, but her bearing exudes confidence and self-assured ease. She eyes Jaye up and down as I make the introductions.

"So," she says, "you're the sexy young soccer player."

Jaye blushes. I don't.

"Stop!" I say to Toni, giving her a scowl of warning. I guide Jaye past her and into the house.

Toni is unapologetic. She closes the door and follows us in. "I'm only quoting you."

"No, you're not."

"Ah, right. I was incomplete. You used the phrase 'hot and sexy young soccer player.'."

Jaye smiles weakly, and thank goodness Paula appears before us. She's a little taller than her wife, her soft curves countering Toni's sharp edges. Some women are obviously butch or femme; Paula sits right in the middle, a bit androgynous but definitely female, graceful and polished and far more diplomatic than her partner.

"Jaye, how nice to meet you," she says, sweetly, smoothly taking the bottle of wine Jaye holds in her hand. "Let's go to the kitchen and get acquainted. I think Toni and Rachel have some book business to take care of before we eat. Ten minutes, you two."

As soon as they round the corner, I lay into Toni. "Are you going to behave or will we have to leave early?"

"Paula made the Hungarian soup."

Paula Harrington's Hungarian mushroom soup is the absolute best edible thing ever created in the galaxy, the only vegetarian dish I would cross a trackless desert for. That she made it for us tonight means she truly wants to welcome Jaye, which is wonderful. But it also means Toni can get away with some bad behavior because she knows I won't leave until the soup has been consumed to the last atom.

Toni smirks in victory and heads down the hall to her office. I follow quietly, but not meekly. I have a trump card to play.

"You still have to be nice, or you'll never get *Triangle*'s happy ending."

She stops. Turns around. "Speaking the truth about someone's sexiness is nice. I bet you haven't had time to write the ending."

Like an Old West gunslinger, I pull the flash drive out of my pocket. "Au contraire, O publisher of mine." Toni raises an eyebrow. "I even did some revision on the key love scene, so bonus."

The smirk returns. "That, I can believe," Toni says as she holds her hand out.

I move the flash drive out of reach. "Best behavior?"

Toni gives me a curt nod and takes the drive. Before we leave the room, I throw out one last admonition.

"Jaye is the good woman you wanted me to find, okay? Don't make me regret bringing her here."

"She'll be fine," Toni says, and on that comforting-but-ambiguous statement, we are off to eat.

The soup is a religious experience. My gastronomic senses go into a paroxysm of pleasure when the first succulent spoonful hits my mouth, and I send up a prayer of thanks to the Universe that I've been blessed to experience such good fortune. Fresh-baked sourdough bread accompanies Paula's master dish, complementing the soup's flavor perfectly.

Jaye likes it, too. "This is amazing," she says to Paula, and, other than me asking for seconds, those are about the only words spoken until this first course is done.

Paula knows I will be happy making the soup my main meal, but in deference to her other guest, she has also prepared some baked chicken and vegetables. Jaye digs into those with a healthy appreciation and more compliments. The usual get-to-know-you small talk begins to flourish. Jaye finds out Toni and Paula met in college and have been together for thirty-plus years, are both happy with what they do, but will be equally happy to retire to Texas once Paula is eligible.

Jaye tells them about falling in love with soccer, relates a few tales about the places she's seen, and the people she's met. I sit quietly and listen, pleased to see my friends and my lover getting along.

We're almost through the main course and totally lulled into a false sense of security when Paula launches a surprise attack.

"So, Jaye," Paula says casually, "you're living with your best friend."

"And her partner, yes. It's a good arrangement."

"I gather there's not a lot of money in soccer?"

My early-warning system pings softly. I cast a quizzical glance at Paula.

"You can make a living," Jaye replies, not seeing anything wrong with the question. "But unless you're at the top, on the US National Team, you have to work hard at it."

"And she does," I chime in, with enough sharpness in my tone to let Paula know I'm paying attention. "Jaye helps Kath Nickerson with her off-season soccer camps and some other stuff."

"But eventually your playing days will end," Paula says. "What are your plans then?"

"I don't know yet," Jaye says cheerfully. "I'm hoping to play another five years or so. I'll worry about it when I have to."

"I take it you like the grasshopper attitude?"

Jaye hesitates for a moment, her fork halfway between plate and mouth. Then she takes her bite, chews and swallows while my now-narrow-eyed stare loads up and shoots daggers at Paula.

"Actually," Jaye says when her mouth is not full, "Becky Kaisershot's husband, Rick, is a financial genius. When I have some extra money, he invests it for me. I'm not going to be rich, but I've got a nest egg to fall back on when the time comes."

Jaye and I have not yet discussed finances, so I had no idea about this. *But yes!* I think when I hear it. Take that, Paula!

I decide to rip the curtain off this little charade. "Okay, Toni," I say, turning my dagger eyes to her. "You can go next now in the Rachel's Girlfriend Inquisition."

Paula has the grace to appear abashed. Toni, damn her, takes my words as permission and dives right in. "The Internet says you and Nickerson were lovers once. Are you still?"

I drop my soup spoon, ready to explode. Before I can say anything Jaye's hand slips below the table and grips my thigh, keeping me quiet. For the moment.

"Wow," she says, perfectly calmly. "You get right to the point."

"Being blunt tends to get answers," Toni says matter-of-factly.

Jaye says, "The Internet is wrong. Nickory and I never dated, and we never slept together. I wanted to once, but she met Bree, her partner, and that was that. I got over it."

"You did?"

"Of course. True friends support each other through thick and thin. Nickory's done that for me, and I try to do the same for her." Jaye cuts up the last of her chicken. "Like you're doing for Rachel, right?"

Jaye says this with complete, casual innocence. Toni appears confused for a second.

"I mean, Rachel's such a great writer, she must be making you a ton of money. So of course you're overpaying her?"

Now I'm confused. Toni and I stare at Jaye blankly while she blithely finishes the last of her chicken.

Paula, meanwhile, bursts out laughing. "Oh, kid," she says to Jaye when she can catch a breath. "You're good. Well played!"

Toni is still clueless, but I watch Jaye give Paula a soft fist bump and I get a glimmer.

"You set this up!?" I exclaim.

"Darn right we did." Paula stands and starts gathering our empty dishes. "It took me thirty seconds of conversation in the kitchen to figure out Jaye's the real deal. I knew Toni was going to give her the third degree, so I told Jaye to follow my lead and she did. Nicely done!"

She disappears into the kitchen. Jaye smiles at me and pats my thigh. Toni sits very still. I can tell she's angry at being fooled. But I can also tell she knows she has to own some of it. She sits there thinking, coming to terms with it, then says about what I thought she might.

"You've got spirit," she tells Jaye, "and you get all the benefit of my doubt. But if you hurt Rachel, if you break her heart, I will hunt you down and haunt you 'til the end of your days."

"Fair enough," Jaye says.

Paula swings back through the kitchen door holding the dessert wine we brought with us. "Honestly, Toni," she says. "Your whole tough Texan thing is such a cliché. Can we change the subject now?"

"When did you guys meet Rachel?" Jaye asks. We're enjoying the after-dinner wine, comfortably seated around the table, all tension gone.

"I actually met Paula first."

"And it's a good story," Paula says. She glances at me. "May I?"

Jaye's eyes light up, and I defer.

Paula sips her wine, and begins. "I came to Denver TRACON—that's the air traffic control facility—as a newly-promoted supervisor. I'd managed to drag Toni out of Houston, and we moved here not knowing anybody. My first day I walk into the control room and see ten people: eight guys, one woman, and one person whose gender I cannot immediately discern."

"I wore my hair super short that year," I say.

"As soon as our eyes met, though, the gaydar pinged, and I knew I'd met family. Not that she let on, of course. That first week I learned Rachel showed up on time, never complained about sector assignments, and was good at the job. Everything else was a blank. I tried dropping some hints, but she never took them. Then one day, one of the guys made a reference to Texas, and I found out she was from there. I mentioned that my partner Toni was from Texas, and it went right over Rachel's head."

I say, "The name Toni was far too ambiguous for me to go there."

Paula rolls her eyes. "I was about to give up when Jesse Tannehill came back from vacation."

"JT was TRACON's resident asshole," I tell Jaye.

Paula talks right on over me. "JT walked into the control room, saw me and Rachel at the desk, and said, 'So it's true? We're changing the name to Dyke TRACON instead of Denver TRACON?' He said it loud enough for everyone to hear. The controllers on sector, who were all men by the way, stopped talking, and the room went dead quiet. I sat there, speechless, but Rachel stared JT down like she was the sheriff and he a pissant little cowboy. Then she said 'Well, I'd rather be one of the dykes than the worst controller in the building.'"

Jaye grins at me in pleased surprise.

"You could hear a pin drop," Paula says. "Until Brian Jones laughed and said 'Call the fire trucks, Tannehill, because you've been burned!' Everybody laughed, except for Rachel, who was still in sheriff mode. JT turned around and left the room. I knew then I was going to have trouble with him—but I also knew I would make a friend of Rachel."

"And here we are," I say.

"Was he that bad a controller?" Jaye asks.

Paula grimaces. "Oh, yeah. Life got so much better when he transferred to Cleveland Center."

"Where he couldn't check out," I say, "so they transferred him again to some little tower on Lake Erie. And he had to take a pay cut."

"Karma's a bitch," Paula says.

"And a blessing," Toni adds. "If it wasn't for Paula you'd never have read The Fyrequeene."

Of course Jaye wants to hear this story, too.

"We're working a mid-shift, the eleven to seven, Rachel, and Beatle and I," Paula begins, but Jaye cuts her off.

"Beatle?"

"Brian Jones," I tell her.

Paula nods. "Because Brian Jones was a Rolling Stone."

Before Jaye can go deeper down this rabbit hole, Toni touches Jaye's arm. "Don't even try to understand ATC nicknames. Quit while you're behind, and let Paula keep talking."

Jaye, bemused, obeys.

Paula says, "Three-thirty a.m., nothing going on, and I did a walk through the room to make sure all was well. Rachel's sitting at her sector with a notebook in front of her, scribbling like mad. I asked her what she was working on, and after some hemming and hawing, she tells me it's a Xena story."

Jaye's face lights up. "Which one?"

Paula says, "The sequel to something called *Follow the Blood*."

"*Popskull*."

"Eventually, yes," Paula says. "I asked her if she'd ever written anything else, and she says her fanfic is on a Xena website. I go back to my desk, hunt it down, read *Follow the Blood*, then go tell her Toni publishes lesbian fiction, and she'd *definitely* be interested in The Fyrequeene's work."

"And," Toni says, "after a couple of years of her hemming and hawing, I finally got a book out of Rachel and a star was born."

Jaye smiles at me proudly and raises her wine glass in salute. Toni watches this, staring at Jaye until she notices and gazes back.

"I'm glad she moved faster with you," Toni says. We gape at her in surprise. "And for the record, she's never complained about her royalties."

Chapter Seven

Fyrequeene's Blog: June 2

"Flight of Fancy"

> *"Hope is the thing with feathers that perches in the soul, sings the tunes without words, and never stops at all."*
> *~Emily Dickinson*

I do not by any means claim to be the writer Emily Dickinson was, but I feel like we have a couple of things in common. She was an introvert, as am I. She had a few people close to her in her life, as do I. She never married, as I never have. And we both write, though her talents and insights far, far surpass mine.

I came across the quote above a few months ago, and since then one particular phrase has taken up residence in my mind. Chop off everything else Dickinson said, and consider "the thing with feathers." Lots of things have feathers. The ancient dinosaurs, certain hairstyles, birds… I focus on the birds. As I've aged I find myself more and more appreciative of birdsong. Something about the music of the birds brings me great comfort. Perhaps it's what I perceive as simple innocence. Birds sing to mate, I know, but often I hallucinate that they sing because it's so damn much fun. Even the simplest two-note chirp is expressive, and whatever the birds are expressing resonates with me. The "tunes without words" do indeed "perch in my soul." If such is also hope, then I'm glad it's there.

In one of my darker moments I once asked for hope to leave me. I believed living without hope meant I would be doing things instead of simply dreaming of doing things, but I was wrong. Living without hope brought me so low, I almost didn't survive. I will never banish hope again. It perches in my soul, yes, but recently hope has expanded its horizons, taking up residence in my life as a whole. I have visions of fully engaging in the world, not simply existing in it. I have visions of fulfilling my purpose here, whatever such purpose may be, not simply marking the days until I die. I have visions of happiness, not merely grateful contentment for a life with little conflict. I have not only hope, but high hope. Though I once tried to reject it, "the thing with feathers" deigned to stay, never stopped singing at all, and at last came to fruition.

I take Jaye to the airport early Tuesday morning, come back, and hit the swimming pool for an hour. If it helps ease the sharp ache of her absence, it's not enough to notice. The hollowness of missing her is almost a living, breathing thing.

Back at my house, after my swim, I try to find something to do. I stand in the loft, thinking how Jaye liked the idea of making the loft into the bedroom. I end up spending the morning completely rearranging my second floor. Lamp, reading chair and side table are moved into the bedroom, while the bed gets disassembled and put together again in the loft. When I get it all done I put fresh sheets on the mattress and clamber in, recline against the headboard, and stare at the mountains. I watch them change color as thunder clouds build up above them. The sight is beautiful, and my mind goes peacefully still as I watch.

Actually, the peace doesn't last for more than a few seconds. My mind never shuts up, ever. But the mélange of thoughts and images swirls through like a lazy Southern creek versus Class V rapids.

A lazy Southern creek, wrapping itself around Jaye. Her eyes as she watches me, her smile as we talk, the incredible tenderness of her touch, the things we're learning about each other. It's everything I've ever dreamed of, except for the distance.

"I want to completely change your life," Jaye had said in Portland. Less than a month later—

Mission accomplished. For the first time in my life, I know I am in love. And with someone who might be in love with me.

Love. I suppose the next step is to tell her. But the thought of uttering those words locks me up like the gold in Fort Knox.

I can love, and love deeply. But saying 'I love you,' letting it be known for sure? Whole other story. Expressing love is baring it all, and I've never done it without getting burned. I wish I could forget the distance and the age difference and the shadow of depression, but those are the tattoos marking me. Those will never go away.

I glance at the clock: Soccer practice is ending. Another hour or so and Jaye will call.

I decide if Jaye says the words, then I will. Does that make me cowardly? Or sensible? Are we both in opposing holding patterns, each waiting for the other to make the move?

I slide off the bed and go downstairs to fix lunch. I know me, I know my patterns. Coward wins.

"Rachel, if this was on real paper, it would catch fire."

I'm having lunch with Toni, and we're discussing the *Triangle* novel. It's Wednesday. Barely thirty hours removed from Jaye, and it's like torture. Our long, affectionate, innuendo-filled conversation on Tuesday night left us both hot and bothered and frustrated. It's good to get out of the house. It's also good to get confirmation that the new, happy ending and the jazzed-up love scene work.

I smile. "Worth keeping?"

"I think so," Toni says. "Is Jaye getting as much out of this as you are?"

"She's the MVP of the league at this point, so yes."

"Not that you're biased."

"You can look up the stats!"

"I know you think I was harsh with her Monday night, but you also know I only want the best for you."

I do know. But I'm still a little miffed at Toni's lack of faith. "You're not going to have to hunt her down, Antoinette. Ever."

Using her full given name earns me a grimace. "I suppose I can put a bug in Paula's ear about Dallas TRACON now."

"Yeah. Why hasn't she applied already? TRACON or Fort Worth Center would jump at the chance to have her. And you'd be home."

"We didn't do it because it would have left you alone."

I stare at her. "What?"

"You need friends, Rachel. Friends nearby. Paula and I wanted to be here for you."

I am stunned. I had never once thought Toni would forego moving back to Texas because of me. "Tell me you're kidding."

Toni's stern expression doesn't change, but there is the love of a friend in her eyes. "No. You're a good woman, Rachel. I know you like being alone, but you can't be alone all the time. I'd've worried too much about you if I went home. Besides, Colorado's been okay." She smiles. "But now that you have Jaye, I can let myself think about it."

Friday evening Jaye's impish smile comes at me from New Jersey. The Blues have an away game against Sky Blue FC (my writer's mind is fraught with pun possibilities), and she's hanging out in the hotel room talking to me.

"Hey," she says, "I need to ask you something."

"Anything."

"I want to change my Facebook status to 'in a relationship.' Is it okay to use your name?"

"Why wouldn't it be?"

As soon as I say the words, though, the implications of Jaye's going public with "us" flood my mind. Despite the marketing advantages for an author, I'm not on Facebook, and I know I'm one of maybe ten people on the planet who isn't. Anything popping up there is available to the known world instantaneously. If Jaye posts that we're a couple, then my little oasis of privacy will essentially be gone.

Am I ready for this?

As an air traffic controller, I had to make quick, accurate decisions. I don't waste time with this one. "Yes, it's all right, but do me a favor. Use my real name for now, and give me a couple of days to think about outing me as The Fyrequeene. Okay?"

"Outing you?"

"Almost no one knows I'm The Fyrequeene. I think I can handle the change, but let me get used to the idea."

"I won't say anything at all if you don't want me to."

I am so *not* going there. "Jaye—we are not a secret. If you want the world to know, tell them. I'm unbelievably lucky to have you. Shout it from the rooftops if you want."

"Wow. Okay. Listen. Is there any way you can come to KC like, on Sunday? We get back from Jersey about four."

My original plan was to leave Denver on Wednesday for the four-day drive to Cape Cod. I would have spent Wednesday night with Jaye, then left. She, as usual, has suggested something much more sensible in terms of our spending time together.

"You don't have any team obligations Sunday night?"

"No. You'll be my obligation."

"I take it you'll want me to get a room."

Jaye's laugh is low and sultry. Pure, smoky Bacall. "Or we can scandalize Nickory and Bree."

"As long as they don't want in on the act." I'm not sure where that thought comes from.

Jaye ignores it anyway. "Won't happen. Come Sunday."

"You promise I'll come Sunday?" I can't do the sultry voice, but I can do the double entendre.

"As many times as you want."

Sounds like a plan.

The Blues beat up on Sky Blue Saturday evening. The home team should have given KC a better game, but nothing works for them, and Nickory plays better than she has all season. She makes three spectacular saves in the first forty-five minutes, while Jaye spreads the wealth in the attack half, assisting on goals by Kirstie Longstreet and Sherry Cavallini. Near the end of the match, Kirstie is tackled ten yards from the goal, which leads to a penalty kick. Jaye takes the kick and buries the ball in the net, extending her scoring streak to five games. Final score, 4-0, Blues. I am one proud girlfriend and happy fan.

The last part of my Sunday drive to Kansas City occurs under cloudy skies and threats of rain. I dodge raindrops east of Salina and end up pulling into the townhome complex a little after five.

I don't have a key to the townhome, and nobody's there when I arrive, so I wait things out in the shade of a tree near the pool, which is full of kids. After twenty-six noisy minutes (yes, I count them), I'm relieved to see Nickory's every-bell-and-whistle Jeep Wrangler finally drive up.

Turns out she and Jaye have just gotten in, too, with bad weather delaying the team's flight by a couple of hours. Nickory, who I've learned barely tolerates flying, is her usual reticent self with a hefty dose of crankiness thrown in. Jaye is marginally more civilized.

After a perfunctory hug, Jaye says, "We had to hold over frickin' Nebraska for forty-five minutes! What is it about puffy white clouds that scares you air traffic controllers so much?"

I give Jaye an unapologetic stare. "Were the puffy white clouds big and anvil-shaped?"

Jaye nods, and Nickory grimaces as she opens the door and lets us all in.

"Those kinds of puffy white clouds hide thunderstorms, which eat airplanes, given the opportunity. The controllers were keeping you safe. Appreciate them."

I slide my arm around Jaye's waist. "Or better yet, appreciate this retired one who's here to make it all better."

Jaye melts into my half-hug. "I missed you," she says softly, right before she kisses me. We don't go overboard with passion, but our lips linger together long enough to draw a comment from Ms. Grumpy.

"Bedroom's right around the corner."

Jaye lifts her head and shoots a glare at her friend. "Yes, it is." She takes my hand. "Promise you won't slam any doors this time?"

I blink at Jaye in astonishment, then risk a glance back at Nickory. There is fire in her eyes and a hard set to her jaw.

"I won't be here," she says. "I'm going to go run."

"See you later." Jaye's response sounds friendly enough, but as soon as we get to her room and close the door, I have to know.

"What's up with you and the warrior queen?"

"Warrior queen?"

Have I not yet said that out loud? "Nickory."

Jaye drops her bag, relieves me of mine, and wraps her arms around my waist. "We had a fight."

"About me."

"I don't want to talk about it."

No, of course not. "Are you two okay?"

"We will be."

Any further discussion is forestalled by the touch of Jaye's lips to mine. And this is perfectly okay.

"Being away from you is getting harder."

Jaye's honesty is borne out by the enthusiasm of this evening's sex. We didn't actually hear Nickory leave, and so were more quiet than usual. This gave things an intensity beyond what we usually experience, which is saying something.

But I'm in complete agreement with her. "Yeah. It is. I don't know how I made it through the week."

"Especially without phone sex."

"Shut up!"

"How did you ever live without me?"

"Oh, it was a war, an absolute war," I say, and we both know I'm only semi-joking.

Jaye pushes herself up so she can meet my eyes. "No more wars."

I kiss her, lightly. "You know, if the depression was something I had to go through to end up with you, it was worth it."

"Nobody should have to go through that."

"True. But I did, and if because I did I was able to have you? I'll take the deal."

"I wish we'd met sooner."

I laugh. "We couldn't have met much sooner. You'd've still been jailbait!"

Jaye gives me a playful push. "Not true. We could have met ten years ago, when I was twenty-one, which is legal everywhere."

I shake my head. "We met when we were meant to. Let's be happy with what is."

"Are you happy?"

I reach out, caress her face. "Indescribably happy."

Not quite *I love you*. But I'm getting closer.

Monday afternoon a thunderstorm rolls through Kansas City. I'm reading outside on the patio when the wind kicks up and thunder rumbles. I put the book down and get lost in scanning the clouds. They are storm clouds, but not the deep dark threatening kind that bring tornados. This will only be rain. The thunder is constant, but after a while I realize there's no lightning—it's all hidden behind the swirling gray masses of moisture. The rumble of thunder with no apparent cause fascinates me. It could be angels, in heaven, bowling. Or the shellfire of distant war.

Or, I think, as raised voices come from inside, salvos from my lover and her best friend arguing in the kitchen. Apparently last week's argument didn't settle anything. With a nonchalance well-feigned, I waltz into the kitchen.

"A fight! Can I play?"

The pair turn to me. I'm surprised at the venom in Nickory's expression. It's all I can do not to take a step back. Words, I think. Buried before she starts.

"Nickory doesn't think we should be together," Jaye says, clearly peeved.

"That's not what I said," Nickory grinds out, her jaw tight.

"You said Rachel's too old for me," Jaye snaps back. "You said we were moving too fast. You said I don't know her. I went to college, Nickory. I can draw my own conclusions."

Nickory opens her mouth, but I beat her to it. "She's right, Jaye."

Both of them gape at me in astonishment. I elaborate.

"It's been less than a month. I'm older than the soccer coach bitch. We haven't even scratched the surface of knowing each other." Before Jaye's head starts to come off, I finish up. "But remember what you told me that night in Portland? When I said we didn't know each other?"

Jaye blanks out. "I said a lot of things then."

"A lot of wonderful things, one of which was, 'isn't that why people get involved? To know each other?' Remember?"

I watch her anger literally pour itself down a drain. "Yeah," Jaye says, glaring back at Nickory. "I do remember."

I turn back to Nickory, too. "That's what we're doing. That's why we're involved. And it would be nice if you'd stop acting like a jealous high schooler and give your best friend some support. After all, it's her call, isn't it?"

The venom does not recede. "Doesn't mean I'm wrong."

"Fine," I say. "You've made your point. But even if you're right, I'm not going to turn away someone as wonderful as Jaye because you disapprove. If Bree was twenty years older than you, would you have turned her down if Jaye didn't like it?"

Nickory sets her jaw and steps toward me, fists clenched. "Don't bring Bree into this."

Fists, I'm toast . . . shit.

Before she can actually raise her hands, Jaye steps between us. "Whoa! That's enough, both of you."

I seize the opportunity and take a small step back. Jaye gapes at her best friend, bewildered. "What the hell, Nickory?"

A host of expressions, all of them dark, play across Nickerson's face. I hallucinate they have something to do with eviscerating me. But I'll never know, thank goodness, because she abruptly turns on her heel and walks away, through the dining area and back toward the bedrooms.

I start breathing again while Jaye watches her go. "I've never seen her like that before." She sounds a little lost.

"Probably a good thing," I say, far more casually than I feel. "Let's get out of this war zone, go to dinner or something, okay? You and me."

Jaye, staring toward the hallway, nods absently. "Okay."

We end up at Carenza's, a nearby pub, lesbian-owned and woman-centric. The pub is a quiet, comfortable place where music actually plays softly in the background, rather than pounding from a million speakers.

Jaye gets a beer, and I indulge with a Bombay Sapphire and tonic, heavy on the lime.

"I've never seen her react like that before," Jaye says.

"Nickory doesn't approve of me."

"She's never approved of anyone I've been with."

"Any idea why?"

Jaye leaks a tiny smile. "Until you, she was right. They weren't worth her approval."

"Did you ever fight her on any of them?"

A sip of beer. A slow shake of her head. "No. They were all one-night stands, remember?"

"But you're fighting her on me."

A glare. "Shouldn't I fight for you?"

I take Jaye's hand. "Absolutely. Because I don't want to go anywhere."

She is slightly mollified. "But you think we're moving too fast?"

"Yeah. But I also feel like we've got something strong." I sip my drink. "Maybe we're blinded by sex right now, but I'm not complaining."

Jaye's brow furrows. "You're not just doing this for the sex?"

My denial is immediate and vehement. "No!" Then I get a glimmer. "Is Nickory telling you that?"

"More or less."

"Do you feel she's right? Because your opinion counts, not hers."

She turns the table on me. "Do you think *I'm* just doing it for the sex?"

I laugh. "No. Because if you were, it wouldn't be with me."

Jaye's hand slams down on the table, loud enough to turn every head our way. "Cut that out!" she says with enough force to make me sit straight up. "Stop putting yourself down. I mean it."

I stare at her, speechless.

"I think you're beautiful, and sexy, and amazing, and *that* counts. Okay?"

Someone in the bar claps quietly. Three or four someones, actually. Tentatively I lift Jaye's hand to my lips, kiss it softly.

"Okay," I say humbly. Maybe I've finally learned a lesson.

Jaye sees something in my demeanor that says she made her point. "Can we agree we're not doing it for the sex?"

I nod. "Yes."

"Good."

We both take healthy hits of our drinks, and the waitress comes up to take our dinner order.

"Don't get me wrong, though," I say after the server leaves. "I love the sex."

"Good." The word is accompanied by a hint of flame in Jaye's eyes.

"But I also love simply being with you, getting to know the woman you are. Finding out what we have in common and what we don't. I'm delighted we read the same books, prefer quiet nights to noisy bars, cats to dogs, whatever. I'm connecting with you like with no one else."

"Why doesn't Nickory see it?"

"I think she does, Jaye. I think she's afraid of losing you."

"She's not going to lose me!"

"Yes, she is. Probably. I mean, if we keep going like we're going, eventually we'll move in together, right?"

"I hope so." Big smile.

"Which means you'll no longer be part of Nickory's everyday life."

"But we'll still be friends."

"True. But it won't be the same for her."

"She's my best friend," Jaye says plaintively. "Why can't she be happy for me?"

I have a suspicion about why, but I'm not about to voice it. So I shrug and play dumb.

"I don't know."

Tuesday morning Jaye and Nickory go to practice together, and when Jaye comes back she tells me they settled some issues. I have my doubts, but Jaye appears to be a lot less worried than she was last night, so I hope it's true and keep my mouth shut.

In complete contrast to yesterday's storms, today is gorgeous and sunny. In lieu of another run-in with Nickory, I suggest we go to a park near the townhome. Jaye eagerly agrees. We pack a picnic lunch, take the short walk, find a lovely shade tree to sit under, and things go fine until she decides she wants to take a picture of us.

I don't waste any time trying to dissuade her of this notion. "What, you have the makeup artists ready? The airbrush expert?"

Jaye glares at me, lowers the iPhone. "I thought we'd agreed. No more putting yourself down."

"Maybe I'm talking about you."

She laughs.

I turn away, hiding a grin. "I'm not photogenic."

"Neither am I, for crying out loud, and there're a million pictures of me on the Internet!"

"Yeah. Pictures of your gorgeous legs, dead-perfect abs, and killer smile."

"My abs? Show me."

Ah-ha. Successful distraction. I grab my own iPhone and tap the screen. With a few quick swipes I find what I want.

Jaye stares at the candid shot, taken during a game, one of those moments where she's lifted her shirt to wipe sweat off her face. I've seen similar pictures of many women players, and male players, too, out there in cyberspace. Even on a four-inch screen one can see the exquisite definition of Jaye's stomach muscles.

"Huh," she says. "I guess you *can* find everything on the Internet."

"Pretty much."

"Dead perfect, you think?"

"Oh, yeah."

"Smile when you say that."

I do, and she's got me. iPhone comes up and photo is snapped before I can react.

"Jaye!"

She's checking out the result. "It's a good picture. Honest."

Reluctantly, I peer over. She's right, I suppose. I've never considered myself at all photogenic. "You're going to put it on Facebook, aren't you?"

"Of course."

I take in her self-satisfied expression, then make a quick grab for the phone. Silly me. Jaye pulls it away, leaps up and takes off, twenty years younger and twenty times more fit. She's halfway across the park before I get to quarter-speed. I stop and throw up my hands in surrender, realizing that deep down, I'm pleased she wants to do this, to show people who her lover is.

Maybe I should at last consider joining Facebook so I can do the same thing.

Tuesday night everyone is home. I've discovered the Musketeers are, like me, on the introverted side and actually enjoy doing stuff around the house. On this evening, rather than watch yet another soccer match, Bree insists on a game of Scrabble.

"Nickory and Jaye against me and Rachel," she announces.

I laugh. "You seriously think the jocks have a chance?"

"I hear you!" Jaye says from the kitchen, where she and Nickory are cleaning up after dinner. "I have an English degree, remember? And you don't!"

"But she's a writer," Bree calls out, winking at me. "And I know all the medical words."

"Like I said," this time aiming my words at the kitchen, "do you think the jocks have a chance?"

I've turned to look that way as well, in time to catch Nickory's expression as she hands Jaye a plate. Her face shines with unguarded desire, longing, and love—lots of love—all aimed at Jaye. A chain reaction, like puzzle pieces falling into place, glides down my spine. It feels right. It feels true. It hits me like a two-by-four in the hands of Bigfoot. Suspicion confirmed.

I glance over at Bree. She's seen it, too. There's no missing the bleakness in her expression. But she's not about to go there. "Rachel, help me set the game up."

I move to comply, a knot of tension twisting my stomach, a whirlwind of emotions spinning in my head. Confusion, fear, and helplessness all congeal into one overriding sensation. Despite my bravado when we were arguing, I'm certain I can't compete with Nickory. If the warrior queen decides to make a play for my girlfriend, I am lost. Lost.

Nobody seems to notice my silence as we take our places. Partners sit opposite each other, which means Jaye ends up sitting to my right. As the game starts she puts her hand on my thigh and keeps it there. Could it be she has no awareness whatsoever of Nickory's feelings? Or is she the best actress in the world?

Her fingers slide idly along my skin, her touch slowly easing some of my tension. No, I decide. Jaye doesn't know. Her open nature couldn't hide such knowledge. All may be lost, but it's not lost yet.

Focusing on the game, I examine the board, then my tiles. A few moves in I spot the perfect place for a killer word. I'm struck, then, by the urge to clobber Nickory at the one thing I know I'm better at. My mood shifts from confusion and fear to cold competitiveness.

"You're trying to distract me," I accuse Jaye, the first words I've spoken since play began.

She smiles, fingers brushing along my thigh from knee to hip. "And it's working."

"Not entirely," I say smugly and lay out ZYGOTE on a triple word score bonus. The Y lands on a double letter, so my team tallies sixty-nine points in one go.

Bree makes a touchdown sign with her arms. "Yes!"

Jaye grimaces, but keeps her hand on me. "Still a lot of game left."

"True," Nickory says in that ebullient way of hers. She's a little too calm as she studies her tiles, examines the board, then glances over at Bree.

Uh-oh.

Still watching Bree, Nickory shakes her head, and plays out "earning" on the Y I just laid down.

YEARNING crosses a double word square, plus Nickory gets fifty points for using all her tiles.

I am trumped, 74-69. Shit.

I bite back the urge to say "How apropos," instead managing a very grudging, "Nicely done." Spoken through clenched teeth.

Jaye squeezes my thigh in delight. Bree is mute with shock.

"I went to college, too," Nickory reminds us. No smugness at all, but there's a hint of yesterday's venom in her dark eyes as they pass across mine.

The game never quite gets cutthroat, but it's obvious Nickory and I are serious about beating each other. I can understand why Bree thinks we are both alpha personalities. And I think Jaye sees the Three Musketeers will never, ever be Four. Bree throws me. I have no idea what she's picking up on—or already knows.

In the end, the letters fall our way, and Bree clinches the match with an obscure medical term, putting us in the lead. I should feel like I'm on top of the mountain, but the victory is hollow. Winning a skirmish is not winning the war, as I well know, and this war is one I neither want nor want to lose.

When Jaye and I finally settle into bed, I want to make love to her with a fierceness that feels like freshly exploded ordnance. I want the walls to rattle like they did at the Hampton Inn, leaving Nickory with no doubts about who can satisfy Jaye best.

But it scares me, this fierceness. This is not loving Jaye, but using her to prove something, and I resist the competitive urge. When I wrap her in my arms, my kisses are as soft and tender as one would bestow on a newborn baby. Full of love, full of wonder, but with passion well banked.

"Are you all right?" Jaye asks.

"I'm always all right when I'm with you."

This leads to some more kisses, but Jaye doesn't let the subject go. "Something's bothering you."

Tears spring up in my eyes. I'm seized with the fear that this closeness is going to end any day now. I start a slow, light, fingertip exploration of

Jaye's body, like I'm trying to memorize the feel of her skin against mine, the gentle touch of her hands, her lips, even her hair.

"Yeah," I say, eventually.

"Tell me?"

I truly don't want to. "Can I think about it for a while?"

Jaye doesn't answer right away. Then she says, "Do you just not want to lie to me?"

Ouch. "I won't ever lie to you, Jaye."

"But you sure want to keep a lot to yourself."

The coward in me has been pulled out of the closet and into the harsh light of day. "Yeah, sorry. I've always kept my thoughts to myself. It's a hard habit to break."

"Are you kidding? Your blogs are full of thoughts and opinions."

"The blogs are The Fyrequeene's. She's much braver than I am."

"She's the same person. Don't you get that?"

"On some level." I lower my head to Jaye's shoulder and wrap my arm around her waist. "But she's also the shield protecting me from the big cruel world."

"And you're using her to protect yourself from me?"

"No. I'm trying my best to be the real me with you."

"Good," Jaye's arm tightens around my back. "I was raised to be honest, Rachel. And I believe in honesty. It can make things hard sometimes, but we've got to have it. You understand, right?"

"Yes. If we're honest, we're true to each other. We make everything real, and I don't want us to be anything else." I slide away from Jaye, enough to get my arm under me, to lift myself up enough to meet her eyes. "I promise never to lie to you."

"But you'll make me ask what's wrong a lot, won't you?"

I look at her sheepishly. "Yes. I'll try to be better. I promise that, too."

Jaye sort of half-laughs and tries again. "What's wrong, Rachel?"

I have, and want, a smart lover, but it comes with a price. I take a breath and plunge in. "Nickory's in love with you."

There is a seriously pregnant pause before Jaye bursts out laughing, which I admit was not on my list of potential reactions.

"Ohhh-kay," she says. "Now I know you're not perfect."

My spirits lift a little, caught up in her mirth. But I'm a little pissed, too. "I never claimed to be."

"What makes you think she's in love with me?"

"The way she observes you. Her expressions when you aren't looking." Particularly in the kitchen, before the Scrabble game. "The way she doesn't like me, like I'm taking you away from her."

Jaye shakes her head. "Nickory and Bree are totally happy, and they have been for ten years. Nickory loves me as a friend, I know. And I love her. But she's not in love with me. She would have said something by now."

Jaye sounds so sure. I don't hear any undercurrent of doubt. My spirits lift a little more.

"Besides, I love *you*. Doesn't matter what Nickory feels."

Her comment comes out so casually neither of us notice at first. But our synchronicity is consistent, and we register the words at exactly the same time.

I go still. Jaye blinks. We stare at each other, a little shocked.

Then she smiles. Weakly. "See? That's how to say things: Blurt them out all of a sudden."

Right. This is the moment for me to blurt "I love you" out, too, but my heart is in my throat and I can't say anything. I fall back on the good old standard of kissing her instead.

She returns my kiss, and God, it feels so wonderful, like it has every time we've been together. The feel of her skin against me, the touch of her hands, the precious miracle of her presence. It feels like—Christ, it feels like home.

Now I'm kissing her both to hide my speechlessness, and to keep from crying

And she knows. "You don't have to say it back," Jaye says when our lips part again. "But give yourself the chance to come around to my point of view. Okay?"

Oh, I'm there. But I'm still too cowardly to say so.

Jaye actually beats me to wakefulness in the morning, gives me a few tender kisses, then gets up at dawn to do some running. When sleep turns itself off, I rise and wander into the kitchen to find Bree sitting at the table by herself, white terry cloth robe contrasting nicely with her dark skin. The iPad is on, her coffee mug securely in her left hand.

"Morning," she says cheerfully. "Chocolate muffins by the toaster."

I smile, a little, grab a muffin, and set water boiling for tea. "No work today?"

"Off today, two weeks of swings starting tomorrow."

I grimace in sympathy. "I always hated those rotating schedules. Nickory sleeping in?"

"She went out with Jaye. I think they were going to practice right after."

Good. I find a teabag and a mug, a saucer for my muffin, pour the water when it boils, and cart my breakfast to the table.

Then I set about ruining Bree's good mood. As my tea steeps, I say, "Bree, how long have you known?"

Bree avoids my eyes; it's obvious she knows exactly what I'm referring to. The question is, will she talk about it?

I have time to doctor up my tea with cream and honey and take a healthy bite of scrumptious chocolate muffin before she comes to a decision.

Tentatively, Bree says, "I'm not sure it's what you think."

I finish chewing and swallow. "I'm open to persuasive evidence against."

Bree gets up for more coffee, a nice delaying tactic, but I'm not going anywhere. She comes back to the table and only now engages me face to face.

"The one constant in Nickory's life, other than soccer and me, has been Jaye. Except for college and the National Team, they've always played on the same teams, took part in the same camps, and Jaye has always roomed with us."

"Always?"

"Except when we were out of town for the Olympics and the World Cups. I wondered about it in the beginning, but Nickory told me about Jaye and the older woman—you know about that?"

"The soccer coach bitch? Yes."

Bree grins for a second at my turn of phrase. "It was a little odd, but I figured Nickory was being a good friend, and I grew to love Jaye like a sister. I hoped she'd find somebody, but I got to where I could live with the idea of us going along as, like you say, the Three Musketeers, sharing apartments and houses, Nickory and Jaye probably coaching the same college team somewhere, until we all ended up in the same nursing home."

"Could still happen."

Bree throws me the patent-worthy laser glare. "You know better than that."

"I can only hope."

Bree rolls her eyes, gets back on point. "Anyway, one day I realized Nickory always made sure, somehow, to turn Jaye off anyone she might have dated."

"Really?"

"Oh, yeah. She was subtle about it, but it always worked. At first I thought she was being over-protective, but then I tried to talk to her one day about how she felt about Jaye, and it turned into the worst fight we ever had. She blew up on me, denied it to the heavens, then ignored me for two days. So I let it go."

"Okay. Seems like it still adds up to Nickory being in love with Jaye."

Bree takes a long sip of coffee. "And Jaye is in love with Nickory?"

I take a long sip of my tea. "She was once, wasn't she?"

"Did she tell you that?"

"Not in so many words."

"Uh-huh. What words did she use?"

"She said she never slept with Nickory—"

"Truth."

"—and I asked, 'but did you ever want to?' And she said yes." Not in so many words, but I don't want to get all caught up in explanations.

Bree takes this in, eyes narrowing. "And where do I fit in this equation?"

Her voice is quiet, but her tone tells me I'm on thin and cracking ice. "What do you mean?"

"Do you think Jaye is honest?"

"Yes," I say unequivocally.

"Good. Because the argument over Jaye turned into a real rough patch for Kat and me. Jaye was the one who finally knocked some sense into our heads. She told me that in all the years she roomed with Nickory on the road, she never once saw her tempted by another woman. She told me more than a few women tried. Fans, coaches, the press, a teammate or two. I still remember Jaye poking me in the chest, saying 'She stayed faithful to you. Who stays faithful, Bree? Someone who loves her partner.'"

I listen, half-hoping a sinkhole will open up and swallow me.

"She clearly said something equally powerful to Kat the same day because Kat apologized to me, even though I was the one who'd screwed up. We had a long talk in bed and worked things out. Now—if Jaye was in love with Nickory—would she have helped us out? And if Nickory was in love with Jaye, wouldn't that have been her moment?"

It's all I can do to meet Bree's eyes. I haven't had a beatdown like this in a long time. And I totally deserve it. "I'm sorry. I can be a real idiot sometimes."

I must sound sincerely forlorn because Bree backs off a little. "A lot of people assume shit about Kat and Jaye that isn't true. I thought you'd know better."

"I should have. But even now it's hard for me to believe someone like Jaye could want someone like me. Doesn't like crowds, doesn't like parties, a lot older—"

"Shut up," Bree says, but she's not quite as grim and hard as she was a second ago. "You can't know this, but I do, and I'm going to tell you. Jaye's not big on parties, either. She doesn't need a lot of people around. Give her a good book or a gym or a soccer ball and she's happy. And she's always had a thing for older women."

"She has?"

"Yes." Bree pauses a moment. "Jaye was sixteen when she got screwed over. She gets a pass there. But in the time I've known her, she's been a good judge of people. If she likes you, you're okay. And she more than likes you." Bree looks now like she wants to poke me in the chest. "Fact: Jaye's in love with you, Rachel. Can you believe that?"

"Yes. She told me last night."

Bree rolls her eyes as if overwhelmed by the idiot in front of her. "Then she means it. Right here, and right now. Her feelings will change only if you fuck it up."

Which I feel infinitely capable of doing.

Chapter Eight

Fyrequeene's Blog   June 11

"This Thing, This Thing, This Amazing Thing."

All my life I have walked through this world alone. Sure, I played intramural sports in college. I have an affectionate if distant family, and I am now part of a sisterhood of writers I value dearly. But none of those ever gave me a sense of truly belonging, none ever closed the distance between me and the rest of the world. As solitude settled in and put down roots I, too, settled down and into the belief that being alone was, for whatever reason, my fate in this lifetime.

I settled. I took the gift of my writing, used it to tell of characters who speak to me and through me, revealing their stories of strength and weakness, bravery and fear. They love and are loved, hurt and are hurt, and they have adventures and journeys to find goodness in life. I took pleasure in chronicling their tales, content to let them partially fill my own heart's emptiness.

The existence I molded was perfectly okay. There was a freedom to being able to make choices without having to consult or get approval from someone else, and that freedom could get me through the rest of my days, keep me safe and occupied, and mostly distracted from the void in my soul. It would be fine.

And then someone came to me. She welcomed me into her life, somehow got me to welcome her into mine, and in the process turned my existence completely upside down. Suddenly I have a place in the world of another, and with each passing day I feel like I've been there all the time. Suddenly this woman, this lover, this treasure belongs in my life, and it feels like we've known each other forever. We are in that first blissful stage where we do not bicker, we do not argue, we both understand the need for the long separations born of living in different cities. We miss each other deeply when we're apart, and we love each other twice as deeply when we're together.

Now I have the freedom to make choices with another, to consider what is best for two, not one. We have the freedom to ponder a future of closeness, comfort, and yes, compromise, but compromise born of togetherness, not solitude.

How empowering this is, how wondrous, to share between us the great gift of connection and caring. I feel as if I have the strength to move mountains, both hers and mine. I want the simple pleasure of walking by her side, and I want the challenges of helping her realize her dreams. I want to keep telling my stories, but I also want to make her life's story be the best it can be. I want to give all I can—and take all I'm given.

I am still who I was. I am also, at last, infinitely more. I have become part of a "We." And I want to keep being "We," for as long as she'll have me.

This evening Jaye and I have the house to ourselves. Bree uses the excuse of being on swing shift for the next two weeks to take a night out and drag Nickory to a club somewhere. The significant glance she gives me as they walk out the door says everything her voice does not.

I'm grateful, even though all Jaye and I end up doing is having a quiet dinner, then sitting on the couch in the living room, me on my computer, her on the iPad, doing that oh-so-21st-Century social media thing. Granted, we are sitting side by side, legs touching from hip to ankle as we use the coffee table for an ottoman. I have been giving the beatdown from Bree a lot of thought, and I'm trying to coalesce my reaction, feelings, and conclusions into something bloggable. It's working, but it's also turning out to be far more honest and raw than I've ever been in public.

Still, I persevere, and as I type the last sentence Jaye breaks the silence.

"Hey," she says quietly.

Her timing, once again, is perfect. "Yes, dear?" My tone is right out of *Father Knows Best*.

Jaye grins. "I'm going to post your photo on Facebook."

I cringe. "Must you?"

"Yes. Face it, Bogart, you're beautiful, and I want everyone to know. But I need a caption."

Too easy. "Not everything you meet in a graveyard is dead," I say, then burst out laughing at my own humor.

After a second, I realize Jaye is not amused. "I'm serious about this, Rachel," she says.

I stop laughing. "I know."

"You're the most important person in my life. I'm a better soccer player for knowing you. I'm a better *woman* for knowing you. I want to tell the world, and it's not a joke. Okay?"

I minimize the blog file, then turn the computer so Jaye can see it. My desktop background is a photo of her, snapped by yours truly before one of her games. The KC Blues uniform brings out the color in her eyes, the sunlight turns her hair into spun gold, and her smile is happy and sexy and oh-so gorgeous.

"When I'm alone in Denver I stare at this picture and think about how much you mean to me, how you've changed my life, how amazing my world is now that you're in it. No, Jaye. It's definitely not a joke."

Jaye puts her arm around my shoulders and kisses my cheek. "Thank you."

"But wait, there's more." I bring the blog file back up. "This is what I've been working on for the last hour. I think I'm ready to post it, but I want you to see it first."

I watch her face as she reads, watch her expression change as she reads what I'm baring to the world. I've said some honest things in my blogs, but I've never been as open as this. She understands that by telling my readers about her, even if I don't yet say her name, I'm revealing how important she is to me.

Jaye has two expressions unique to her. One shows her vulnerability and the other is a secret smile which, despite our sometimes telepathic familiarity, I never quite fathom. When I see the vulnerability I know she's unsure, maybe suffering a little, but I might not understand why. When I see the smile, I know I've pleased her in some way, touched some chord that harmonizes with her soul, but again, I might not know why.

Tonight, as she reads my blog, I get both expressions. Only this time I know exactly what she's feeling. This evening, the chord strikes through both of us.

Tears shimmer in her eyes. Mine, too. This is where I tell her I love her. The moment's right, the emotion is there, and I'm sure she wants to hear it. But I'm terrified of saying the words, even if Jaye already has, terrified of losing my grip on this gossamer thread.

Before the silence goes too long, I take her iPad and put it on the coffee table, then do the same with my MacBook. Device free, I enfold her hands in mine and kiss first her palms, then the backs of them. I stand and move her gently down onto the couch, then follow her there, my face above hers, my eyes willing the message to her.

I love you, Jaye . . .

I brush our lips together, lingering at the taste of her, savoring each cell. Her mouth opens to me. I slide in to meet her tongue, still lingering, intense rather than passionate, embers rather than flames.

I break off and move to her neck, kiss the points of her collarbones, the hollow of her throat, the skin over the shield of bone guarding her heart. I open the buttons of her shirt to free her breasts, then kiss each one as slowly and thoroughly as I did her mouth.

A low moan of pleasure escapes her. She has one hand in my hair now, another trying to get the rest of the buttons open while I tease each nipple to rock-hard stiffness.

I love you, Jaye . . .

Somehow I manage to keep my lips on her as I still her hand and finish the job myself, getting the shirt buttons out of the way as well as the one on her jeans. The zipper is easy, and I sit up again to pull the jeans off her legs. She lifts her hips, our choreography is perfect, and she is naked before me.

I let myself get lost in her beauty. My hand traces a pattern from her sternum to her ribs to her navel and around, then back up the other side, to finish with a soft caress of each breast.

I begin the kisses again, starting at her solar plexus. A kiss to the center, the left, the right, a quiet slide down to her navel, a triplicate of kisses there, a further move down to her pubis, and another three kisses—to the center, to the curve where her left thigh meets her hip, to the curve on the opposite right side.

I love you, Jaye . . .

And then below.

I take the swelling of her clit into my mouth. She cries out my name, the first real word we've spoken since this started. Tears spring from my eyes as my lips envelop her. I taste her wetness, lap up her arousal, worship her in a slow partaking of total devotion.

Her flesh grows firm under my touch. It's hard to stay slow, but I keep my movements deliberate and steady. Jaye opens her hips to me, asks me for more with the movement. I slip my fingers into her depths, increase the rhythm slightly, build embers into fire into explosion.

I love you, Jaye.

When the fulfillment comes, it rockets through her, all of her, a convulsion of orgasm that almost takes us both to the floor. I stay with her, inside and out, ride her through wave after wave after wave. Her cries keen of release and joy, and

I love you, Rachel.

She doesn't say the words, but I literally feel them course through me. I *know* she is thinking them as I have thought them to her, here and now. My tears burst out in earnest, but I try to stay in tune with her body as the orgasm subsides.

She comes down from the crest, and I slip my fingers free after the last small spasms, brush one last kiss around her center; then I kiss my way up her body, ending not with my lips to hers, but with a gentle kiss to her cheek.

I watch her eyes come back into focus. Her fingers touch my tears, and then she slides her hand behind my head to pull me down and bring our lips together.

I feel the words again.

I love you Rachel.

I love you, Jaye.

The power of this, the strength of this, raises me to new levels. For the first time in my life, on a warm Kansas evening, I know the feeling of commitment.

And then I leave. The very next morning I leave the cocoon of love and warmth and connection and make my way along the interstate, across the Midwest and New England, to Cape Cod. I'm not even to Saint Louis when I realize I have company.

Depression has decided to launch an offensive of sorts, hovering over my senses, lurking in the background of every move I make. Why has it come now? Everything to do with my deeply rooted insecurities, perhaps, combined with what I think I know about Nickory. I don't mention it to Jaye when we FaceTime each night, and I tell myself it's because I'm so accustomed to living with this alone. I can survive it, I always have. I will again. But deep down, I know it's because I'm scared.

I have high hopes for my mood improving when I arrive in Provincetown, my favorite place in the world, a place that, as Lee Lynch once wrote, "wraps itself around you like a lover." I arrive, and the arms encircle me and it's good, but even feeling the metaphorical hug of acceptance isn't enough to stave off the gorilla.

Guerilla.

Whatever.

I walk the streets, breathe in the sea air, note the amazing variety of lesbians, gay men, straight couples, and families doing the same thing, and I see it all as if draped in a shroud. The magic of P-Town is still present, the draw still palpable, but on this visit, peace is elusive. I hope it's because, for the first time in my life, I have someone with whom I want to share this magic. And she's not here.

One evening, seriously out of sorts, I do something out of character to make myself feel better. After hanging out at Herring Cove Beach, watching the sun set, vainly hoping for the ocean to soothe me, I drive back into town, park my car near the hotel, and walk over to Commercial Street and up the stairs to the only bar in the world where people know my name.

"Rachel!" comes a greeting as I crest the stairs. Bartender Marie's voice is a welcome touch of the familiar, a balm to soothe my newly-hated solitude. If the ocean can't help me, maybe alcohol can. Usually I limit myself to two drinks. Not tonight.

Three hours and some unknown number of Cosmopolitans later it's closing time. I stagger out of the bar, turn away from the street, and stumble down to the harbor. The night is too beautiful to be inside yet, and if I walk along the water, the cops won't notice my lopsided gait.

The tide is low, so low that small boats close to the shoreline are resting on sand. I drift out onto the strand, ambling along, in no hurry. When the moon starts to rise behind the distant curve of the cape, I stop walking to watch it with awed fascination. It is huge, hanging there low in the sky, this amazing crescent of another world.

And I'm watching it alone.

I pull out my phone, too agitated to go another minute without talking to Jaye, too agitated to consider the consequences if I drop the thing. I'm too sloshed to figure out FaceTime, and almost too sloshed to find Jaye in my "favorites" section on the phone, though she's the only one there. I take a couple of deep breaths, letting the salt-and-fish-tinged air sharpen my senses, then focus my eyes on the iPhone's screen. Finally, my alcohol-fogged brain finds the right combination of swipes and taps.

Jaye answers on the first ring. She is quick on the uptake. "Have you been drinking?"

"Oh, yeah. I miss you so much, Jaye. How I wish you were here." I think of the Pink Floyd song and try not to cry.

"Are you okay?"

"Oh, yeah." Except for the emptiness of being fifteen hundred miles from her. Except for the damned gorilla. "I'm standing in the middle of Provincetown Harbor, at low tide. There are stars above me. The moon has come out. I saw a shooting star, and I wished for you. There's something wonderful about this place, Jaye, something magical. I wish you were here so you could feel it, too, and understand."

"Understand what, Bogart?"

"Understand, understand." I lose my train of thought. Actually, my train of thought pulled out of the "Cosmopolitan" station a couple of hours ago. But its absence doesn't stop me from rambling on in a way only someone with several drinks in them can.

"Being here fills my soul like nothing else. Well, nothing until I met you. You fill my soul, too. Like nothing else. Like the sun and the moon. The moon's hanging over the water tonight, it's amazing. I love this place, Jaye. I love you, too, you know, but I hope when you come you can feel the magic here. It's okay if you don't. But I hope you give it a chance."

Finally I stop talking, and while I'm waiting for Jaye to reply, I start to sit down on the sand, realize what I'm doing as my knees bend, and somehow (comically, I'm sure), manage to maintain a Leaning-Tower-of-Pisa upright stance.

"Is it really that wonderful?" Jaye asks quietly.

"Oh, yeah. It's magic to me, I want it to be magic for you, too. But it might not be, Jaye. It might not be. But I hope you give it a chance."

Another pause, like the two-second delay one gets on satellite broadcasts. "It must be special, Rachel, because you just said you love me."

I laugh, my drunken giggle swallowing a lurch of terror. Have I suddenly cursed the whole beautiful wonder of Jaye and me? "Well, I do, you know," I say, blowing the whole thing open. "I do love you."

"I love you, too. Are you home now?"

"No, no. I'm still standing in the harbor. It's so beautiful, it's so cool, except I'm all by myself."

The next day, in hindsight, I see why she ended up a little perturbed. Jaye thought "standing in the harbor" meant I was standing in water when I was merely on the sand with the tide out. When I FaceTime her again, in the late morning after the Tylenol has kicked in, I clear up the confusion. And maybe a couple of other things as well.

"Honest, I never get that drunk anymore," I say in response to Jaye's worried query. "Honest, the Rachel you've seen since Portland is the real one. Last night was an aberration."

"Why? We've been apart before, and you haven't done this."

"It's getting harder to be apart from you."

I see empathy in her eyes. "I know. But there's more to it this time. So tell me."

She knows me too well. Six weeks, and she knows me better than anyone in my life ever has.

"I'm fighting off depression, and I'm pissed about it."

"Why are you depressed?"

"I don't know. Part of it may be because you're not here. I can't wait to share this place with you—"

"—Rachel, stop. It's about Nickory, isn't it?"

I massage the dull throbbing bones of my forehead. "I'm sorry. I promised you I'd be more open, didn't I?"

She nods. "I guess that's a long-term project."

I close my eyes, then open them again. "You didn't see her expression. Naked, raw desire, Jaye. More than lust. Love, too."

"Okay, so what? Remember what I said? I love you, *you*, Rachel, and I meant it." Even over the wavering distance of FaceTime, Jaye locks me down with her stare. "And what did you tell me last night?"

"That I love you."

"Right. Say it again. Say it now."

I barely hesitate, the faintest catch of air as I breathe the words. "I love you, Jaye."

Her face suffuses with radiance, and I swear the screen starts to glow. "See?" she says. "It gets easier with practice."

I manage a wan but sincere smile. "I wish you were here. It's amazing how good I feel, when you're with me."

"Like nothing in the world can get to us."

"You feel it, too?"

Jaye laughs and shakes her head at the surprise in my voice. "Why do you think I'm so crazy about you? When we're together I feel like the best player in the world, like I can score fifty goals in a game." Her laughter fades to quiet affection. "I love you, Rachel. Stop worrying about Nickory."

Somehow I ration out my sanity over the next five days. I do my Provincetown thing, play tourist, walk the beaches, eat seafood, catch up on my reading. I limit myself to two drinks a day, if I drink at all. Depression hangs over everything, though, like it did in days of yore. My nightly talks with Jaye become my lifeline. Her voice recharges me, relights the shadows in my mind. I can't imagine how bad this would be without her to talk to. I've been fairly stable since my last rock-bottom point seven years ago, the details of which I've yet to tell Jaye. I have to wonder why it's coming back now. I finally conclude it's not only Nickory. It's Jaye, too. I've opened myself up to her, I'm vulnerable in a way I've never been before, and I can't simply "live in the moment" and enjoy it.

People who don't have depressions may wonder how I could be this way when I'm so in love. Truth, I don't get it, either. When I was younger I thought falling in love with someone who fell in love back would solve all my problems, and while I know that's way too Pollyanna for the real world, I still believed love could conquer all.

And it has, but at the same time it hasn't, which makes me wonder how fair I'm being. Can Jaye honestly want someone who can get like this at the best time in her life?

She keeps saying Yes.

"I know it's not going to be all sweetness and light," she tells me during our Thursday night talk. "We're going to have our challenges. I'm up for that."

"I don't see you ever being a challenge for me."

"Wait until I can't play soccer anymore and I don't know what to do with my life."

"Not a problem. We'll travel the world filling in every inch of your family tree, and then you can help me do research for my books."

She laughs, and knowing I've pleased her keeps the shadows at bay for another few hours.

Friday tests everything positive I have in me. I can't shake the sadness, despite knowing each passing hour brings me closer to being in Jaye's arms again. She's flying to Boston with the team today, and the scheduling means we won't talk until late.

I've booked a room at a Hilton by the airport for Saturday night and bought tickets on the puddle jumper that flies between Logan and the P-Town Municipal Airport. A little pricey, but quicker than the sea ferry, and it will give Jaye and me more time together. We've arranged to meet on Saturday in Copley Square, get some together time before her game. It will be great. If I survive Friday.

Most of the day is torture. I'm full of irrational fear. Darkness. Melancholy. Friday means weekend which means more tourists in town. Finding a quiet spot is almost impossible. I end up going out to the harbor at low tide, shortly before sunset, like I did the night I got drunk. This time there's no alcohol in me, just the gorilla/guerilla. I walk out onto the sand, as far out as I can get without going into the water, and stand out there to listen to the quiet of the evening.

I'm at the far east end of town, away from the heart of human activity. There is the occasional sound of a car passing by on the highway behind me, but mostly all I hear are birds, a whisper of breeze, and after some long moments of no thinking, peace.

There is peace here.

The bay is millpond calm, and I become calm with it. Even fifty yards offshore where I'm standing, the seawater is barely an inch deep. The tide is gradually, very gradually coming in, and I watch as seaweed, shells, bird tracks, and sand succumb to the slow, gentle creep of the water. An old, old Elton John song comes to my mind, one I haven't heard or thought of in years. I gaze out at the twilight as the chorus quietly plays in my head.

"Oh, my soul . . . oh, my soul . . . oh, my soul . . ."

My soul is troubled yes, but does, temporarily, find solace.

This lasts until a car horn blares behind me, three short blasts of anger. The peace shatters. I stick it out for a few minutes, but my mood is broken. I turn to walk back to the little hotel and wait for Jaye's call.

Which I discover I've missed because I left my phone in the room. She's left an affectionate voicemail, says she's tired from the flight but invites me to call back as long as it's before lights out at ten p.m. She can't wait to see me tomorrow in town. She loves me.

I check the clock: one minute to ten, I hit the call back button but get voicemail right away. Jaye's turned off her phone already. I know she needs her rest for the game, but a lurch of disquiet floods my heart, something on top of the ache of missing her.

Stop worrying, I tell myself, in twelve hours we'll be together. I can handle twelve hours. I play back her message to hear those precious last words.

"I love you, Rachel. See you soon."

The twelve hours crawl, but they do pass. I park my car at P-Town's tiny airport, fly over to Boston, ride the T to Copley Square, walk half a block, and see Jaye standing on the grass in front of Trinity Church.

Our eyes meet, and immediately I know something is different. Jaye smiles as she sees me. It's not the nine-thousand watts of brilliance I've grown used to, but a muted, almost wistful turn of her lips. I try to prevent my own happy expression from faltering.

We slide into each other's arms with ease, hold each other close. The pleasure of our hug is unchanged, though Jaye hangs on a little more tightly than normal, and the overall sense of safety and belonging I get in her arms feels muted.

"God, it feels good to hold you," Jaye whispers into my ear.

I lift my head to meet her eyes. The glow that always radiates from them isn't there, has been replaced by a scary sort of blank darkness. No, wait— the darkness is not blank at all, but swirls with something I can't puzzle out.

"Jaye?" My voice is soft, inquiring. "What's happened?"

She pulls away from me and holds out her hand. "Let's walk."

Oh, boy. I fight down my own little storm of clouds and uncertainty, accept Jaye's hand, and let her lead the way. She takes us away from the square, over a couple of streets to Commonwealth Avenue. Here the lanes of traffic are separated by a long mall, an attractive little park area with statues, trees, benches. The mall goes on for blocks, all the way to Boston Common. We only walk a little way, though, before she picks a bench in the shade and sits us down.

Jaye turns to face me. "I love you, you know."

"Yes." Even now, even with her weird demeanor, I feel the truth of her words.

"Something happened last night that made me sure, but I don't think you're going to like it."

A tremor passes through me. "I guess we won't know unless you tell me."

Jaye hesitates, like she's screwing up her courage. When she finally comes out with it, the words are jarring, a thunderclap from a clear blue sky "You were right about Nickory, maybe."

Jarring—and confusing as well. "Maybe?"

She bites her lower lip. "We hadn't talked much since you left, and last night I finally told her I was going to get my own apartment because I needed a place where you'd be welcome. She threw the same shit back at me—the age difference, you not being in a relationship before, yadda yadda. We went back and forth on it, and I finally said something like 'Rachel thinks you're in love with me, so maybe you're jealous.' Nickory got real still and stared at me, and I right then I thought it was true. I thought you were right."

Jaye is far from done, but she stops talking. We sit there, me waiting, her not meeting my eyes, until finally I blink.

"And then?" I ask.

"She got up and came over to me, pulled me up. She put her arms around me and said, 'Maybe I don't want to lose my family.'"

Now Jaye digresses a little. "Nickory doesn't have any contact with her parents. Bree and I, and my folks, we've become her family since her parents disowned her. So I understood that, and I let her hold me, and when she kissed me, I let her."

Something inside of me freezes up. Jaye doesn't notice.

"It was like I was sixteen again. Something came over me, and I wanted to know how she felt, so I kissed her back. I let myself get lost in it for a while. I honestly can't say if it was one minute, or ten."

The pain in Jaye's expression is clear as she admits this. Cold spreads out from my core, icing over my heart. "How far did it go?"

"My brain woke up when she pulled my shirt off and she started to touch—"

Jaye cuts herself off, takes a deep breath. "She wasn't going to stop at kissing me. All I could think was if I let this happen, I'd lose you. The message was so clear, 'You'll lose Rachel!' Almost like someone was shouting it at me."

I'm watching her in profile, and abruptly I recognize the darkness emanating from her. Fear. Jaye is not angry, not even guilty, much. She's afraid.

"I pushed Nickory away, hard," Jaye says. "I didn't let her say anything, I packed up my gear and switched rooms."

I give a fleeting thought to the rumors undoubtedly galloping through the team grapevine right now, but keep it to myself. So okay, the cold has not reached my brain. Not yet.

Jaye exhales. "I spent the whole night angry at Nickory, then angry at me for kissing her, then wondering if I've screwed things up, if it's already too late."

Her expression is hollow, haunted. "Please tell me it's not too late."

She's so sad, so bereft, sitting there with slumped shoulders. All I want to do is take her in my arms and make it better. And the beauty of it? Taking her in my arms *will* make her feel better. It's a win-win, right? But the cold within me is a solid ice wall, it won't thaw quickly. Still, I can do something. Instead of wrapping Jaye up in a hug, I take her hand in mine and interlock our fingers. My grip is firm, and I hope there's some comfort in it.

"I don't think ten minutes is a deal breaker, Jaye."

Her response is tentative, her tone beyond subdued. "I wish you sounded more sure."

Me, too. I keep hold of her hand as we fall into silence, get lost in my own head. Why *don't* I sound more sure? I love Jaye, right? The worst happened, right? She chose me in the end, right? So what's wrong?

I must be lost in my head for longer than I realize, because Jaye asks, "Where are you, Rachel?"

The little girl quality of her voice spears right through the ice in me. I want to comfort that little girl. I want everything to be all right for her.

"I'm trying to figure out what's wrong with me."

"There's nothing wrong with you."

My perfect lover strikes again. "Yes, there is. I love you, Jaye. Deeply. And my almost-worst nightmare came true, but you chose me in the end, right?"

"That's why I'm here now."

"Then why am I not dancing down the grass? Why am I not ecstatic and hugging you and kissing you? Why did my emotions bury themselves in a deep freeze?"

"I don't know. Do you want me to go?"

"No." My answer is immediate and unequivocal. There's hope for me yet. I tighten the grip on Jaye's hand so she doesn't try to get up anyway. "Can I ask you something?"

"Sure."

"If this were reversed, if I were the one coming to you saying I'd kissed another woman and almost went to bed with her, how would you feel?"

Little girl graduates to simple, clear, adult certainty. "You're not going to do that."

"You weren't going to either, were you?"

Jaye hangs her head. I touch her chin, raise her eyes to mine. "I'm not blaming you, Jaye. It happened, and I'm not angry. Honest."

"But you're something."

Too true. "Please humor me. How would you feel, say, if I met someone at the writer's convention I'm going to later in July. If something clicked, and I didn't go to bed with her, but we maybe slow-danced a few times and made out in a dark corner. And I told you about it and was genuinely apologetic and said it would never happen again."

She won't go there. "It wouldn't happen in the first place."

"How do you know?"

"I just do. You would never do it."

We're gazing into each other's eyes, and Jaye's are full of faith. She believes what she's saying. She is totally sure. Her expression and simple declarations combine to crack my ice. The frozen wall doesn't fly apart and shatter into tiny little shards, but I think part of my spirit does.

I let go of her hand, turn away and face the sidewalk. "But I thought you would. I thought if Nickory made her play you'd jump for it and be gone." I squeeze my eyes shut, ready to fall into complete and utter despair. "I don't deserve you."

I feel Jaye rest my head on her shoulder. "I don't deserve you, Rachel," she says softly. "So if we don't deserve each other, can that cancel things out and make it all okay?"

Now I'm fighting back tears. Ten days ago I made a commitment in my mind. Or so I thought. Faced with a bump in the road of my first relationship I sit here now confused, unsure, and stupid. If I'm committed to Jaye, then where is my certainty? The worst has happened, and we've passed with flying colors.

Or at least Jaye has. I seem to be tangled up in the flag.

"Please tell me what you're thinking," she asks.

A mélange of debris in the eye of a tornado. "A mess of stuff," I say out loud. "Can we walk again? For a bit?"

Jaye pulls me to my feet, keeps hold of my hand, and we saunter slowly down the mall toward Boston Common. The day is absolutely gorgeous, slightly cool, but sunny and full of positive energy. There are people around, but not huge crowds, and we move easily along the pathway. I try not to think about nearly melting down in public, but let the positive energy flow through me, try to put my soul back together. It works a little. I'm glad Jaye is with me. I'm so lucky Jaye is with me.

"If I could take back last night I would," Jaye says after a while.

"No, it needed to happen. At least now there's no what if."

"You're not acting like there's no what if."

"I know. But I don't know why."

We cover almost another block before Jaye speaks again. "Would it have been easier if I'd had sex with her?"

Wow, what a question. "No."

"Are you sure? If Nickory and I had sex, then I showed up begging your forgiveness, wouldn't it be easier for you to believe me? To believe I really want you?"

I stop walking because I'm too stunned to move. "I need to sit down again."

Benches abound, and I collapse on one. Jaye has no choice but to join me or lose a limb, since I'm still gripping her hand. The morning has been a roller coaster ride beyond Coney Island's wildest pretensions. I have no idea what the ups and downs are, but I'm sure I'm hitting every peak and every valley.

"I need to think a minute," I say.

"Do you want me to go?"

"Absolutely not."

"Okay." There's a calmness in her tone, a sort of peace I'm suddenly envious of. She sits back and turns away a little, as if to give me space to do exactly what I asked for. Think.

But thinking is not the answer. I blank out instead, let it all go unconscious, see what floats up from the depths. This takes one minute, or ten. I have no idea. But something does eventually surface.

"You're right about last night," I say at last. Jaye shifts back toward me.

"Right about what?"

"If you'd slept with Nickory, you'd have lost me."

"Okay." Her tone is still calm, but also carefully neutral. "I haven't lost you? Is that what you're saying?"

"I hope so. You deserve someone who wants you heart and soul, Jaye. I want to be that someone, but . . ." My words trail off, slinking away with my ever-tenuous confidence.

"You *do* want me heart and soul. I just have to get you to believe it."

I heave a deep cliché of a sigh. "I have to get me to believe it."

Jaye pauses, then nods firmly, intense and serious, like she's found solid ground again. "Do you promise to try?" she asks, fervor in her voice. "Do you promise not to give up on yourself and go away?"

An image sears through me suddenly, a flashback through the thirty years of darkness marking my prime years. And a flash forward to what I can expect without Jaye in my life. The guerrilla surges inside me, ready to fire IEDs all over the place. But this time, I know, if I let it, there will be no other side, no second chance. I will exist in hell until death takes me away.

Jaye will not wreck me. I will wreck myself.

I face her and meet her gaze. "Yes, I promise to try. Anything for you, Jaye."

She stands, pulls me up with her. "Okay. Come on."

Now it's me who has to move or lose a limb. Jaye's energy has done a complete one-eighty, and her stride is full of purpose. The roller coaster is moving again.

"Where are we going?" I ask.

"You'll see."

All the way back to Copley Square, as it turns out. Right near the T-station are some street vendors selling things like paintings, hand-woven scarves, trinkets of Boston-related minutiae. I had not noticed them earlier, but clearly Jaye did, because she goes right up to the one selling jewelry.

The table has earrings, necklaces, pins, and two long boxes full of rings. Jaye gestures toward them. "Remember what you said the day we talked about tattoos?"

I glance at the rings, then at her. "Yes."

"Good. Pick one."

Moment. Momentous. Monumental. I try to swallow, but my throat has gone dry.

"Not marriage," she says before I can protest. "Not yet. But a commitment to try. To try for us."

Jaye is calm on the surface, but something in me knows this is a turning point. This is my chance to get untangled from the flag, find my own flying colors.

I examine the rings. Some have inset jewels, but most are simple bands of metal. Like wedding rings, for sure. I'm drawn to those, the ones that imply you are married, probably because deep down I always wanted to be. I've always wanted a partner, and now I have the chance.

My eyes fall on a thick band with a Celtic-like pattern of engraving. Simple but not plain. And there are two of them, actually, a pair amongst a bunch of different single designs or unadorned rings. I catch the vendor's eye. She's watching us with an amused expression.

"Those two, please," I say, pointing, "are they silver?"

"Stainless steel," she tells me. A surprise, but a workable one. Not marriage, not yet.

"Can we try them on?"

"Of course."

I pull both rings out of their slots. They are different sizes, a good thing since Jaye's fingers are larger than mine.

"Give me one," she says, and I hand her the smaller one. "Hold out your hand." I obey, and she slides the band onto my right ring finger (not my left hand, not yet . . .). It fits like a custom-made Tiffany special. For the first time since we met this morning, I smile.

"Your turn," I say to Jaye, and when she holds up her hand I slide on the larger ring. It, too, fits like a custom-made Tiffany special. My ice wall evaporates, replaced by the first building block of certainty. Of knowing Jaye and I are meant to be.

I hear clapping then. Startled, I realize we have a small audience. And they are all smiling. I love Boston.

"I do good work," the vendor says. Several people laugh, and Jaye and I both reach for our wallets.

"You buy one, I buy one," she says, and we do. Thanking the vendor, we head toward the T to go back to Jaye's hotel, to meet up with the team. It is the same day, the same sun, the same city it was an hour ago. But everything, for us, is different.

Chapter Nine

We get back to the hotel in time for Jaye to catch the team bus. She wants me to accompany her, but that's way out of my comfort zone.

"I'll take a cab or something," I say, my hands clasped around hers. "I promise I'll be there."

"I got you a field pass. I want you to use it." The serious, intent side of Jaye I saw earlier is still present. "I want you close to me."

"Okay. I promise," I say again. She's satisfied.

I save cab fare by using a public transportation route I'd mapped out last night. The T, then a bus, then a short walk takes about an hour to get me to the high school stadium the Breakers call home field. I spend the T and bus time staring at the ring adorning my right hand, and the walk doing a lot of thinking about what happened today, and where it will take my relationship with Jaye Stokes.

Do I trust her? Yes. I could not possibly ask for anything more right than how Jaye has behaved with me from minute one. And I owe her the same, want to give her the same.

Do I trust me? I'm full of apprehension about measuring up to this. Am I honestly ready to commit to building a life with Jaye?

After the last evening in Kansas City I would have said yes, no question. But something about my own process, how quickly I built the ice wall, how I couldn't take her in my arms and declare my love, gives me pause. Is it fair to Jaye that I'm having these issues?

I approach the stadium, idly sliding my thumb along the metal of the ring. She may be twenty years younger than I, but Jaye is mature beyond her years. All this most wonderful woman is asking of me is to try. And try I will.

I walk through the stadium gates, show my ticket, and let the noise of the entering fans distract me. I go down to the sidelines near the KC bench and hang out until Jaye, doing her warmup on the pitch, sees me. Immediately she breaks off and heads my way.

"Here." She hands me a lanyard with the field pass attached. "Come on."

I climb over the railing and she wraps me up in a quick hug. "Becky's husband is here. He's a cool guy. Are you okay watching the match with him?"

No problem. As we make our way over Jaye tells me Becky Kaisershot, an Olympian and long-time National Team member, switched rooms with her last night. She introduces me to Rick Kaisershot, who greets me amiably.

Before Jaye heads back out I take her aside. "We're still on for Provincetown, right?"

Her intent expression comes back again. "Absolutely."

I smile, bravely, still awash in my unworthiness but doing my best to hide it. "Good."

Rick does indeed turn out to be a cool guy. He is low key and soft-spoken, a perfect foil for Becky's fierce on-field persona. He confirms that rumors are indeed flying about Jaye and Nickory's "split," but he doesn't press me for details and alludes to seeing this all before on the National Team stage, a whole different level of soap opera. He doesn't go into detail, either, and my respect for him goes up a notch. I'm going to ask him what it's like to be a financial genius, but he beats me to the punch and asks me how long I've been a Rockies' fan. I'm thrown until I remember the Colorado baseball cap I donned on my walk to the stadium to save me from sunburn. Turns out we are both serious baseball fans, and we get into a discussion about the DH rule which kills the minutes until the match starts. From then on, it's all soccer.

I have my fingers crossed that the events of the last twenty-four hours won't follow Jaye to the soccer field, but before long it's obvious they have—in a good way. Jaye is channeling into her game the intensity I saw earlier, and it pays off almost immediately.

The Blues earn a corner kick five minutes into the first half. The teams set up near the goal, and Jaye takes her place in the corner. She's always the one who kicks the ball toward the goal, the idea being to connect with one of her teammates to get the ball in the net.

Tonight, though, she spins a beautiful, arcing ball that curves like something in *Bend it Like Beckham*, sailing right above all the players and the goalkeeper, but underneath the crossbar and into the net. It's a rare feat, something I've only seen once before. Rick and I stand there amazed for a second, then whoop like banshees.

Kansas City 1, Boston 0.

Nickory, surprise surprise, isn't on her game tonight, and the early lead slips away. The Breakers score two goals, at least one of which the warrior queen should have prevented, and the teams go into halftime with Boston up, 2-1.

The Blues walk past us to go to the locker room. Becky nods at Rick, while Jaye gives me a quick smile. The determination in her eyes tells me she's not worried about being behind. She's not anywhere near done tonight.

Nickory sees me, too, and Rick can't help but notice the fiery, venomous glare she aims my way.

"So it was all about you," he says quietly.

I shrug. "Kinda."

"I sure wouldn't want that woman mad at me." I shrug, and only then notice something—I'm not scared. Nickory could do her worst with me, but she's already lost. Jaye has spoken, Jaye is sure, and Jaye is who counts. Another block of certainty falls into place in my head.

The second half starts with a Boston possession, cut off in mid-break with an audacious steal by Becky Kaisershot. She's got room to run, takes the ball all the way past midfield, moving like Mia Hamm in her prime. At first I think she's going to go all the way and try to score, but she slows up, sees Jaye breaking for the goal, and lofts a perfect pass. Jaye redirects the ball with her head and nails her second goal of the night.

Kansas City 2, Boston 2.

Rick and I give each other a rousing high five. "She has mad dribbling skills!" I joke.

Rick shakes his head. "She's a defender to the core. I want her to score an international goal before she retires, but she doesn't much care."

"I guess I relate."

"You can?"

"Yeah. She's the best at what she does—defense. My job was about that, too. She's okay being under the radar."

Rick nods thoughtfully as we refocus on the action. Both teams settle down after the goal, and the next thirty-five minutes of playing time pass without either team getting a chance to score. The match is shaping up to be a draw, which is the soccer version of lukewarm beer and cold pizza. Palatable, but not preferred.

Then, in the eighty-sixth minute, Boston commits a foul. Kansas City is awarded a free kick, some ten yards in front of where Rick and I are standing. Jaye, the Blues' go-to player for these kicks, strides up to the mark, and something in the way she moves gets my attention.

She stops over the ball and stands facing the goal, some twenty-five yards away. There is a moment's stillness, a moment of repose. Her back to me, her legs are slightly apart, her strong sturdy calves supporting even sturdier thighs supporting a torso I know for sure ripples with muscle, front and back. Shoulders on top of torso, graceful and defined, complete the whole package of a body of such beauty and presence that it stops my breath. This is Jaye Stokes, in her element, in her moment, confident and capable.

This is the woman I love.

I focus on her, and everything else drops away. I don't hear the crowd or Rick or the players calling out to one another on the field. In utter stillness, I feel love so strong, it spasms through me.

Jaye steps back and turns toward me. Her expression is neutral, but her eyes are on fire. She knows what I'm thinking. She knows what I'm feeling.

She faces the ball again, re-immerses herself in the game. She's taken my love and its sizzling energy from me, I swear, and I can see it surge through her as the whistle blows. She kicks the ball over everyone on the field, a line-drive rocket perfectly on target, just above the goalkeeper's outstretched arms, just below the crossbar. Indefensible.

Goal. Hat trick. Kansas City 3, Boston 2. The Blues go crazy. Jaye's teammates bury her under a mass of hugs and shouts. The Boston crowd hushes for a moment, then a few clap with respect. Jaye accepts the hugs, the high-fives, the celebration, and meets my eyes again.

That, she communicates to me in total silence, but with every fiber of her being, *was for you.*

The win puts Kansas City two games up on Portland for first place in the NWSL. Jaye is the woman of the moment, the week, the month, the season. She takes in the congratulations of her teammates and coaches, even gets a salute from the opposing fans who stick around for autographs. She signs for everyone, very much the perfect representative for her league and her sport.

When she finally gets to me, we both feel the energy flare up again.

"Wow," I say, inadequately.

"It's because of you."

"I know. It's because of us."

We're standing maybe a foot apart, facing one another. The incandescence is back in her eyes. Jaye moves closer. We smile at one another as a camera clicks.

The photographer jumped the gun and missed a real opportunity, because we were milliseconds from kissing each other. The click stops us. Still, this is our moment, our time, and we stand there oblivious to our surroundings. I focus on Jaye, and now, in her, I see a knight, clear of the shadow of her queen, free to be herself. She is beautiful. Powerful. Wondrous.

The camera clicks again, or maybe it's another one, and now I do acknowledge where we are. "Coming soon to a Facebook account near you."

"Twitter and Instagram." Jaye puts her arm around my shoulders. "Let's go."

We walk off the pitch. I don't worry anymore about who will see, who might not approve. I'm in love. I can totally live with everyone knowing it.

This time I do take the bus back with the team. Rick had mentioned he rode the bus out, and as Jaye had insisted, it's not a big deal. Riding along means she and I can be together from now until she flies home on Tuesday.

And that's everything I want.

It's late Sunday afternoon, and we stroll down Commercial Street, the heart of Provincetown. Jaye and I are two of many people enjoying the sunshine and the energy on this day, one of many lesbian pairs mixed in with the gay guys and the straight couples and the occasional family with kids. There's a little bit of everyone here, sexually, racially, whatever-ly, and we're all getting along and smiling at each other and having a good time. Feels like magic.

I revel in Jaye's presence, pleased to be showing her the town at last, absolutely jazzed about walking down the street hand in hand, and yes, more than a little pleased when she gets so many appreciative stares. Even a couple of outright recognitions.

"Hey, aren't you a soccer player?" two baby dykes say to her as we walk by the City Hall. She smiles, stops long enough to sign autographs for them.

"Nice hat trick, Stokes!" comes another shout, up by Bayside Betsy's. We never did see who the shouter was. She had a nice contralto voice, though.

Jaye grins at the words and says, "Okay, I see why you like this place."

"It's even better with you here," I say. We've reached the residential section of Commercial, and I take Jaye along a narrow path leading down to the bay. We find a convenient bench and sit. There are not so many people here, and the buildings block most of the town noise, leaving us almost alone with the birds and the water.

"This is wonderful," Jaye says. "Thank you for bringing me here."

My answer is a soft kiss to her lips and love in my eyes. The gorilla in me is gone again, buried so deep I can pretend it will never return. We sit in blissful contentment for a while, but now, away from the crowds and under Jaye's calm, I sense sadness.

"What's up?" I ask her.

"I'm fine."

"Not completely."

She sighs. "I was thinking about Nickory, about how we probably aren't friends anymore."

At a team dinner the night before, Nickory and Jaye seated themselves as far apart as the restaurant could manage and still keep everybody in one room. It was as if there were two royal courts, Jaye's on one end and Nickory's on the other, though the game victory successfully drowned out most of the tension. I was next to Jaye, naturally, which meant Nickory's eyes and mine met only once or twice. Good thing, because our mutual dislike showed every time.

I say, "I think you two may work it out eventually."

"You do?"

"Yeah. If you're right, and she's afraid of losing her 'family,' then I can see you forgiving her actions."

Jaye raises a skeptical eyebrow. "Really?"

"Yes. I doubt she and I will ever be friends, but if you all find a way, I won't stand in it."

Jaye puzzles that one out. Shrugs. "Maybe. I do know I'll be getting my own place as soon as we get back to Kansas City." She puts her arm around my shoulders and draws me to her for a kiss. "Want to move in with me?"

The same disbelieving question I always have pops up, but I manage not to say it aloud. Jaye, though, reads my mind.

"Yes, I'm sure," she says and kisses me again. "Why do you keep underestimating yourself? Why can't you see how wonderful you are?"

"There was never anyone to show me before."

Both her arms encircle me then, and the feeling between us is pure love. "There is now. So listen to me, okay?"

"Okay. I promise." This time our kiss goes on almost to the point of indecency. But we're in Provincetown. We can do this, at least until the bench threatens to spontaneously combust.

"You want to walk some more?" Jaye asks when we cave to the need for oxygen.

"I'm fine. I'm fine anywhere as long as you're with me."

She cocks her head. "How about Kansas City?"

"Is this the U-Haul discussion?"

Jaye nods. "Yes. Kirstie says there are a bunch of apartments open in the complex she and her boyfriend live in. We could get a short-term rental, like three months, to get us through the season."

Three months would also be a good measure of how well Jaye and I handle being under the same roof. "And then?"

"I'm hoping to move to Denver."

The truth of what we're proposing comes crashing down on me. "Jaye, I haven't lived with anyone since my parents. More than thirty years ago."

"So?"

"What if I can't? What if I'm so used to being alone that I screw us up?"

"I'm an expert at sharing spaces with people. I'll talk you through it." Jaye gives me yet another kiss, a quick one this time. "Remember, you promised to try?"

The unfamiliar weight on my ring finger reminds me I did, indeed, make a promise. I wait a beat, keeping a neutral expression. "It would have to be a big enough apartment for each of us to have our own space if I need to escape sometimes."

"I'll get a two-bedroom."

"With a balcony. If I have to live on one floor, I don't want to be on the ground."

"That's doable. Oh, there's a big pool in the complex, too, so you can swim."

"Okay. Deal."

Jaye blinks, not sure if I'm kidding or not. "You mean it?"

Only then do I break out the shit-eating grin. "Absolutely."

Jaye stands and pulls me up with her, wraps me in a crushing bear hug. "I love you, Rachel. I love you, love you, love you!"

She spends the rest of the weekend proving it.

Honestly, I'm not sure I'm ready for this. But the Universe clearly is, because Paula calls the day I get back to Denver, telling me Brian Jones needs a place to live while he and his wife have a house built. Toni had told her about my U-Haul moment, and perhaps I'd be willing to rent to him while I'm in Kansas City?

I smile. Beatle. Good controller, better person. I know he'll respect my place and my stuff while he's there. I think he can get his two kids to do the same. And with his rent to cover my mortgage? It's too perfect. I call Paula and tell her to give him my number. Ten minutes later he calls me, thirty minutes after that we have an arrangement, and my path to KC is wide open.

Okay, Universe, this is happening.

I spend the next week packing up my clothes, computer, a few books and DVDs, and kitchen stuff. "The pots and pans are all Bree's," Jaye had said. "Bring whatever you've got." I box up my breakables and a few other things I don't want children messing with. Then I'm off to Kansas City to what I'm thinking of as "The Great Experiment."

Can I live with Jaye? Can I live with anybody? Is the connection I have with this oh-so-special woman something meant for the ages? Or a cool hit song that stays in my head for a while before inevitably fading? What if I'm only *her* cool hit song?

The questions won't go away, playing in my head like an old, scratched phonograph record. When I'm on the road to Kansas City I finally call Toni for a second opinion. I ramble out all my doubts, and when I finally shut up, I'm rewarded with silence. Did the call drop?

"Rachel." Ah, there's the blunt tone I know so well. "Are you happy?"

Easy, instantaneous answer. "Yes. Like, I-never-knew-I-could-feel-this-way happy."

"Good. Because Jaye loves you."

"Yeah, I think you're right."

"No, I know I'm right. There's a picture of you two on Tumblr. I'd check it out if I were you."

"What?"

"There's a Tumblr account devoted to Stokes," Toni says. "I'd check it out if I were you."

The car flies down half a mile of freeway before I say anything. "You were on the Internet hunting down pictures of my girlfriend?"

"Not me. Paula," Toni says without the slightest hint of defensiveness. "There's a photo of the two of you together. Jaye's in uniform, and you're not. But you're standing on a field, like a game's ended."

It takes me a second, but I get there. "Boston. The night she scored the hat trick." I'm distracted now, thinking about how to find the website. Tumblr, she said? "Tell me, Toni, do I look like I love her?"

"You're gazing at each other like there's no one else in the world. So, yes. All right?"

All right.

GPS gets me to the complex in the late afternoon. After a few minutes of wandering around the multi-structure layout, I finally locate the right building and park. We're up on the third floor—yes, there's a balcony—and I'm glad I didn't have to move furniture. Jaye had gotten Rick and Shawn, Kirstie Longstreet's boyfriend, to help her with the few things she took from the townhome and rented the rest. After all, if this works out, Jaye's coming back with me to Denver. No need to purchase anything new right now.

I grab two bags of luggage and the backpack holding my computer and head up the stairs. Jaye must have been watching because she opens the door, meets me halfway, and takes one of the bags. When we get inside she drops the stuff by the door, relieves me of my own load, then wraps her arms around me. "Welcome home." Her breathy voice and ardent kiss make for a most lovely greeting, though we break off way too soon because we have to get the rest of my things.

After hauling everything up to the apartment, I'm ready for a grand tour, but Jaye demurs. "Leave everything here," she says, gesturing to a spot by the front closet. "We'll get it later."

"I need to use the bathroom."

"Oh, right. But come right back out."

Okay. As I follow her commands I notice the master bedroom door is closed. "What are you up to?"

"Nothing," she says in a tone indicating the exact opposite.

I'm curious but play along. "Can I get my computer out and check something, or do you want to have mad passionate sex before dinner?"

Jaye appears honestly torn by the choices. "Umm, dinner first. For energy. Sex later."

The flat is arranged so the living room and kitchen are divided by a tall bar/counter. The dining table is already set, so I pull out my MacBook and settle on the couch. Jaye goes into the kitchen area. I hear her open the refrigerator door, and suddenly it hits me. I'm in Kansas City with my lover, in our own apartment. She's doing one thing, I'm doing another, but we're still sort of doing it together. We're like any other happy couple getting ready for a quiet evening in—unless she's hiding a mariachi band in the bedroom.

We'd sort of done this at the townhome, but now it's our space, mine and Jaye's. I go still for a moment.

"Do you prefer goat cheese or feta?" Jaye calls from about eight feet behind me.

"Whatever you think works best."

"Goat cheese it is."

Such a simple thing, but I blink back tears. I open up the Mac, glad Jaye can't see me getting emotional over a silly thing like happiness, and go hunting for the Tumblr site Toni mentioned. I find it easily, because whoever set it up used Jaye's full name in the title.

My turn to call out. "Did you know there's a Tumblr site devoted completely to you?"

"You're kidding."

"Nope." Jaye comes up behind me. She hands me a glass of iced tea, which I put on the coffee table before leaning back. Jaye rests her hands on my shoulders, and a wave of pleasure washes over me.

"There'd be more probably," I say as I click on the link, "if you took your own photos and posted them on Twitter or Instagram or whatever."

"You won't let me take pictures of you," Jaye says.

"And don't expect that to change."

The site comes up, and the lead posting is the picture taken in Boston. The photo shuts us both up.

I remember the moment, and I remember the click of the camera. I also remember seeing nothing but Jaye, feeling nothing but her love emanating out in waves. I never thought a photograph could capture that. But this one does, radiating the whole wonderful aura of us. Spielberg couldn't have done it better.

My stomach does a solid professional diver routine. How right this is, I think. We fit together. We belong together.

"Oh, my God," Jaye says from behind me. "That's, that's it, isn't it?"

I glance over my shoulder. "I think we're stuck with each other."

Jaye wraps her arms around my neck. "Good."

I turn my head so she can kiss my lips, and we get fairly hot and bothered before I reluctantly opt to break it off. "Dinner first, remember?"

Jaye pulls back. "Okay."

Ten minutes later we are seated at the table, partaking of Jaye's genius creation of a salad.

"This is fantastic," I rave as I devour the most intriguing mix of lettuce, chicken, cheese, and fruit I've ever eaten. "How can you say you don't cook?"

"I don't. Bree can do anything involving a grill or a stove, so I learned how to do this stuff. It's not hard."

No mention of Nickory. "What about the chicken?"

"Kirstie and Shawn grilled last night and let me have some leftovers."

"We'll have to return the favor."

"By taking them out to dinner, right?"

"Maybe. But I can grill a little, too." I wave my fork at the now-empty plate. "This was delicious, Jaye. Thank you."

She takes my hand, and we do some soppy gazing into one another's eyes. Then Jaye stands up. "Let's do the dishes and go to bed."

There is no mariachi band in the bedroom. But a dozen long-stemmed roses sit in a vase on the dresser, and candles glow from the tops of both bedside tables and the chest of drawers. Jaye has put some gauzy material over the window that enhances the candlelight. This is romance central.

"I see you're not settling for the couch this time," I joke, very weakly.

"We're going to want a little more space." She runs her hands down my back. I shiver.

Jaye's iPad is hiding behind the flowers, connected to a tiny set of speakers. She reaches over, hits a button, and one of the most romantic songs I know, the perfect slow dance song, begins to play: Fleetwood Mac's "Crystal."

Jaye pulls me to her, and we stand at the foot of the bed swaying back and forth, like high school kids at the prom.

"I love you, Rachel," she murmurs in my ear.

"I love you, Jaye," I whisper back.

The song ends, another equally romantic and slow piece starts, and Jaye moves her lips from my ear to my mouth. As we kiss I feel like I've been released from confinement, like dungeon walls have fallen away and Jaye, the sunshine and the light, is there to take me home.

Our kisses are long, deep, slow, and intense, a restrained passion building from embers. Truly, madly, deeply . . . as the second, or maybe third, song ends we help each other get our clothes off, and then, naked, we start kissing once more, feeling the contact not just of lips upon lips, but flesh upon flesh. And the embers burn hotter, and glow.

I sit on the edge of the bed, put my hands on Jaye's hips, and bring her to me.

I kiss her stomach, her navel, work my way down to the center of her. I partake of the depths there, slowly, thoroughly, reverently, conveying with every touch the love I have and need to share.

I feel her legs grow rigid with tension, hear her breath get deeper and faster. She continues to say my name, quietly, gently almost, as she takes my love, lets it run over her in waves of pleasure.

When Jaye comes, she lets out a short sharp cry of release, and her hands grip my shoulders for support. My own hands cup her from behind as her legs give way under the strength of the orgasm. All the while my mouth stays on her, draws the climax out of her, takes her from storm to calm.

"Lie back," she gasps, and when I do, she collapses on top of me, wraps her arms around me as my own encircle her. We hold each other tight as she recovers. I'm in heaven. I have my angel.

And my angel has me. When Jaye raises her head again I see fire in her eyes, and I know it's my turn for pleasure. She steals a kiss, then slides down my body and off the bed, kneeling between my legs.

She worships me then, as I have just done to her. My cries are not so brief, nor so quiet. I let my release be the release not only of orgasm, but of the tension and fear that I nearly lost this. When I call Jaye's name, cry out Jaye's name, scream out Jaye's name, there is no question what is happening and who is creating the happiness.

When at last I am still, Jaye comes up and kisses me, lets me taste myself on her, and then we take to the whole of the bed and, having worshipped, we sleep, holding each other as we lie side by side.

I like this living together thing.

Chapter Ten

Three weeks into The Great Experiment, I'm immersed in a blur of happiness. My worries that Jaye and I would constantly trip over each other turn out to be groundless, because she's almost never home.

Pro soccer players, it turns out, work *very* hard at what they do. A typical day for Jaye includes some light stretching after she wakes up, breakfast, a five-mile run or the gym—or a five-mile run *and* the gym—practice with the team, practice with various teammates before and after the team session, individual drills, lunch somewhere in the midst of it, then maybe another run before dinner. I would be exhausted. She thrives, and it shows during the games.

Her stellar play peaked with the hat trick, but this means she's on top of the mountain now. Jaye continues to score goals or assist on goals. She and Kirstie Longstreet are the league leaders in scoring. Jaye works magic on the field and leads the Blues to win after win. Kansas City has not lost since that long ago game against the Flash, and people who know soccer are giving Jaye Stokes much of the credit. She is far and away the front runner for league MVP, and a couple of websites are floating rumors she is at last being considered for the National Team.

"I'm trying not to get my hopes up," Jaye tells me after I point this out. "But I can't help it."

"Keep doing what you're doing, because your best is top of the table right now."

"I know." Jaye isn't bragging, isn't copping attitude. The phrase isn't humble, but the tone is, like she's surprising even herself.

All this positive energy infuses my own work. The editing stage of *Triangle* is going smoothly, and I'm casting about for another disaster to hang a book around, homing in on the 1928 collapse of Saint Francis Dam in California. When I run it by Jaye, she congratulates me for moving into "modern times."

On the home front we are meshing together quite well. We talk out everything, from who does what chores to how we budget funds to whether we eat in—which means salad—or out, since Jaye knows tons of good restaurants in KC. We finally watch Bogart and Bacall in *To*

Have and Have Not. We make full use of the tiny balcony and sit outside in the evenings, talking. And we make full use of our bed, too.

But I find, to my surprise, my life in Kansas City encompasses more than Jaye. We have the Kaisershots and Kirstie and Shawn over for dinner one evening as a thank you for helping Jaye move. The dinner party goes so well Rick and I talk everyone into a Royals' game the following week, and we all enjoy the night out. Rick Kaisershot and I have become fast friends, bonding over a love of baseball and mutual free schedules—apparently day traders work when they feel like it.

I introduce him to the history of baseball, thrilled to have an eager student. He helps me understand why some of those insanely esoteric stats are actually interesting. We agree to disagree on the importance of the Yankee dynasty. We take Jaye and Becky to the Negro Leagues Museum.

Rick and I don't even realize how much we're hanging out together until one day at my apartment when we're watching World Series highlights courtesy of a DVD set I've brought from Denver. We replay the scene from the 1956 Series, where Jackie Robinson steals home.

"Safe," I insist. "He's safe!"

"Too close to tell," Rick counters. "Where's HD when you need it?"

Rewind. Play again. "Safe!"

"Maybe," says Rick, ever the Yankee fan. "Yogi still says he got him, though, and you can't discount that."

Rewind. Play again. Freeze frame. I vaguely hear the apartment door open behind us.

"Safe!" I say for the third time.

Jaye's voice rings out loud and clear. "I *told* you he'd be here!"

Rick and I look up to see Jaye and Becky. Is afternoon practice over already? Jaye winks at me, pleased with herself, while Becky glares at her husband.

Rick pats down his pockets. "I forgot my phone again, didn't I?"

Becky shakes her head in mock disgust, and we all get a good laugh out of it.

"Admit it—you are *so* not a recluse," Jaye says to me the next morning. She's back from her run and not quite out the door to practice. "You're having too much fun with the people you've met here."

True. But Jaye has also been more than accommodating about my very acute need for alone time, time to recharge, time to still be a writer. I know this is the honeymoon stage, but we definitely have promise for the future.

Our only break from togetherness, other than Blues' road games, comes when I go to the Golden Crown Literary Society's yearly convention. I still go as The Fyrequeene, but a few of my readers are on to me.

"You're dating a soccer player, aren't you?" one woman asks as I'm signing books on the penultimate day.

"What makes you think that?"

"I'm a soccer fan, too," the woman says. "You've always blogged about soccer. Then I saw an interview with Jaye Stokes, MVP-to-be, saying she was playing well because she's in love. Then you blog about being in love and about soccer. One plus one equals couple!"

Intrigued, I hunt down Jaye's interview and find it on YouTube. Sure enough, when the local TV station asks her why she's playing so well, Jaye flat out says, "I'm in love. I never knew life could feel this good, and my soccer is better for it."

The reporter, used to canned responses, can only manage a strangled "Congratulations." His befuddled response amuses me, and prompts a visit to another website, Facebook, which I've finally joined so I can check Jaye's postings. I want to know if it's possible to connect Rachel Johnston and The Fyrequeene.

The answer, I discover, is yes, and I spend a restless night coming to terms with the knowledge that I can't hide any more, can no longer be Rachel the Recluse.

When morning comes I'm surprised to discover my anxiety is gone, and I feel truly at peace with being "outed." Wow.

When I get back to KC, I tell Jaye, wrapped around her body after a thorough welcome home greeting. "You think it's working out, yeah?" she asks.

"So far, so great."

"Are you ready for the next step?"

"Next step?"

"I want to invite my parents down next weekend."

Yikes. On some level this is totally expected, but I still freeze up enough for Jaye to notice.

"Don't worry," she says. "They'll like you."

"Yeah, we're from the same generation," I observe wryly. "We'll have lots in common."

"Actually," Jaye says, "you have a guaranteed 'in' with my dad, which I'll tell you about later."

"Tell me now!"

"Nope. Don't want to spoil the surprise."

Abruptly she gets out of bed and throws some clothes on. Turns out she's late for soccer practice, and her rush to get out the door neatly forestalls me finding out what the hell me and her father have in common. I'll just have to wait, darn it.

Meanwhile: Meet the parents. Yippee.

Over the next three days I learn a lot about Jaye's family. Tom and Marcia Stokes own a small farm near Cedar Rapids, Iowa. Jaye describes to me a childhood of playing in creeks, doing morning chores, and learning to drive a tractor before she drove a car. From what she says, her parents strike me as fairly typical Midwest people, what they used to call salt of the Earth types.

With one little quirk. "My older brother Jonh, J-O-N-H, lives in Cedar Rapids. Jeena, my kid sister, and her husband Troy live on the farm with Mom and Dad, and Jeena will take over when they finally retire. Thank goodness."

"Jonh, J-O-N-H?"

"Yes. His baptismal name and all. He hated it growing up, swore he was going to change it legally when he turned eighteen, but he never did."

"Why did they spell it that way?"

"No clue. But they named me Jaye, and my younger sister Jeena, J-E-E-N-A, so they definitely have a 'J' thing going."

All I can think is they had to have lost a bet with some family member. Uncle Jim, or Aunt Jill, maybe. "I think you came out on top in the name department."

Jaye winks. "Me, too."

"What is this 'in' I supposedly have with your father?"

"You'll see."

"You said you'd tell me."

"All in good time."

Mildly put out, I throw the age thing at her again. "You realize you'll be spending the weekend with people who will reminisce about the '60s and '70s because we lived through them?"

Jaye's bright mood abruptly fades. "Actually, they don't talk much about the '70s. Dad was in Canada for most of those years, and Mom wasn't. They didn't get married until he came back."

"Why was he in Canada?" I ask, but as soon as I say "why" the answer comes to me.

Jaye pauses, then tells me what I already guessed. "He refused to fight in Vietnam."

"Oh."

Jaye takes my even tone the wrong way and gets defensive. "He says a lot of people went to Canada back then. That it was a popular thing to do."

"He's right," I say calmly. "Going to Canada was a hell of a lot more popular than going into the Army. At least, that's how I remember it."

"Really?"

"Yes. I was a kid, but I could still tell the mood of the country was ugly. Even my mother, who was mega-conservative and mega-Republican and a mega-Nixon supporter, said Vietnam was an immoral war. Your father was doing what he thought was right. He sounds like a man of conscience and conviction, and I can understand why he did what he did."

"I think he's going to like you."

"I hope so."

Jaye's parents arrive early Friday evening. They prove to be what I expected, but taller. Thomas Stokes is well over six feet, a lean, spare man whose eyes match Jaye's to a T. Marcia Stokes is right at Jaye's height, and they share strong sturdy builds. The two appear well-grounded, a little reserved, and clearly loving and protective of their daughter. I watch their ease with each other, envious. My parents and I didn't have any sort of close relationship.

Their reaction to me is mixed. Jaye's mother greets me politely but coolly, while her father—"call me Tom"—is more willing to give me a chance. We exchange the usual pleasantries as we haul the Stokes' luggage up the stairs and into the second bedroom. I'm in a space with four people again. Thank goodness it's only for a couple of nights.

Dinner is takeout barbecue plus one of Jaye's gourmet salads, with key lime pie for dessert. I may try grilling steaks on Sunday, but only if I haven't been filleted myself by then. The food is great, the chemistry less so. In an odd move, Jaye has put on some music, a soft pop playlist providing an unobtrusive backdrop to the slight tensions between us all. I'm soon wishing I could up the volume because Jaye's mother does not waste any time showing where her loyalties lie.

"I talked to Kathleen this week, dear. She misses you."

It takes me a second to remember Nickory's given name is Kathleen. I should also have remembered Jaye telling me her parents were part of Nickory's 'family.'

"That's nice." Jaye says neutrally, calmly shredding the chicken sitting on her plate. "Did she tell you why we're not talking?"

"Not in so many words. It's a shame since you two have always been such good friends."

"Friends support one another, Mom. She stopped supporting me."

"So, Rachel," Jaye's father says to me in a blatant attempt to change the subject. "You're a writer, I understand?"

"My second career, yes. I was an air traffic controller until a couple of years ago."

Mrs. Stokes—I'm not even daring to think of her as Marcia yet—allows this diversion, but she's clearly not done with the topic of Nickory. She's merely biding her time.

"Exciting," Tom Stokes says. "You must have some stories."

"Maybe a few the flying public wouldn't want to hear."

"Try me. I don't fly much."

"Jaye does."

This earns me a playful tap on my arm from the woman in question. "Fifty million people can't be wrong."

I relate a fun but harmless story about the time a certain billionaire pilot tried to cut the holding pattern at Aspen. Bad weather, lots of planes trying to land, he wanted to be first, and the controller working the airspace (not me) essentially told him to shut up and wait his turn.

"His jet was like, fifteenth in line to land, which meant at least two hours because it was snowing so hard at Aspen. So, after several minutes of whining and griping, he finally gets that we weren't going to give him special privileges, and changes his destination to Grand Junction. He lands there, goes to the local Jeep dealership, pays cash for four Grand Cherokees, and the whole party drives to Aspen."

Jaye and her father laugh. Mrs. Stokes gives a polite smile.

"Does anybody get special privileges in the air?" Jaye asks.

"The President," I say with a grin. "A few secret things I can't tell you about." Then, more seriously, "And emergencies. Emergencies always get priority."

Which must click something in Jaye's father's memory. He asks, "Were you working on 9/11?"

A pall of sadness seems to drop over us, and it takes a moment for me to answer. "Yes," I say. "One of the weirdest days of my life."

Mr. Stokes, who I really do want to call Tom, asks a couple of astute questions about that fateful day, and we all recount where we were when we heard the news. I discover Jaye is the only one of us who actually ever went to the World Trade Center.

"You remember," she says to her parents. "In 2000. The last U-20 tourney I was in. The team went up to Windows on the World for lunch." Her eyes drift back into memory and cloud a little. "The view was incredible."

She falls silent, and for a moment the lost towers and her lost dream juxtapose. The iPhone music maestro seems to know it because the playlist chooses an Al Stewart song next, a song which talks about, among other things, the aftermath of 9/11.

"Go figure," Tom Stokes says softly.

I gape at Jaye in puzzlement. "I didn't know you had Al Stewart in your iTunes."

She snaps back to the present, glances first at her father, then at me. "I don't. That's *your* phone."

I nod, knowing now why every song was familiar. I'm ready to let the moment go until I see Tom Stokes staring at me with surprise.

"You're an Al Stewart fan?" he asks, and lo, I discover my 'in.'

Al Stewart is a Scottish singer who had a couple of big pop hits back in the '70s. To most people he disappeared after "Year of the Cat," but in reality, he kept putting out albums, good ones, for the next thirty years. He still plays shows in small venues here and there to a devoted, loyal group of hard-core followers. I like his songs because a lot of them deal with his take on historical events. Not your typical pop/rock singer at all.

"Yes, I bought all his records, then replaced them with all his CDs."

"I still have the records," Tom Stokes says, with a slight sense of wonder. "Do you know I've never met another Al Stewart fan until now?"

I steal a glance at Jaye, who's smiling like a canary-stuffed cat. I also notice Mrs. Stokes rolling her eyes.

"Neither have I," I say to Tom. "He's always been a secret treasure."

"Exactly," he says, and for the first time since we carried in the luggage, I can believe things might work out with at least one future in-law.

I awake the next morning to the aroma of bacon and—could it be?—waffles coming from the kitchen.

"Jaye, somebody's cooking."

My lover burbles incoherently and slumbers on. I slide out of bed and get dressed, then venture out. As soon as I open the bedroom door a plethora of heavenly smells washes over me. Someone is engaged in major breakfast building.

Two someones, actually. I pop my head out of the hall to see both Mr. and Mrs. Stokes working in the kitchen. They move around the tiny area in a graceful dance bespeaking of long familiarity with each other, and comfort in small places. While he mixes eggs in a bowl, Tom also oversees the bacon. Mrs. Stokes stands over another bowl, samples the waffle batter within it, and adds something to the mix.

I observe this for a moment. This is what Jaye grew up with. This is the kind of marital harmony Jaye saw all her childhood years. Comfort, affection, closeness. No wonder she believes she can have it with me.

"Good morning?" I say as I come into the living area.

Tom Stokes gives me a very Jaye-like grin. "Morning, Rachel! I hope you're a breakfast person."

I respond with a vigorous nod. "Smells wonderful."

"It'll wake up Jaye in a minute," Mrs. Stokes says with confidence. "Waffles are her favorite."

I smile. "She told me she's had her waffle iron since college. We haven't used it yet."

"We'll start it off right for you," Tom says. "Marcia's waffles are the best."

I stop short at the profusion of items spread across the kitchen counter. "Um, we didn't have any of this stuff last night."

"We got up early, went and got groceries," Marcia says.

Tom is still grinning. "Farmers, remember? Want some coffee?"

"Thanks, no. I prefer tea."

"Coming right up." He fills a mug with water and pops it in the microwave.

"How about I set the table?" I have to do something to help me feel useful amidst all this efficiency.

"Already done," Tom says. "Have a seat."

I bow out to the breakfast experts and obey. "You didn't have to do this, you know. You're the guests."

"Oh, we always make breakfast for the girls." Tom opens the microwave and presents me with tea, gestures to cream and honey already on the table. "You know, when Jaye lived with Nickory and Bree. Got to be a habit."

"Thank you. I'm sure Jaye's told you I'm not much of a cook."

"Neither is she," Jaye's mom says with a sigh. "She was always busy playing soccer or practicing to play soccer or away at tournaments playing soccer."

"She's still busy doing that," I say with affection.

I watch as the eggs go into the skillet for scrambling, and the first waffle starts cooking in the iron.

"I guess I'll go wake Jaye."

Tom glances over my shoulder. "No need."

I turn around and see Jaye walk out of the little hallway.

"Waffles!" she says with delight. She enters the kitchen and gives each of her parents a hug. I get a nice kiss on the cheek, then Jaye sits down next to me. "Isn't this great to wake up to?"

"So far, so great," I say, meaning it.

And it is, all of us digging in with gusto, right up until Marcia brings up the evening's plans, which involve Jaye's ex-roommates. "Tom and I are having dinner with them after the game."

"You are?" Jaye and I say in unison. My peripheral vision, still honed to ATC standards, catches Jaye's father covering a smile as he bites into his waffle.

"Of course we are," Mrs. Stokes continues. "Kathleen and Bree are like our own kids, and we have to do something to make you all friends again."

Lovely. Jaye sits there, stone-faced, but says nothing before going back to her breakfast.

"It wouldn't be the worst thing in the world," I venture then, somewhat timidly. Jaye glares at me. "Well, I miss Bree."

"You haven't seen her at the games?" Jaye asks.

"No. Either she's avoiding me or she's been working. Have you talked to her?"

"No."

"See, Jaye?" Mom says. "That's simply not right."

Jaye puts her fork down. "Mom, I have my reasons, okay? Nickory basically told me it was her or Rachel. And Rachel wins. Every time."

The words are nice, even if Jaye snaps them out like muted rifle shots.

"I'm sure Kathleen wants what's best for you, dear."

"Rachel is what's best for me." Jaye puts her arm around my shoulder. "I love this woman. She's good and kind and smart, and I'll never find anyone better. You heard her. Even she thinks Nickory and I should be friends again."

"If they can work it out," I say. "But it's their choice."

Jaye starts in again. "See? And all Nickory did from day one was try to tear us down. I'm not willing to be friends with someone who tries to undermine my happiness. So, go do what you want tonight, but when you guys come back, Rachel and I will be here, together. Like we're meant to be."

Breakfast breaks up, but the tension lingers. Jaye goes off to do a short run, and Mrs. Stokes grabs the empty bathroom for a shower. I opt to do the dishes and try to dissuade Tom from helping me.

"You guys made a great breakfast. The least I can do is clean up."

"Thanks," he says and grabs a dishtowel, "but it's quicker with two."

He's right, and he's so relaxed that I make no protest as he brings the dishes over from the table. I rinse them before loading them in the dishwasher. The skillets and waffle iron we tackle at the sink. I wash, Tom dries, and we find a comfortable rhythm, chatting at first about Al Stewart songs, then moving on to something more serious.

"Jaye says she told you I was in Canada years ago, and you guessed why."

"I was only a kid then, but I remember the times."

Tom finishes drying the last of the skillets, hands it to me to put away. "You said I had conscience and conviction. Did you mean it or were you just buttering her up?"

His tone is light, but I see what he's getting at. I put the skillet with the others in a cabinet, pour the last of the coffee, and give the cup to Tom.

"I don't know what your true motives were," I say while making another cup of tea, "but I like to think the best. And either way, noble intentions or running away, it has to be a hard decision when you're eighteen years old."

"I was nineteen. And I wasn't running away." Tom Stokes pauses for a long moment, probably deciding how much to tell me. Then he says "My father fought in World War II, and he won medals, and I thought I could do it, too. But it wasn't the same kind of war."

"No, it wasn't, not at all." We reseat ourselves at the table, doctor our drinks with cream and, in my case, a generous dollop of honey.

"World War II, there was a cause there," Tom says, "a good reason for fighting. Vietnam was a waste. And when push came to shove, I couldn't sacrifice myself for an immoral war."

"That's what my mother called it. Immoral."

Tom nods. "I spent almost six years in Canada. Worked on a farm in Saskatchewan. After the war ended I could have stayed, the government there was granting citizenship to the conscientious objectors, but it never felt like home to me. And Marcia didn't want to leave the U.S. or live that far north. I came back in 1977."

"After Carter pardoned everybody." President Jimmy Carter had offered all the Vietnam era draft dodgers a pardon shortly after he took office in 1977.

"Well," Tom clarifies, "you had to ask for the pardon. You had to admit you'd broken the law. And I did, so I could come back."

"Home to marriage, another farm, and at least one wonderful kid."

He smiles. "All our kids are wonderful. You'll get to meet Jonh and Jeena soon, and you'll see."

"And will I learn why you named your son Jonh, J-O-N-H?"

He laughs. "If we haven't told him, what makes you think we'll tell you?"

We fall into a comfortable silence. I think over what he's shared with me and what I remember about my own childhood. And my own father.

"Can I say something, sir?"

"Please do. And call me Tom."

"My father served in World War II, like yours did. He was in the Pacific theater, at Iwo Jima and Okinawa, and he never talked about what he went through or what he saw. Awful things, I'm sure."

"My dad was in Europe. D-Day, then all the way to Germany. He never talked about it either."

"I was a history major. I tried to get him to open up a couple of times. But he never did. We were never close. My father was a good person, but he was always distant, and I believe whatever he went through during the war helped make him that way."

"You can't know for sure."

"True. But there were all these people at his funeral who kept talking about what he was like before World War II—and after. It changed him. I may be out of line here, but when I see the way you interact with your wife and with Jaye, how close you are, I think you did the right thing. If you had chosen to go to war, especially a war you didn't believe in, it would have changed you, too. And maybe you wouldn't be as close to your family as you are now."

Over the next few seconds Tom's whole demeanor opens up. He gives me a smile just like Jaye's, but before he can say anything, there's a noise from behind us, and Marcia Stokes comes out of the hallway to stand behind her husband.

"Do you mean that?" she asks me. "Do you truly think Tom did the right thing?"

"Yes. I don't say things I don't mean."

Mrs. Stokes isn't ready to melt yet. "Jaye had some trouble a long time ago with an older woman."

"The soccer coach bitch? Jaye told me about her."

"Yes," Tom says, suppressing a smile. "Her."

Mrs. Stokes gives not an inch. "You can see why we'd be concerned then."

"Yes, ma'am, I can. But I promise you, I'll never do to Jaye what that woman did. I love your daughter very much, and I want to be with her for as long as she'll have me. I hope it's for the rest of my life."

This whole time Jaye's mother's expression has been one of, shall we say, thoughtful suspicion. But she lets my words roll around in her brain, and I see her make a decision.

"Good," she says, and it sounds so like Jaye I have to bite back a laugh.

"Jaye says it exactly the same way," I tell her before I negate the good will. "Now I know where she gets it from."

Mrs. Stokes actually smiles, and Tom says "I think Jaye's found the right woman, honey."

The three of us are now surrounded by, at worst, an amiable willingness to compromise. When Jaye chooses that moment to walk through the front door, she doesn't see it at all.

"Mom, I want to show you something," she says without preamble, then stalks off to the bedroom. She comes back with her iPad and sets it on the table so we all have a view.

Jaye brings the device to life, opens up YouTube, makes a couple of entries, and plays a clip from the old Johnny Carson show. The guest is Lauren Bacall, and she's on the show to promote her memoir. I had found this clip a couple of years ago and showed it to Jaye during one of our Bogart-Bacall discussions. Bacall and Carson clearly get along great, joking back and forth, and Carson asks her a few questions about Humphrey Bogart, including what it was like to introduce the much older Bogart to her mother. Bacall says it worked because she and Bogie were "two honest people," and her mother could see that.

When the clip is over, Jaye takes my hand and stares her mother down. "We're two honest people, Mom, like Bogart and Bacall. We're two honest people who love each other. I know she's older, and I don't care. Rachel and I belong together. Okay?"

Marcia Stokes—I'm almost there with the first name—puts a hand on Jaye's shoulder, then her other hand on my shoulder.

"Okay," she says. "I got it."

Jaye is flummoxed this has gone so smoothly, and it shows on her face. Tom laughs, as do I, and her mom smiles.

I lean over and stage-whisper in Jaye's ear. "We talked things out while you were running."

"You did?"

"Yes. As long as I treat you like royalty and make you my sole heir, they'll be nice to me."

Jaye looks around at all of us, then smiles. "Good."

The game tonight is the Blues versus the Washington Spirit, a good team, but nowhere near the level of play Kansas City is enjoying right now. There's a little bit of suspense in the first half, though. The Blues take several open shots but fail to find the net, while Washington squeaks one past Nickory to take a 1-0 lead. But Jaye is doing her best, as are her teammates. One can sense the crowd is not worried. There's a lot of soccer left to play.

Jaye's parents have dinner plans with Nickory and Bree after the game, and Bree joins us shortly before halftime, fresh off her work shift. She sits on the other side of Tom and Marcia, and that plus our focus on the game keeps the tension under wraps. But at the half, when the elder Stokes go off in search of refreshment, Bree and I finally have to talk to each other.

"Hey, Bree."

Since we sat down, it's been obvious she's ambivalent about me being there. When I at last force the issue, she settles on politeness.

"Hi, Rachel. How're you doing?"

"Great, actually. How about you?"

"It's been rough lately."

I have no idea what Nickory has told Bree about Jaye's departure. Jaye herself had only told Bree she had to move out, leaving the bitter details to her ex-best friend. My usual tendency to bluntness collides with my genuine affection for this particular Musketeer, which collides with my lack of knowledge about how much she knows. Maybe I should have kept quiet and left Bree alone.

Sincerely, I say, "I'm sorry to hear that."

"What did Jaye tell you? About what happened?"

I decide to obfuscate. "She and Nickory disagreed about their relationship."

Bree smiles bitterly. "Did she tell you they slept together?"

The words jolt a bit, but I'm not totally surprised. "No. Jaye told me they didn't sleep together."

"And you believed her?"

"Yes, I did." I meet her eyes and don't waver. "Like you did when she said Nickory never cheated on you."

Bree frowns and to my surprise blinks back tears. "Nickory won't tell me anything."

I process this. I've watched every game the Blues have played this season, and since the rift, Nickory's goalkeeper play has definitely declined. She's still good, still a pro, but Kathleen Nickerson is nowhere near the best at her position right now. And I guess I know why.

Tom and Marcia come back at this point, a good thing, because I'm not sure what I would or could say to Bree. We go into polite/detached mode, and the second half starts.

KC's luck finally shows up in the seventy-sixth minute. Jaye and Kirstie Longstreet exchange passes up the field and confuse the Spirit defense until Jaye can finish it. Another goal, another notch on the MVP belt. But though Nickory holds firm, with some help from her defensive cohorts, that ends up being KC's only score, and the game ends in a draw. Not the result the Blues wanted, but they still haven't outright lost a match since April. An impressive streak.

After the usual interactions with fans, Jaye and Nickory join the four of us outside the locker room.

"Are you sure you won't come to dinner?" Marcia asks her daughter.

Nickory still glares daggers at me when she can, but I notice tonight's blades have no venom. The warrior queen is a little ragged at the edges. And it's not because she's finished a hard game. She's confused on some level, and hurting. I, secure at last in the cocoon of Jaye's love, can have some sympathy.

But I don't have to show it. "What do you want to do, Jaye?"

"Go home with you," she says. No sympathy there. Her next words are aimed at her parents. "You guys have a good time. We'll wait up."

Tom laughs, Marcia is disappointed, Bree resigned, Nickory sullen. And maybe a little pained.

"All right then," Tom says. "We'll see you two later."

Jaye and I grab takeout on the way home. After we settle in on the couch with Chinese and a baseball game on TV, I learn a little bit about Kathleen Nickerson's past.

"Nickory's parents kicked her out when she was seventeen because she was gay," Jaye tells me. "She hasn't had anything to do with them since."

This would have been in the late 1990s. "I didn't think people did that anymore."

"They definitely do. We were friends by then, so I started asking Nickory to the farm for vacations. After she met and fell in love with Bree, she was invited, too. My parents treated them like me and my brother and sister. They really are part of my family."

Hmm. "Maybe Nickory meant what she said, in Boston."

"What do you mean?"

"When she told you she didn't want to lose her family. Maybe she meant it."

Jaye sets her jaw. "Then why did she kiss me? There was nothing familial about the kiss."

Jaye has a point. And she's not done yet. "Do you remember I told you I had a crush on Nickory, way back when?"

I raise an eyebrow. "Yeah?"

"I was going to tell her. I was a sophomore at North Carolina, and I went up to Penn State for spring break, specifically to tell her how I felt. Turns out she'd met Bree a couple of weeks before. So I swallowed my feelings, told her I was happy for her, and stayed a friend. Eventually, I got over my horrible timing."

"I bet that took a while."

"It did. But Bree's story was just like Nickory's: her parents kicked her out of the house for being gay, completely cut her off. In the middle of the winter. In Chicago. One of her teachers took her under his wing, and she says she'd probably be dead if not for him. She doesn't have anything to do with her family, either."

"Sounds like they're perfect for each other."

"Yes. They are. And I could see it, back then, even with my crush. So I got over it."

"You're a good person, Jaye."

"Then why did I kiss her back, in Boston? You know I wish I hadn't."

"Yes." I hand Jaye the fried rice container and take the Moo goo gai pan. "Water under the bridge. I haven't thought about it since then."

"Nickory probably hasn't either. She's not exactly the contemplative type. She's always left the thinking to Bree."

"And you."

"Yeah . . . if I could see how good Nickory and Bree are for each other, shouldn't she be able to see the same for me?"

"I think you know that answer," I say. "And maybe you were simply being a good friend, despite wanting her and all."

"Yes. I *was* a good friend. She should be, too."

"Point taken." I lean over and give Jaye a kiss. "I don't know that we're perfect for each other. We're just crazy in love."

"What's wrong with that?"

"Nothing. Nothing at all."

"You still think it's too soon?"

"Too soon for what?"

"To be thinking forever."

I hark back to what I'd told "the parents" earlier. *I hope it's for the rest of my life.*

"No, Jaye. It's not too soon. Being with you feels so right I can't put it into words."

Jaye swallows her last bite of rice and graces me with a soppy romantic grin. "You don't have to. I feel it, too."

The parents get in around ten o'clock, and the four of us finish off the key lime pie from last night (yes, key lime pie goes with Chinese). Dinner had been a little strained, I gather, and Marcia once again tries to persuade Jaye to make amends with Nickory. Jaye fends her off with proper deference of daughter to mother, firm in her stance nonetheless. Tom and I listen, somewhat amused.

At one point he leans over and says to me, sotto voce, "Marcia thinks Nickory walks on water."

I lean back and respond, equally softly, "Nickory thinks Nickory walks on water."

Our eyes meet, and we burst out laughing. Jaye and her mom raise their heads in surprise, but Tom says nothing, and I adopt a mock-innocent expression.

"Marcia," Tom says then, "let it go? Nickory dug this hole herself, and she's the one who has to fill it in again."

"Dad's right," Jaye says, and her pronouncement closes the conversation, and the evening.

The elder Stokes opt to leave early the next morning for Iowa, and I put off grilling steaks for next time. Jaye considers their visit a great success, and I'm pleased to agree. I'm more pleased, though, to have her all to myself again.

Except for soccer, of course. We fall back into our usual routine. Jaye goes to practice, or the gym, or to do drills, and I mull over the rough outline for my next book. There are two games left in the regular season, followed by the playoffs. Then the future.

One morning I'm in the bathroom, standing in front of the mirror, freshly showered, struck by a sense of *déjà vu*. Hair, still brunette thanks to a good-but-not-as-good-as-Krystal stylist. Face, still mostly unlined. Body, unchanged—on the outside. Still not Playboy material. I certainly don't feel like I'm fifty-two.

Jaye comes up from behind me, misreads my pensive gaze at the mirror. She puts her hands under my breasts and raises them up.

"Better?" she says, not bothering to hide her amusement. Before I can answer, she runs her thumbs over my nipples.

"Yes," I gasp and lean back into her. She runs a series of kisses along my neck.

"It's what's underneath that counts, you know."

"Ah. The flab."

Jaye squeezes my breasts. "No, silly. The heart, the soul, the mind."

"Don't forget the liver."

"And the liver." She lets go of my business and turns me to face her. "I love you no matter what, Rachel. I always will."

I press my body against hers. "I know. And I love you too, no matter what."

"Good."

A minute later the mirror is steamy again and not from my recent shower. I spend a long moment admiring Jaye's wondrous gray eyes.

"Come to Denver with me after the playoffs?"

"I thought you'd never ask."

Chapter Eleven

On a hot Friday evening in August comes the long-awaited rematch with Portland. Kansas City is still in first place, but Portland has managed to stay close. If the Blues win tonight they will clinch the regular season title, but a Thorns win, or a tie, will leave things in doubt for another week. Finishing first means home-field advantage in the playoffs, and like every team, KC wants that badly.

There's something full-circle about the matchup for Jaye and me. We became lovers after the first game in Portland. And she has something planned for this one, too, though she won't tell me what.

I say, "I can guess."

"You could. But I won't confirm it, so you may as well be surprised."

Fine.

Jaye's run to MVP also started in the Rose City. I have no doubt now she'll win the award. Soccer aficionados are calling her season the best since Mia Hamm's breakouts in the early 2000s. Tonight's game is being televised on a national cable network, so Jaye has a chance to showcase her skills to the whole country.

She's psyched. So are her teammates. Victory is in the air.

But Portland didn't get to second place without effort, and tonight their team fights hard. Literally. Soccer is a beautiful game, but it can also involve lots of contact, incidental and otherwise. Tonight's match is not for sissies. Both teams use their bodies to move opponents off the ball and go for position. Before long, not even midway through the first half, tempers are flaring. I imagine the TV commentators using the word "chippy" to describe the atmosphere.

"Do you suppose a hockey game's going to break out?" I joke to Rick as we watch from the sidelines.

"I think it already has," he remarks as one of the Thorn players bowls over Becky Kaisershot. The Blues defender jumps up and gets in her opponent's face as the referee stops play, calls the foul, and issues a yellow card against Portland. Five minutes later, KC returns the favor when Kirstie Longstreet angles for a pass and takes out a Thorn defender. She argues with the ref and is rewarded with a yellow card of her own.

The chippy trend continues right up to halftime, both sides seeming to prefer running into each other over scoring. It's 0-0, points-wise, 1-1 in yellow cards. If the strategy is to keep the elite players in check—Stokes for KC, Conway for Portland—it's working.

Rick analyzes the first half play during the break, but I listen with only half an ear, bothered by a vague sense of worry. Jaye is tall and strong and more than capable of mixing it up if necessary. It's not her game, though, not her style, and I saw the frustration in her eyes as she walked past me toward the locker room. We're both hoping the TV exposure, coupled with a good performance, will solidify Jaye's chances for the national squad. So far, though, all anyone's seeing is each team's "fighting" spirit.

The second half brings more of the same. KC's coach makes a substitution which brings in one of their biggest, toughest players and puts her right in the middle of the defense. A few minutes later, Portland's coach does the same, bringing in Celia Green, a defender with a take-no-prisoners reputation.

"It's a pity they're settling for brawl mentality," Rick says. "We should just get the ball up to Jaye and Kirstie and let them run."

I agree, but I'm not the coach. "Yeah, but that lets Sandra Conway do the same thing, right?"

Rick turns to me, shocked. "Conway's never been able to get by Becky."

"True," comes a voice from behind us. "Kat's always had her number, too."

We turn to greet Bree who fist bumps Rick and gives me a neutral glance. Then we all go back to the match.

Kansas City, at its best, is a passing machine, moving the ball with precision from player to player, seeking the open woman, getting up the field, and setting up scoring chances. Portland works much the same, but with tonight's emphasis on blocking the middle, the game stalls into a series of takeaways and out-of-bounds kicks and not much going on. This frustrates both sides, and the tempers are evident, though no one gets any more yellow cards.

No one gets any real chance to score, either.

Then, as soccer is wont to do, one little opening shows itself and everything shifts. Ten minutes into the second half, Becky Kaisershot steals a ball from the Thorns' Sandra Conway and kicks it out to Sherry Cavallini, who spots Jaye near midfield and lays a perfect pass at her feet. Jaye takes it in stride, and all of a sudden the pitch is open for her. She starts moving like she's done all season long, weaving between opponents. Longstreet comes along, paralleling her. The crowd senses the opportunity and cheers.

The two Blues get close to the Portland goal, and Jaye has two choices: take it in herself or pass it off to Longstreet for the shot. The action is far enough from me that I can't see her face, but I catch the little bit of hesitation as she sets up her next move.

No one sees Green coming at all. As Jaye, decision made, starts to pivot toward the goal, the Thorn defender slides in from the side, hard, and slams right into Jaye's leg. Jaye shrieks as her knee snaps and bends in a direction nature never intended. She falls heavily to the ground. In an instant the crowd falls silent. Someone immediately kicks the ball out of bounds to stop play.

In the stunned hush, Jaye tries to sit up and fails. She collapses back to the ground. Her scream this time is a shriek of both pain and devastation. The agony of it slams into my ears and my brain and shudders its way down my spine.

This is no simple injury.

I run toward her, getting a few feet out onto the field before Rick's quick reaction stops me. "Rachel! You can't." He wraps his arms around my waist. I fight him, but he's younger and stronger, and I get nowhere. Jaye is still screaming, and I can't reach her. I will remember her cries for the rest of my life. Remember the hopelessness echoing there, and my helplessness.

I vaguely register the referee as she blows her whistle, the Blues players as they move toward Jaye, the Portland side congregating awkwardly nearby. I want to close my eyes, but I don't. The least I can do for Jaye is watch. As Kansas City's trainers run out on the pitch, Jaye's teammates are waving for a stretcher. Sherry and Kirstie kneel beside their teammate, and the others stand close, looking grim.

"Fuck," Rick says under his breath. I couldn't agree more. He's managed to get me back on the sidelines, where Bree puts a supportive hand on my shoulder.

The crowd starts to murmur when the ref approaches Celia Green, then they boo wholeheartedly as the red card, for a blatant or reckless penalty, comes out. Green is out of the game, and Portland will play the rest of the way one woman short, ten instead of eleven.

Nickory, meanwhile, has come up from her position at the far goal, close enough to check out the damage. She watches the trainers tending to Jaye, then turns and says something to the referee, who says something back. She scans the Thorns players and spots Green, who is only now starting a slow walk off the field. Nickory heads over in her direction.

"Fuck," Rick says again.

"Oh, Kat, no," Bree echoes him.

Everyone in the stands and on national TV sees what happens next. Nickerson stands in front of the Thorn, blatantly blocking her way. The two exchange words, Nickory's expression hard as granite, Green's defiant and taunting. Then the *coup de gras* as Nickory suddenly balls her gloved fist and punches Green in the face.

Now there are two players lying on the pitch. Green holds her face and curls up into a fetal position. The referee stares at Nickory in shock, but pauses only for a moment before pulling out the red card again. A few in the stands start cheering. It's a crazy mix, then, of cheers, boos, and hushed words. Jaye is lifted into the stretcher, Green continues to lie on the field, and Kathleen Nickerson, warrior queen, walks toward the locker rooms, not an ounce of regret in her stride.

"Rick, get me over to the ambulance," I say, and then he and I are moving, too, running toward a future that has changed in the blink of an eye.

I don't get to see Jaye before the ambulance takes her away. Rick drives us to the hospital. By the time we get there I'm too late to see Jaye in the emergency room. Cursing the bad timing, I go to the reception desk to find out her condition and run into an unexpected obstacle.

"Are you a relative?" the nurse asks.

"No, a good friend."

"I can only give out information to relatives or approved next of kin," the nurse says.

Next of kin? "I'm the closest thing to family she has in Kansas City."

"Name?" I give the nurse my name, my brows knitting together in puzzlement. She checks something on her computer screen, then tells me primly "You're not on the list."

"She's her partner," Rick interjects. "If you check they're wearing the same rings."

We're in Missouri. The nurse is less than impressed. I see her reaction and wish Rick had kept quiet.

"I'm sorry," the nurse says, curtly. "If you're not on the approved list, I can't tell you anything."

I take a mental step back and count to ten. "Who is on the list?" I ask when I can do it without exploding.

"I can't tell you that."

A stare-down ensues. Despite my age, I've rarely run into blatant prejudice against my sexuality. I watch the nurse's expression shift from coolly neutral to triumphant in her power over me, and it's all I can do to keep my hands from forming fists and punching her out.

My eyes narrow. "Is there actually a list?"

"Of course."

"And do you have any intention of notifying anyone on it?"

"That's not in my job description."

"So this seriously injured patient will have to go through this entire experience alone?"

"Not if family shows up."

"Her family is here," Rick says, his voice low with a touch of menace.

I touch his arm to silence him, then check out the badge around the nurse's neck. The letters are small, but I can make out her last name, Meade. Now I know who to file a complaint against later. "You skipped the class where they told you nurses were supposed to be kind and compassionate, didn't you?" I say. The nurse's expression doesn't change at all. I turn my back on the hate.

"Come on, Rick." I stalk away from the desk, through the waiting area, and out the door. Standing at the entrance, I breathe in the warm night air and try to find some calm. When I was working I never panicked. I try to remember how I managed. I'm about there when I hear my name.

"Rachel!"

Bree and Nickory come quickly up the steps. "How's Jaye?" Bree asks me, agitated. "Why aren't you in there?"

"I'm not family. They won't tell me anything."

"Are you kidding?" Nickory's is a growl of disbelief.

"As soon as the desk nurse found out I was Jaye's partner, she totally froze me out."

"Bullshit," Bree says.

Nickory goes into warrior queen mode. "Come on." We all follow her back inside. She walks right up to the nurse and asks about Jaye.

"Are you on the next of kin list?" the nurse says primly.

"Yes," Nickory replies in a tone that would freeze molten lava. "Nickerson, Kathleen."

The nurse checks something, and must find the name there because she is visibly disappointed. "Do you have ID?"

How nice to see Nickory's dagger eyes aimed at someone else. With deliberate calm she pulls out her wallet and presents a driver's license.

Nurse Meade examines it, eyes Nickory, and smiles.

"This picture is of a blonde," the nurse says. "You're not blonde."

Indeed, Nickory's hair has been dyed mourning black since Boston.

"Listen, lady," Nickory says, "I've already broken someone's nose tonight. I don't mind going two for two. If you don't let us in to see our friend, I'll make sure you're the next patient in the ER."

Nurse Ratched's—sorry, Meade's—eyes narrow. "Are you threatening me?"

Out comes the venom glare. If it was even half real, the nurse would be shriveled into crusty particles of skin. "No," Nickory says. "I'm making a solemn promise."

I don't normally condone violence of any kind, but if Nickory makes good on her words I'm tempted to provide an alibi later. She and the nurse stare each other down, neither inclined to give an inch. Nickory's hand clenches and starts to come up, and at the last second, I change my mind and grab her fist with both my hands.

"Nickory, no. Sanctimonious, homophobic, narrow-minded little twerps are not worth going to jail over." The warrior queen stares at me like I've lost my mind. Nurse Ratched's face wrinkles in puzzlement. Guess I used too many big words for her.

We'll never know what would have happened next because the ER doors open with a swish, and a huge, dark oak tree of a man comes striding through them. He's at least six foot six and three hundred pounds, most of it muscle. He's in scrubs with a name tag very similar to Meade's.

"Bree!" he says with a voice that escaped from the basso profundo section of a choir. "Glad you texted me."

The cavalry has arrived.

"Hi, Neil," Bree says calmly.

I turn to see Nurse Meade shrinking visibly into her chair. I would, too, if Neil was the enemy coming my way. He lumbers majestically over to the desk and around to Meade's side of it. There's not much room back there, and she has to shrink even more to avoid being crushed. Paybacks are hell.

Neil twitches his nose, like he's smelling three-day-old fish. "Figures it's you," he rumbles, then ignores her as he checks a computer screen. "Stokes, Jaye. Knee injury. Right?"

"Right," Nickory says.

"Okay. I can bring one of you back there."

Nickory, to my surprise, gestures at me. "Her."

Neil nods at me. "Come on."

And it's my turn to walk through the swinging doors.

Neil leads me to a cubicle with the curtain closed. Before he pushes it aside, he gives me some information.

"The doctor says you can come in for five minutes or so. She's stable, and she's been given medication for the pain. Don't expect her to make too much sense."

"Thank you, Neil," I say from my heart.

"You're welcome," he says as he lifts the curtain aside, and motions me in. "I'll wait here. Five minutes." He pulls the curtain closed. He'll hear all we have to say, but we have at least a pretense of privacy.

The first thing I notice is that Jaye still wears her uniform. The second observation is her eyes. Her pupils are the size of saucers. Neil wasn't kidding when he said she was medicated.

"Bogart," she says raggedly.

I take her hand, lean over, and kiss her lips. "Hey, Bacall. I'm sorry it took me so long to get here."

"S'okay." Jaye sounds like a little girl fighting sleep. She's high as a kite. "Stay with me, Bogart. Stay with me, please."

I bring her hand to my chest, to my heart. "I'll stay as close as I can. You're going to get X-rays soon. I can't go with you there. But I'll be here. I'll be close by."

She rolls her head from side to side on the pillow. "It's gone, Rachel. My knee is gone."

"No, Jaye. You're hurt, but you're going to get better."

"It's all gone." Then a sudden moment of lucidity. "Did we win?"

Fuck. "I don't know. I left as soon as they put you in the ambulance."

The basso profundo rumbles from the other side of the curtain. "Yeah, KC won. 2-1."

Did Bree tell him? It doesn't matter. Jaye relaxes a little. "Good." She watches me, but her eyes blur like she's fading out again. Those scary dark pupils are desolate. "I'm done, Rachel. My career is over."

"Shh. We don't know that yet."

"My body knows." The hollowness of her voice is chilling. I lean down and kiss her again, then rest my cheek against hers. Her despair washes over me, and I feel it mingle with my helplessness to settle in for the long haul.

"We'll get through this, Jaye," I murmur. "Let the doctors take care of you. We'll get you healed."

I hear a clatter outside the curtain. I brush one last kiss against her cheek and straighten up.

Neil opens the curtain. "X-rays, round one."

"You'll stay here, Rachel?" Jaye beseeches me, wide-eyed.

"I'll be back with you as soon they let me, Jaye. I promise."

"I love you."

"Love you, too." Reluctantly I loosen her grip and let the ER people do their jobs. Jaye is wheeled off, and Neil guides me back to the swinging doors.

"Do they know anything yet," I ask him. "Is it as bad she thinks?" When he doesn't answer right away I try a lame joke. "Be honest with me, Hawkeye. I can take it."

Neil graces me with a ghost of a smile and a full house of sympathy. "It's bad. I'll tell the doctors to bypass Meade, and they'll give you the details when they can."

My heart clenches in my chest, but I keep walking. As we reach the doors, I touch his arm. "Thank you for your kindness, sir."

He nods in acknowledgment, then lets me back out into the waiting room.

Turns out Neil is a charge nurse in the ICU at this hospital, but he worked with Bree a couple of years earlier, and they stayed in touch. I'm eternally grateful.

In the waiting room, several of Jaye's teammates have joined Rick, Bree, and Nickory. All eyes turn to me, and I give them what little I learned, including Jaye's belief that her knee is ruined.

"She's right," Nickory says. "I saw it before they got her on the stretcher. It's wrecked."

There's no venom in her eyes, or her voice. She's simply being matter of fact. I try not to start crying.

"Your season is wrecked too, you know," Rick says to her, and he's right. Nickory will certainly be suspended, probably fined. Maybe arrested?

Nickory shrugs. "Green's is, too."

"Kat," Bree says with resignation.

And so, I think silently, is Kansas City's. In one fell swoop, the team has lost two of its best players. Will Jaye's amazing season all go for nothing?

"It wasn't worth it, Nickory," I say.

She shakes her head in disagreement, her face bearing the expression of someone who's lost the battle but is still sure of winning the war. "Green did it on purpose. So did I. Fair is fair."

Warrior queen to the end, even as she's falling on her sword.

The swinging doors fly open, and we put the Blues' wake on hiatus. An average-sized man, not a tree this time, comes into the lobby.

"Who's with Stokes?" he asks. Ten people stand up. He gives us the bad news.

"Shredded" is the word he uses. Green's swift kick has snapped the Anterior and Medial Cruciate ligaments in Jaye's left knee and torn her meniscus as well.

"You can't tell without an MRI though," Bree says, trying to find an out.

"True," the doctor says, "but from the movement of the knee, and the severity of the pain, it's a good bet. Vegas quality."

The air leaves the room. Jaye's dream season is indeed over. In the blink of an eye, in one eighth of a second, she has gone from MVP and probable National Team member to not even being able to walk. Life is a cruel game sometimes, and yeah, yeah, bad things do happen to good people. But this seems particularly sadistic.

The doctor finishes up. "I can release her in about thirty minutes, but she'll have to come back Tuesday for the MRI. She needs to keep the leg elevated, iced, and move as little as possible. I've written a couple of prescriptions for the pain, and the nurse at the desk will arrange for a wheelchair and crutches."

No, she won't. I can guarantee that one. "Better get Neil again," I say to Bree, but she's one step ahead of me.

"I'm texting him now."

Jaye sleeps most of the way home. Rick takes us back to the stadium to get my car, then follows us back to the apartment complex. He helps me get Jaye up the three flights of stairs to our apartment. I take it from there, settling Jaye into our bed, then taking my place beside her, away from the injured knee. Tentatively I lay my head on her shoulder, feeling the relief when she wraps her arm around my back, holds me close. Her grip is so tight, I have trouble breathing, but I don't care. She is here, she is with me, and she's letting me be with her.

As the week passes, however, things go downhill fast. The Tuesday MRI does indeed confirm the doctors' suspicions. Jaye's knee has suffered the "unhappy triad": fully torn ACL and MCL, plus tears in the meniscus. All three require surgery, and because of the meniscus damage, she won't be able to put any weight on the knee for six weeks after the operation. Rehabbing the ACL could take up to a year. Best case scenario, she's fully healthy again when next year's season is ending and plays pro soccer again when she's thirty-three, about the age most players start thinking retirement.

Jaye takes this news with a weird, defeated sort of calm. She knew it anyway. "I'm done," she'd said that night in the hospital. When I try to tell her the doctors can't know her full prognosis until she starts her recovery and rehab, she stares at me, eyes devoid of hope.

"I'm done. It will never be the same."

Plenty of athletes have had injuries like this, a startling number of them women. Even Nickory lost a season in college with a torn ACL and made a full recovery. Most of the athletes who came back good as new, though, were in their teens or twenties. Jaye is older, and she already believes the worst.

I try to stay upbeat but realistic. Jaye doesn't notice. She won't talk about what happened. I try to raise the subject of her injury a couple of times, but she brushes me off.

"I can't talk about it, Rachel. It hurts too much."

The only words with any real substance are still spare. And devastating.

"I feel empty inside," she tells me. "Like there's nothing there."

Soccer's only a game, sure. But Jaye truly, madly, deeply loved the sport, loved to play, and the cruelty of her exit from the field, on the cusp of finally achieving her ultimate goal, begins to appear like it will be too much for her to handle.

I find her state of mind terrifying. I'm willing to deal with tough times, but how? I keep silent about my own fears because this isn't about me. I fight my helplessness against her silence by trying to let my love seep out of me, by osmosis, every time I hold her.

Maybe it works. Jaye is silent and closed, but she's not completely disengaged. She's able to get around well enough to attend her team's final regular season game on the Saturday after the disaster. She sits on the bench and puts on a good face, smiling at her teammates and shouting encouragement. But it's clear the Blues are not the same team without Jaye at center. Nickory, to no one's surprise, has been suspended indefinitely for punching Celia Green. Her statement to the press is solidly in character: "I was absolutely out of line with my actions. I accept the suspension. I will do my best to ensure it doesn't happen again." Twenty-four words, and not one of them an apology.

The backup goalie, a Canadian named Rheaume Delacroix, holds the Houston Dash scoreless even as Houston's goalie does the same to the Blues. The 0-0 draw makes no difference in the standings. Kansas City still finishes "at the top of the table," first in the league. But their playoff opponent, Wendy Allerton's NY Flash, undoubtedly smells blood in the water.

Jaye's teammates make sure she's part of the post-game ceremony where the Blues are presented with a league "Shield" for finishing with the best record. To watch her then, see her interact with players and fans alike, no one would know what she's going through at home. She even does an interview with local TV, and it gives me hope that her emotional recovery has begun.

My hope lasts only until we're in the car, driving back to the apartment.

"I know it was hard for you, but you did great tonight," I say. "The Blues were happy to see you there."

"I never knew how much it could hurt not being able to play. I was laughing to keep from crying."

I take her hand, give it a good squeeze.

"I wasn't ready to stop." I hear the tears in her voice. "I'm not ready for this."

"It's still too early to know for sure."

She lets out a deep sigh. "My body knows," she says softly, exactly like she had in the emergency room. I cringe inside, and Jaye keeps talking. "I never told you the worst thing."

Worse than shredding three crucial pieces of your knee? "What?"

"Hatfield called me the Thursday before the game, before I got hurt." Linda Hatfield is the U.S. National Team head coach. "She told me she was naming me to the team."

We're stopped at a traffic light, and I turn to meet Jaye's gaze. I'm shocked. Jaye's eyes are dull, devoid of any expression at all. No light, no dark, no life.

"I wasn't even going to have to try out," Jaye says. "I was in."

I recall the secret she was waiting to tell me, something that had her excited and happy. It was the last time I saw the brilliant light in her eyes.

She doesn't cry then, but I do, as if all her emotion is routed through me now. Only the honk of a car horn behind us brings me back to the moment, to driving. To getting us home.

Soccer is just a job, only a game.

Yeah, right.

Chapter Twelve

Fyrequeene's Blog: September 13

"To Strive or not to Strive"

I've never been much of a goal-setter. Don't know why, but throughout my life I tended to let things come as they would or stay away as they saw fit. I fell into a college degree, a job, a life. And it's been okay.

As most of you readers have figured out by now, I, The Fyrequeene, the ultimate hermit, have become romantically involved with a professional soccer player. Her name is Jaye Stokes, and she is the wonder of my life. I never thought a love like this would be possible for me. I have never been so glad to be proven wrong.

Jaye is a world-class athlete. She's played soccer since she was five; the game is her first and perhaps still strongest love. Early in our acquaintance she told me her goals as a child were to make the National Team, to play in the World Cup and the Olympics, and to win. And she was almost good enough to do it.

Almost.

Jaye made the "U" teams, the Under-17, Under-18, Under-20 squads from which members of the main, National Team, are eventually chosen. When she got to college, though, Jaye discovered she wasn't quite good enough, wasn't quite fast enough, to keep progressing up the ranks.

"It's an eighth of a step," she told me once. "An eighth of a step separating the excellent from the great."

Jaye is an excellent professional soccer player. Until recently, she had never been a great one.

Learning this raises a question for me: How many "Jayes" are there? How many swimmers are there for every one Janet Evans? How many baseball players for every one Derek Jeter? How many soccer players for every one Wendy Allerton or Mia Hamm? Thousands, no doubt. And perhaps even hundreds like Jaye, who can claim excellence—but not greatness.

This year circumstances changed for her. Somehow Jaye Stokes found an eighth of a step, found the difference that makes good players elite. For four glorious months, she glided across the soccer pitches of the NWSL, excelling in every aspect of the game she loves, knowing, at long last, how it felt to be the best of the best. Her childhood dream was rekindled, burning brighter and brighter, buoying her to greatness.

And in one-eighth of a second it was taken away. In one-eighth of a second, her dream got snuffed out like a match. An injury to her knee on a deliberate foul ended her hopes, her dreams, made mincemeat of her goals.

Maybe that's why I never set goals. If one doesn't set goals, one can't fail. One can't feel the bitter devastation of coming up short. Granted, one can't feel the exhilaration of achievement either, but is that worth shooting for when its opposite always lurks?

I'm not sure it is. Does this make me a coward, or a sensible survivor?

Many, I think, would say coward, and I may have to agree. But many of those same many have never had to watch what happens when, through no fault of her own, a loved one's dream dies.

Three and a half weeks after she was injured, three and a half weeks into my sincere and soul-deep efforts to take care of Jaye, I find out I'm terrible at it.

How else to explain the slow unraveling of our relationship? One week of fraying, okay. Jaye's in pain, in shock, numbed by painkillers and reeling from the blow that turned her life upside down.

Two weeks, and the threads of our connection fray a little bit more. I'm considering what happened to her as a kind of death, the death of someone loved and close, someone who wasn't expected to die for quite a while yet, whose sudden loss leaves a void so large nothing can fill it.

Not even grief, though grief tries, spreading out, seeking the limits of the void until everything else is blocked. And I mean *everything*. Jaye's grief takes her appetite, her interest in books and TV, her friends, her attention to hygiene and appearance—and her love for me. The happy young woman with the incandescent smile is buried so deep within the void that soon I cannot find her. I'm left with a silent, brooding automaton, a parody of a human.

She rustles up enough energy, barely, to attend the playoff against the Flash. The game is a disaster: Rheaume Delacroix is no match for the skill and experience of Wendy Allerton, and KC's offense is aimless and impotent without Jaye. The Blues fall hard, 4-1, and their season ends.

Two days later, Jaye has surgery, which goes well. Or so everyone says. Jaye will be in bed for a few days, on crutches for six weeks, then face months of rehab. The prognosis is good, unless you're a top-notch athlete. Then it's much more nebulous.

"You should walk without limping," the surgeon tells Jaye. "We'll reevaluate when you start rehab, gauge your scale of recovery. There was a lot of damage, and each person heals differently."

He should have been a politician. Jaye hears what I do: there's no way to know if she can play soccer again. If, up to that point, I held some faint hope she could empty the void of grief, the surgeon's ambiguity chops the hope right off. At the knees.

Two days after, she is, as expected, named MVP of the league, which is a mixed blessing at best. Everyone involved in the NWSL makes happy sound bites and tweets about how she deserves the award, hands down, but what a shame her season was cut short.

She hears and reads none of this. Jaye is lucid enough to record a very simple "thank you for the honor" press release, but there is no spark there. She literally switches off her smile when the recording is done, and goes back to lying in bed, taking her pain pills on schedule, and saying as little as possible to me.

Three and a half weeks after the injury, Jaye uses the excuse of post-surgical discomfort to ask me to sleep separately from her.

"You toss and turn sometimes, and I don't want to risk the knee. It's only for a little while."

There's a logic to this, so I accept it, but it cuts me to the core. Now, finally, I grasp the extent of the disconnect between us, Jaye's shift from grief to depression, her own version of the dreaded guerrilla/gorilla.

When depression ruled me, I, too, had days where I couldn't get out of bed, periods where the only reason I left the house was because something such as work made me, long stretches of believing nobody cared or would miss me if I was gone.

Like Jaye, I didn't fight it. I let the depression be my bully slave master, let it block out the light, let it take my body over and plunge me into a darkness and sadness so bleak I knew I could never escape. Throughout those times, I always wished deeply for someone to hold me in her arms, to love me and help me endure. I was certain a partner and her love would be enough to overcome my captor.

The big difference, though, between Jaye and me? She has the partner. She has the love. I'm the one holding Jaye (well, until she kicked me out of our bed), trying to help her endure, trying to be what she needs. Three and a half weeks in, I realize it's not enough. Nothing is okay.

This discovery is so shocking that the darkness pulls me in, too.

And the discovery *is* a shock, not creeping up on me slowly, but hitting all at once late one evening after Jaye has drugged herself to sleep. I'm watching some Blues' soccer highlights, including a replay of the game where Jaye was injured. I rewind the awful moment a couple of times, and the evidence is clear: the Portland player fully intended to hit Jaye rather than the ball. She purposely set out to put Jaye on the ground. If I'm charitable, she couldn't have known she would succeed so spectacularly. If I'm not charitable, she deserves more than the broken nose Nickory gave her.

Portland won their playoff game and advanced to the finals. At least Nickory's punch literally knocked Green out of the playoffs, too. I feel no guilt over the petty pleasure this gives me.

The replay isn't what stuns me, though. The shock comes when I watch Jaye's interview with local TV after the last regular season game. I had watched her do the interview and saw only her polite, "We're all doing this for the team" face, complete with clichés and smiles. I didn't listen to what she said, though. I listen now.

The reporter asks the usual questions about KC's chances in the playoffs, listens to Jaye give the usual answers. He then asks if it's hard to watch and not be able to play, and Jaye replies with what at first seems like another typical cliché.

"Oh, it's killing me," she says, with a smile even. But I know Jaye. Underneath the smile, I see the despair. She means it. Not being able to play is killing her. Literally.

I sit there, numb. Surely it can't be that bad? How can someone who has so much light inside, so much intelligence, plus a partner who lived through her own darkness and talks about it, how can someone so innately positive feel so hopeless?

The answer floats up from deep inside me. *She's never felt anything like this before.*

But what about the soccer coach bitch? Jaye told me herself how devastated she was when the woman dumped her.

Another floater: *Jaye knew, deep down, something was wrong with her teenage love affair. There was nothing wrong with her soccer dream, nothing wrong with the goal of playing for her country.*

Thus, all the more shattering to have it taken away.

I get up and go into the bedroom, stand over Jaye's sleeping form. She has been silent today, as usual. I check on her now, making sure her injured leg is stable. I listen to her quiet breathing, watch the peaceful face slumber brings. A small thing to be grateful for. She is not so tortured that sleep provides no escape. For the hundredth time, I wish I could take on some of the pain.

After a somewhat heated inner argument, I take a chance and lean my head down, gently kiss her forehead.

"I love you, Bacall," I breathe, far too softly for her to hear. "If I could take away this grief and roll back time I would. If I could take on your pain, pull it away from you, I would. Please don't give in. Please don't turn into me."

I stand and walk out of the room, a gorilla following gleefully in my wake.

Over the next few days, no matter my intentions, no matter how simple or complex a task, I do everything wrong.

The problems start innocuously enough. Because of the surgery, Jaye has to keep weight off her knee for six weeks. This puts us in the middle of October before she can even think about walking unaided again. Our lease is up at the end of September. I make what I think is a logical decision.

"We should stay another month here," I say to Jaye one morning. I have managed to get her out of bed and parked over a bowl of cereal. She's clearly lost weight; every time I get her to eat is a small victory.

She gives me a blank stare. "Why? Don't you still want me to go to Denver?"

Where did that come from? "Of course I do. I thought we'd wait until you can put weight on the knee again, when you don't need the crutches." I attempt a grin. "It's not like Kansas City's the worst place in the world."

"Part of me died here, Rachel."

Well, shit. I'm behind the eight ball, and the cue shot is coming hard. I apologize, and she shrugs.

"Whatever you think is best."

Crash. That little incident sends me flying into the air without a gyro, blind and tumbling. A couple of days later, I come back from my usual early morning swim to find Jaye up, balanced on a crutch and her good leg, standing at the countertop separating kitchen and living area. She turns my way, holding something.

"I thought you were going to wear this all the time."

I draw closer and see the ring Jaye bought in Boston. I gently take the steel band from her fingers.

"I do wear it all the time. Except in water. I take it off when I swim, and I take it off to shower. Then I put it back on." I slide the ring onto my finger. "See?"

I'm puzzled. I've been doing this since we got the rings. Did Jaye never notice? Why should she care now?

"So you're still trying," she says, reminding me of what we said that day.

"With all my might."

She leans against the countertop, as if her energy has suddenly deserted her. "Why?"

It's a tiny little word to instill such utter terror in me. I'm knocked back on my heels for a fateful moment.

"Because I love you, Jaye. Because I made you a promise, and I'll always keep my promises to you."

She acknowledges this with an even tinier little word, a sharp little needle which shoves the terror right through my soul. "Oh." No inflection, no emotion. Nothing except detachment, like I'm talking about something she has nothing to do with.

I touch her shoulder. "Jaye? You believe me, right?"

She looks at me with empty eyes. "I believe you'll keep your promises."

I hear a roaring in my ears as the gorilla screams in triumph.

This is depression's third major victory in its war with my soul. The first was the nervous breakdown in my mid-thirties. The second was a few years ago, when I was close to retirement but not close enough, and the stresses of my job and my solitude combined to put me on the brink of suicide.

I think back to the second episode, remember how I acted then, and realize with a sick pain how closely Jaye's current behavior matches it. I spoke to people only when necessary, cut myself off from all and sundry life whenever possible. I stopped eating, stopped exercising, stopped caring. I let myself sink almost to the brink of oblivion.

Now I'm watching the love of my life do the same things.

I suppress the terror bubbling inside me and take action, doing as much as I can, without being obvious, to make the desperate next step more difficult. I keep the doors locked. I hide the kitchen knives—I'm the only one preparing food now anyway. I take much shorter swims. I stop sleeping. But there's one thing she is bound to notice.

"Where's the Percocet?" Jaye asks me the morning after I move the pill bottle to my car.

I pull a little case out of my pocket. "Here." I hand her the morning dose.

Jaye may be blank and hollow right now, but she's still smart. "You don't trust me."

"I'm beginning to worry, yes."

Part of me hopes she'll lash out a defense or at least get angry at me for treating her like a child. But no. She pauses a moment, then takes the pill from me and disappears into the bathroom.

We don't speak for the rest of the day.

The next day I ask Bree to come visit and bring Nickory. If my brain were working better, I might have thought of this sooner. But my brain is fogged from worry and sleeplessness and also clouded by my normal tendency to let people do what they want. I don't force my will on people. I don't arbitrarily decide I'm right and bull ahead against others' wishes, especially when my lover and partner is the one I'm defying. But hiding the pain pills starts that very process in motion, and once moving, I decide I may as well continue it.

Jaye has been extremely reclusive since the injury. Other than the two Blues games and the brief recorded press release, she has seen no one other than me and the doctors. She told her parents not to come down, she would be fine, a decision I disagreed with. Most of the team, including Rick and Becky, scattered to off-season homes and distant jobs after the playoff loss. The only ones left here are Bree and Nickory, and even they will be moving to their home base in Chicago when September ends.

Since the night in the ER, Bree and Nickory have repaired their relationship. I don't have the details, but something is working again that wasn't before. I know this because Bree has kept in touch with me, both to build back our own nascent friendship and to check on Jaye. She and Nickory have tried to come over a couple of times already, but the new dark version of my lover refuses to see them.

I keep my promises, yes, but I never actually promised Jaye I wouldn't let the pair drop by unannounced. After her listless little "oh" and the pain pill incident, I call Bree and we make plans.

What ensues is an unqualified disaster. I manage to get Jaye to shower and dress in clean clothes, and I tidy up the apartment so at least we are presentable. But as soon as the doorbell rings, Jaye, brain still fully functional when she chooses to use it, knows what's up.

"You called Nickory, didn't you?"

For the first time in weeks I don't kowtow to the ice in her voice. "No. I called Bree." I get up to open the door.

The two Musketeers walk in to see their former third standing on her good leg, reaching for the crutches at her side.

"Jaye," Bree begins, but gets no further before she's cut off.

"Have a nice visit," Jaye says and clomps off to the bedroom, making sure to slam the door.

Nickory takes action and stalks after her friend. She opens the bedroom door and goes inside, slamming it shut behind her.

Bree stares at me, wide-eyed. "Jesus, she looks terrible!"

"And this is a good day."

She gestures toward the hallway. "Shall we put our ears on the door and listen in?"

I'm half-tempted, but I'm also overloaded with Jaye's bullshit. "No. I'm tired of dealing with this." And since I'm sure Jaye won't jump out a window with Nickory here, I add "Take a walk with me?"

We exit through the front door, close it quietly, head down the stairs and out of the parking lot. There's no park nearby, but the sidewalk on the street is nice and wide, and the traffic is light. It'll do.

Bree is naturally full of questions. "Is she eating?"

"Not enough. I try."

"You're not eating either. And you're not sleeping, are you?"

"Jaye sleeps, if she's taken a painkiller. I get a few hours here and there."

"What pain killer?"

"Percocet. And yes, I'm being careful she doesn't take too many."

"She should be cutting down by now."

"I'm hiding the pills, so she doesn't have access. I started giving her half doses a couple of days ago. Next week I'll cut it back a little more."

"She's not complaining about pain?"

"No."

"Are you guys talking at all?"

"If you count one-word sentences, maybe."

Bree puffs out a breath. "How long has she been like this?"

"Since the surgery."

"You look pretty ragged yourself," she says, with sympathy.

"I'm at the end of my tether, Bree." I choke up a little, hope I can keep a meltdown at bay. "I thought love could conquer all. I thought we could handle bad times, thought we'd be able to talk things through. But my love's not enough. Jaye doesn't give a shit about anything now, and I don't know how to change it."

"Have you suggested a therapist?"

"Once. She completely ignored me."

"You're hiding her pills. Are you afraid she's suicidal?"

I debate how much to reveal and settle on a simple but certain, "Yes."

Bree stops walking. I stop one step beyond her, turn to face her with bleak eyes, and say it again. "Yes."

Bree measures her next words carefully. "There's something called a seventy-two-hour hold."

"I know what that is."

Because my therapist threatened me with it once. A seventy-two-hour hold is when a potential suicide victim is deemed to be so close to attempting death she's essentially arrested and placed in hospital care—*mental* hospital care—monitored and locked up for three days. The tactic is intended as a life-saving action, but I considered it a threat because I didn't want people to know how bad off I was. In my case, the threat was enough.

"As a nurse I can authorize it, Rachel. If you think I should."

Wow—a truly drastic step. And if it became public? Jaye's celebrity in soccer circles would make her troubles news in the gossip world. News enough to ruin her? Gossip aside, it would almost certainly ruin our own relationship. Is Jaye far enough gone?

"God, I don't know what to do anymore." We reach an intersection, and I turn around and head back toward the apartments.

"Tell her you're thinking about it," Bree says. "It might get her to talk."

Before I can reply, a Jeep Wrangler pulls up alongside us.

Nickory barks out the window, "Get in!" Wordy as ever. Bree climbs in the back, and I take the passenger seat.

"You left Jaye alone?" I ask with more than a hint of alarm.

Nickory pops the clutch and starts back toward the Gates of Hell. "She threw me out."

"Was she angry?"

Nickory's lips are a tight thin line. "Furious."

I take this in, decide it might actually be a good thing. We get back to the complex about a minute later, and I climb out of the Jeep.

"Remember what I said, Rachel," Bree says. Nickory nods at me with actual sympathy, and I close the Jeep door, waving a half-hearted goodbye.

When I get back up to the apartment, the door is locked. And my key is inside. I put my fingers to the doorbell, then screw that wimpy move, form a fist instead and pound on the wood. I pause, listen for movement, hear none, and pound some more.

"Jaye!" I shout, not caring who else might hear. "Jaye!"

I pause, listen again. Nothing. I raise my arm and start round three.

"I'll break the door down, Jaye!" The door is solid, but I'm solidly angry, and its destruction is well within my capabilities.

At the next pause, I finally hear the lock snick. The love of my life opens the door and yes, Jaye is furious. Anger blazes through her eyes and right into my psyche. I still think it's a good sign.

"Let me in," I say, in my best I'm-the-boss-don't-mess-with-me ATC voice. Jaye, on one crutch, backs aside awkwardly, enough for me to slip through. Keeping with the tone of her day, she slams the door. I walk into the living area and hear the crutch clunk behind me.

"Why did you do that?" Jaye shouts.

"I didn't have my keys."

An incendiary glare. "Why did you let Nickory come over?"

"Because I thought it would help."

"Help what?"

"Help you come back to life."

Jaye falters in her stance and I move toward her. "Don't touch me," she says.

Three little needles. I opt for a sledge hammer. "Then sit down before you collapse and wreck your knee all over again."

Jaye flinches, but I have swallowed harsh words for almost a month now. I won't swallow them anymore. She moves toward the couch, flops onto the cushions, and throws the crutch to the floor. She looks up at me like a petulant child. "Are you happy?"

There's enough room to sit next to her, so I do. "No, I'm not happy. I'm worried sick. It's like you're dead inside and it scares me. I don't know what to do to make it better."

"Calling Nickory wasn't the answer."

"Okay. What is?"

I get what I expect. Silence. But I think the anger has receded some, so I chance taking her hand. She lets me do it. My own anger dies in the wake of this small victory.

"Jaye, my love," I say tenderly, "I can't bring soccer back." Her eyes close in pain, but I keep going. "You told me part of you died here, and you may be right But you're not dead, not by a long shot. You're at the bottom of the well. It's dark, and it's fucking awful. But you're not dead."

"Might be easier if I was."

The words run down my spine like nails on a chalkboard. Finally it's out in the open. Does she mean it? So many times people don't. So many times people throw those words around in jest, in frustration, in whining. "I wish I was dead," they say. "This is killing me." Or "I can't go on like this."

"I don't know if I can do this," she says then, echoing my last thought. "I can't get away from the pain."

I take Jaye's chin in my hand, make her meet my eyes. She's not talking about the pain in her knee. "You can. You absolutely can."

"How do you know?"

"Because you're stronger than me, and I did it."

She takes this in. "But you said you never tried to kill yourself."

Jaye has spoken the words. I swallow, hard. "I didn't. But I came really fucking close. I felt pain and despair so bad that ending it all seemed like a good idea. I stood at the edge of oblivion for a whole fucking afternoon and thought about jumping in."

"You're not making this up, are you?"

"No, I'm not making it up." I sit up straight, gather my courage. "It was seven years ago, the first time I went to Provincetown."

Where, as it happened, I was far enough away from my therapist to avoid a seventy-two-hour hold.

Skepticism plays all over Jaye's face. "But you love Provincetown."

"I do, I did, then, too. The first time there, I walked the streets, checked out the beaches, met some lesbian couples who were totally cool and totally in love. I felt the energy of Provincetown calling to me, but I also felt my own loneliness, heard my own darkness telling me all this positive could never be mine. I didn't believe I could ever be happy."

I drop my gaze toward the floor. I can't tell this story otherwise. "The irony would have been funny if it hadn't hurt so much. I finally found a place that welcomed me for who I was, yet I never felt more alone, or isolated. With each day I got more depressed, more hopeless, and the emotional pain got worse and worse until one day I thought if I couldn't find a home, I could at least find death."

Jaye's breath catches slightly after I say 'death.' Okay. She's listening.

"It was November, way past tourist season. I went down to the breakwater at the edge of town and walked across it, out to Long Point."

We hadn't taken that walk, Jaye and I, but I'd pointed it out to her while we were there, and I thought she'd remember.

"It's about a mile across those rocks, and another five minutes or so over the dunes to get to the beach facing the bay. I went right down to the water, maybe four feet from the waves, and sat down on the sand. I had it all to myself, like I thought I would, and I knew if I went into the water, swam out far enough, the cold would get me. Nobody would see me, no one could rescue me. I'd be gone, and all the misery and darkness and pain would be gone, too." I pause. "God, it was awful. The idea of suicide felt so wrong but at the same time the idea of living with all the pain I was carrying felt just as bad."

I lift my eyes. "You know how it feels, don't you?"

Her eyes meet mine, raw with despair, and for the first time since the injury I feel true connection with the woman I love. Jaye bursts into tears, collapses against my shoulder. I put my arms around her, hold her close.

We lose time, minutes and minutes of it, buried in misery both current and remembered. Eventually Jaye's crying subsides, and I worry she'll pull away, but she doesn't. Not right then.

"Why didn't you do it?" She asks me, face still buried against my neck. "What stopped you?"

I bite my lip and wish I had a better answer. "I don't know. To this day I don't know. Except . . . there were these two seagulls, one on either side of me, standing there like sentinels. I watched them looking at me, and suddenly I thought, 'They're sentinels to the making of a decision.' And the decision was mine. Live, or die."

And because I'm honest, I opt for full disclosure. "Live? Die? Neither felt good. There was no right thing to do that day. There was only choice. Eventually I chose to get up and walk back into town."

Now the memories and the strain of dealing with Jaye all come together and crash down on me. My tears flow uncontrollably, and the more I try to rein them in the more they rush out. Jaye pulls my head onto her shoulder, and her arms encircle me while I cry. Finally, the comfort I'd longed for over so many empty years. If anything, the comfort makes me cry harder.

At some point the dam reseals itself, and the jag subsides from sobs to snuffles.

Jaye says, softly, "I wish I had been there for you."

I pick my head up. The Jaye I love peeks out from the shadows. I put my hands on her cheeks. "All I've wanted since you got hurt was to be there for you. I love you so much, Jaye."

"I know you're trying."

Here come the tears again. "I may not know much, but I know this: Every good thing that's ever happened to me happened after I chose to walk back into Provincetown. Writing the books, meeting you, everything. I don't want a world without you in it. I promise you it gets better. Please promise me you'll stay."

Chapter Thirteen

"When you're going through Hell, keep going."
~*Winston Churchill*

Jaye makes the promise, and slowly, very slowly in days to come, the pressure eases. I stop worrying about her overdosing on Percocet or trying hari-kari with a kitchen knife. She addresses me in complete sentences, with nouns and verbs and adjectives. She begins to eat again, almost to the level of an active athlete, and she reacquaints herself with the shower and clean clothes.

Jaye stops short of allowing any discussion of the injury or her emotional state. If I touch on those subjects she shuts down. I venture some words about how therapy helped me overcome my depression and get nothing. I ask if she's going to try to play for the Blues when she's healed, and she leaves the room.

Even a semi-innocent subject goes only so far. "Do Bree and Nickory always go to Chicago in the off-season?" I ask one evening.

"Yep. They like it there. Bree works here and in Chicago, splitting time between two hospitals in the same network. Nickory does soccer camps and National Team events, and with the big airport, Chicago's a good base."

"They don't mind harsh winters?"

Jaye actually brings out a genuine smile. "A Chicago girl and a New Hampshire girl? Winters are nothing to them."

"Did you usually stay with them?"

"Yes," Jaye says. "I do—did—the grunt work for the soccer camps. You know, all the off-field coordinating and organizing."

"You'll keep doing the soccer camps, right?"

Wrong words. Jaye stands up. "I need to get ready for bed," she announces, then clunks off, an expert now with one crutch.

Crap.

After that I avoid the subject of soccer completely, mentally tabling it for later. After all, there's still the subject of the move to Denver. We agree to extend the apartment lease for one month, leaving us the choice of going to Colorado as soon as Jaye feels her knee is ready, with no pressure to do so too soon.

One day I'm out in parking lot, standing like a statue before our two cars. Jaye has a nice Subaru Outback, and I have my Toyota Solara with a generous trunk and back seat. I'm mentally calculating the space available between the two, what we can pack in each for the trip west.

"Rachel!" Jaye calls at me from the third-floor landing. "What are you doing?"

I wave, then come up the stairs to talk without shouting. "I think we can get all our stuff into the cars," I say when we're back in the flat.

Jaye ponders this. "Everything except the bed."

"Yes. Everything except the bed." There's an edge to my tone, but apparently Jaye doesn't hear.

"Will I need the bed in Denver?"

Jaye has yet to allow me to sleep with her again, let alone be intimate, and it's become, like the soccer, a subject best avoided.

But I don't avoid it all the time. "I don't know," I say, making the edge obvious. "Will you?"

Her eyes harden. "I don't want to risk hurting my knee."

Whatever. "Okay. Unless it's a family heirloom or something, maybe you can sell it before we leave. If you're still not ready to sleep with me in Denver, my house has plenty of room for a bed we can buy there."

Wrong words, but I know this. The hardness in Jaye's eyes spreads to all of her. She stalks off into the bedroom—step *clunk*, step *clunk*—and slams the door. I, in turn, go into the office, close its door gently, and sit. There has been an undercurrent of anger in many of Jaye's actions these past few days, but this is the first time I deliberately provoked it.

Why? I'm not angry at Jaye, and I know she has a lot of healing to do still. Perhaps I simply wish I'd see some evidence of progress. Sure, she's moved on from suicide, but how about moving on from the injury? Or how about some sign she still wants me around? Because I still want *her* around. Don't I?

A pang of guilt shoots through me. *Of course* I want her around. I know I'm not dealing with the real Jaye Stokes here. I'm dealing with a traumatized woman, someone whose whole way of life may be changing—and changing in a way she did not choose or want.

"When life throws you lemons, make lemonade." I hate that platitude and can understand Jaye would probably prefer to make lemon bombs at this point. Frankly, I wish she would, metaphorically at least, because it might help her express and dissipate the anger which, I abruptly realize, has replaced the depression.

Or, more accurately, has joined the depression. The two often go together, and they don't need lemons in the mix. They can be perfectly explosive on their own.

"Why, Jaye?" I say out loud, to the air, to the universe. "Why won't you let me in?"

I open my Mac to write, but can't think of anything but an old quote from Winston Churchill, one sentence running through my head over and over. Frustrated, I type it out, with proper attribution, and upload it as my blog for the week.

Five minutes later my phone rings.

"Rachel."

"Toni."

"I read your blog. All one sentence of it. Do I have to come out there?"

"What? No."

"Are you sure?"

It doesn't take much imagination to see Toni running roughshod over Jaye, permanently "fixing" our relationship by shattering it completely.

"I'm sure. Jaye and I will work out, one way or another."

"You're not easing my mind."

I sigh. "That's the best I can do right now."

After a brief pause, Toni says, "Will you keep going until you're out of Hell? No matter what? Rachel?"

A flash of intuition strikes, and I don't censor it. "Did you guys ever go through this? Did Paula ever not let you in?"

"Umm, no." Toni's answer is quick, but not unequivocal. I'm puzzled, but only for a second.

"Did you ever not let *her* in?"

"Maybe."

"How did she finally get through to you?"

Toni hesitates. "I don't recommend it."

"Don't recommend what?"

Apparently, I've hit a nerve. "Let's just say I learned my lesson. Jaye will learn hers."

I recognize by her tone that I'm not going to get anything further out of Toni on the subject. Not today, anyway. "Maybe I'm the one who needs to learn a lesson."

"You both do. Guess I'm not much help."

"I'm glad you tried. I really am."

My take from the frustrating and somewhat confusing chat with Toni is to avoid provoking Jaye. Over the course of the next week, I go out of my way to be solicitous and kind. I don't back down completely when we disagree, but I back down a lot, hoping something of my behavior will get through.

No such luck. If anything, Jaye grows even more irritable. The moments of connection we had when we talked about suicide are long gone. One night, ensconced in the office, computer open but blank, I think back to the early days of our romance, trying to relive the kindness, the sex, the love.

"It's happening too fast," Nickory had said. She meant it as an accusation. Jaye and I took it as something meant to be. Now, though, I wonder if what we have is nothing more than a shooting star, a meteor breaking up in the heat of the atmosphere as it falls to Earth.

A crashing noise comes from the kitchen. I get up to see what's happened and find Jaye staring at the shards of a large glass serving bowl. It's not a family heirloom, not anything super special. But that bowl held many of Jaye's fantastic salad creations, and its loss is a symbol, for sure.

I scan the counter top, clear of cutting board and salad ingredients. Perhaps Jaye was getting ready to make salad.

"It slipped out of my hands," she says. Her voice is back to flat and uninflected. "I'll get the broom."

"I've got it," I tell her. "Don't risk your knee."

I mean this. She's so close to being able to use the leg again, there's no point in taking chances.

I get the broom and a dustpan from the laundry closet. When I come back to the kitchen, Jaye is bent over, picking up the larger shards and throwing them in the trash.

"I broke the bowl."

"Yes, and I'll clean it up. It's okay." Funny how one says things, sometimes. How one small thing gets blown up into a larger thing, suddenly representing an issue it was never meant to refer to at all.

"You don't have to clean up after me."

"No, I don't. But I choose to. It makes sense for me to do this. Don't worry about it." I move to sweep up the mess, but Jaye's next words stop me cold.

"Rachel, can you just not be perfect right now?"

Slowly I swivel my head to face Jaye. She stares at me, a little irritated, a lot distant. Uncompromising. I've been watching this expression for weeks, but suddenly my resolve to be patient, my resolve to be kind, my resolve to trust in Jaye's certainty about us, and my certainty in her, yadda yadda yadda . . . my resolve snaps.

With one simple sentence I have found out what my breaking point is.

I lean the broom against the counter and step back. My own tightly packed anger now simmers over. It doesn't explode, it doesn't break anything, it merely vibrates the lid holding it down inside me and steams out the edges.

"Yes, I can definitely not be perfect right now. I can definitely not be perfect for the rest of our fucking lives. And I can definitely not be perfect by myself."

I go back into the office and close up my computer, put it in its carrying case along with the power cord and other accessories. Back in the living area, I grab my keys and wallet, search for my iPhone, spot it and pick it up, too. Jaye is still standing in the kitchen. She hasn't moved an inch. There may be a hint of consternation in her expression, but I've been hoping for something other than flat and blank for weeks now and am sure I'm imagining this.

"Have a nice life," I say in parting, to fling something out and get the last word. I open and walk out the front door. I think Jaye calls out as the door shuts, but I'm not stopping.

I stomp down three flights of stairs, cross the parking lot, unlock my car. Get in the front seat, close the door, put the keys in the ignition.

Then, only then, does what I'm doing hit me. I'm leaving. I'm walking out on the love of my life. I'm going, and I'm alone again.

But wait, there's more: I'm breaking my promise to Jaye's parents. I'm as bad as the soccer coach bitch from all those years ago.

My brain goes numb. I drop my hand from the keys and fall back against the seat. Some unconscious part of me knows that not starting the car is a good thing. As strung out as I am, as upset as I am, I shouldn't be driving. But if I don't drive away, what do I do?

At first the answer is "sit there." I stare into space, seeing nothing. Hearing nothing. Thinking nothing. This goes on for a while. Then the nothingness in my head becomes interspersed with images of Jaye, from those first glorious days and weeks. The gorgeous stranger in the cemetery, the confident soccer player, the enthusiastic lover in my bed, the tender protector of my trust.

One image gets stuck on repeat, and it shatters me. Jaye, about to take the free kick in Boston, stepping back from the ball, her eyes burning into mine, reading my thoughts, feeling my love, interlocking my soul with hers.

My eyes, so blessed to see such a vision three months ago, squeeze themselves shut on this warm Kansas City night, squeeze tight against the sudden flood of tears roiling up from my psyche.

The tears win, bursting out of me. I put my face in my hands and cry.

Tears, I learned very early in life, did not impress my parents. My older cousins would make fun of me too if I cried, so when I was six, I made a conscious effort to hide my tears. In the darker moments of my depression I'd occasionally break down, but by then I couldn't cry for very long. A minute, maybe two, was all I could ever manage before the waterworks dried up.

Since I met Jaye, crying has come back to me, mostly in the expression of tears of joy. On this night it's the opposite, and the heaving, gulping sobs of despair don't stop after a minute or two. The earlier images rewind and play again, faster now, with newly remembered scenes and memories. Jaye taking my picture in the park, Jaye awed at the grandeur of the Rocky Mountains, Jaye calling my name as orgasm envelops her. Jaye simply being with me. I cry through them all. And when at long last I believe I can rein it in, my cruel little mind throws out one more thing.

I'd predicted an May-December affair. I'd told myself this could never last—Jaye was too young and too beautiful to stick with the likes of me. And goddamn me, I was right. The six weeks before the fateful last game, the six weeks we shared an apartment and made two lives one, were the happiest of my life. Now they always will be.

The tears gush out again.

Eventually I dry out. Or maybe I wear out. When that happens I simply stare straight ahead again, blind, deaf, still numb, trying to find the energy to move.

But to move where? Start the car and drive away? Go back up to the apartment? Throw myself into the pool and refuse to swim? Nothing has any appeal. Nothing is worth the effort.

Time passes. The night deepens. I'm vaguely aware of cars coming and going. Perhaps some of their drivers see me. Who knows, who cares. My eyes are open, my body is breathing, but there isn't anybody home inside. There isn't anything at all.

When the phone rings I'm so blank it doesn't even startle me. Jaye's ringtone plays, a clip from one of the most mushy, romantic songs I've ever heard. Slowly the tune registers in my brain, the blankness lifts. I close my eyes tight against a new sheen of tears while I decide if I'm going to answer. Yes, or no?

One second before the call would go to voicemail, I choose yes, and hit "Accept."

It takes me a moment to get my mouth working. "Hey."

"Rachel? Where are you?" Jaye's tone is full-on scared little girl.

Another moment. "I'm in my car."

A long, long pause. "Are you going back to Denver?"

I match the pause with one of my own. "No. I'm still in Kansas City."

"Can—can you come home?"

A whole long string of moments passes while I ponder this question. Eventually I say, "You can keep anything I left, and throw away what you don't want. I don't care."

Now I hear what sounds like a muffled sob. "Rachel, please. Please come back. I don't want you to leave. Please?"

The last "please" is cut off by another sob. This cracks through some of my numb veneer, and a small part of my mind grasps the fact that Jaye's pain is as great as mine. How, by the gods, have we done this to each other?

When I don't answer Jaye tries again. "Bogart, are you there? Please don't hang up."

The nickname keeps me on the line. "I'm here," I say quietly. "I'm not far away. I'll be there in a few minutes."

I click off the phone, check the display and see the time. It's one-thirty a.m. I've been sitting in my car for something like six hours. Whoa. How long did I cry? How long was I staring into space? And was Jaye doing the same thing?

I take a few deep breaths, get out of the Toyota, slam the door, and walk the walk.

As I get to the third-floor landing the apartment door opens. Jaye stands there with one crutch, her face tired and haunted. Her hair is a mess, her skin is flushed and sallow at the same time, and her eyes have a shiny glaze, like someone with a fever. My neutral façade cracks, and my heart thumps hard in my chest. For all the mess Jaye is right now, I see only her beauty. I see only the love of my life. The pain accompanying the image of Jaye, real this time, is almost unbearable. I bite my lip, blink back tears (surely I must be out of tears?), and walk in.

Jaye closes the door behind me. As it clicks into place, I move to let her pass me. She collapses onto the couch. I watch, and I keep my distance. She sees me standing there, unmoving, and her body slumps, deflates, and takes on the air of someone defeated.

Still, she speaks first. "Where did you go?"

"The parking lot."

She frowns, like she thinks I'm being deliberately difficult. "And then?"

"I never left. I sat in my car. I was going to leave, but after I stopped crying, I had nothing left."

"You were crying?"

Suddenly I'm too tired to dance around whatever new reality we're creating. "Are we done, Jaye? Is this it?"

I watch her dissolve into tears, the epitome of utter defeat, and I feel what remains of my hope dissolve, too.

But the sight brings back some of my humanity. Moving like I'm a hundred years old, I go to the couch and sit right next to the most important person in my life. She's close enough to touch, but in this moment she seems a thousand galaxies away. Despite her anger, and mine, and the distance of the last few weeks, I *still* want to hold Jaye, comfort Jaye, make everything better. But I've wanted that since she got hurt and haven't gotten it right yet. Why should now be any different?

"I'm sorry," I murmur, maybe too quietly to be heard above the tears. "I'm sorry I'm so bad at this. All I wanted was to love you, help you heal. I don't know how. And I don't know if I have anything left."

With a gasping shudder Jaye pulls herself together. She faces me. "I talked to my mom tonight."

About fucking time. If anyone can get through to Jaye, it has to be her mother, right? Of course, I've never been convinced Marcia Stokes was truly in favor of me at all. Tonight was her perfect chance to get me out of Jaye's life.

"I should have called her sooner," Jaye says, in synch, yet again, with my mind. "She always sees things differently."

I swallow hard. "What did she say?"

"She said deep down I know what I want. So I need to listen to deep down."

Simple advice. Good advice. Maybe. "And what did 'deep down' say?"

Jaye meets my eyes. Decision time. "I want you with me."

The words sound good, thank you, Mrs. Stokes, but I'm can't let hope back in quite yet. "As what? Your friend? Your caretaker? Your whipping girl?"

Jaye closes her eyes. Opens them again. She tentatively puts her hand on my shoulder. "I want my lover. I can't lose you and soccer both. I didn't see that until Mom pointed it out. I think it would kill me. For real. Without me even helping." Her eyes, glittering with a feverish shine, bore into mine. "Please tell me we can try?"

She desperately seeks the comfort I desperately want to give. My heart thumps hard again, and my mind lets out the me who also wants her lover back. I bring my fingers up to Jaye's cheek. She leans into the touch, drawn to the thread of hope I'm offering.

"Oh, Jaye, I love you so much." I brush her lips with mine, a feather-light touch. "Is the woman who smiles all the time still in there? Is the woman who loves life, and living, and me, still in there? Can I have you back, too?"

She turns away and stares at the floor for a long time. Maybe one minute, maybe ten. My emotions, my hopes and dreams, run the complete gamut from A to Z and back again.

Then Jaye lays her head on my shoulder. "We can find her if you stay with me, Rachel. She's there, and she still loves you."

I slide one arm around her back, use the other to take her right hand and hold it up. The ring is there. Unlike me, Jaye never took it off at all, not for water or soccer or anything. She wanted this so badly, once; she was so sure. Does she truly want it still?

"Do you promise to try?" I ask her. "It's hard what you're going through, it's hard to heal. You're going to need more help than I can give you. But do you promise to try? To try for us?"

Jaye slides her fingers through mine, turns my hand so the ring I wear faces her, and kisses it fervently. "Yes, Rachel. I promise to try."

I lean over and gently kiss her lips. "Good."

She smiles, and for the first time in forever, I see light in her expression. But it also emphasizes the exhaustion in her eyes.

"You need to get some sleep," I say. She lets me pull her to her feet and leans heavily against me as she stands.

"Sleep with me tonight, Rachel. Please?"

I wrap my arms around her waist and hold her tight. We have a long way to go if we want to get back what we had, but her words tell me that now, finally, the tide has turned, and nourishing waters are coming in again.

Despite the god-awful bitchy late night, my eyes pop open at half past seven feeling more than a little sand-filled, but I'm awake and that's not changing. What makes it bearable is once again, at long last, I'm waking up next to Jaye. The woman I love sleeps beside me, and I have real hope this will continue, that we can somehow recapture the ease of our first months together.

We're not snuggling. In deference to her injury we simply held hands all night, but now I roll over, put my head on her shoulder and my arm across her waist. I know I won't be going back to sleep and risk aggravating her injured knee, so we're safe. Jaye slumbers on, oblivious. While she sleeps I take the chance to enjoy the simple contact of our bodies, to try to pass some of the tremendous love I have from my soul to hers. To begin the healing process of our relationship.

We have a lot of work ahead, but it can wait. Right now, all I want—need—to do is lie here against Jaye and get reacquainted with the feel of her, the scent of her, the sound of her breathing. Oh, how I missed this.

Maybe an hour passes before she stirs, probably because her arm, lying underneath me, has gone completely dead.

"Rachel?" she murmurs.

"I'm here."

Her arm moves, so okay, not completely dead, and I lift myself up enough for her to slide it around my back. I kiss her neck, then settle into her embrace and wonderful, warm contact.

"What time is it?" she asks.

"I don't know, maybe nine o'clock?"

"I'm sorry I've been so awful to you."

My first impulse is to say "It's okay," but it isn't; I keep hold of the words and choose something else.

"It's been a rough time for you."

"I'm glad you're here. I'm glad you didn't drive away."

"Me, too."

We fall quiet again for several minutes. Then Jaye says, "I still feel empty, like, there's this big hole where my life used to be."

"A void."

"Yeah. Is that how you felt?"

"Sometimes. When the depression was at its worst, yes. Mostly I was angry, and sad, and disconnected."

"How did you survive?"

"With some difficulty." I pull away from Jaye's body and slide up to a sitting position. Time to get down to the nitty-gritty. "Can I be honest?"

A hint of fear flashes across her face. "You're not going to leave, are you?"

"No," I say gently. "I love you. I love you more than I ever thought possible, and I'm staying right by your side. But it's clear, Jaye, my love's not enough to heal you, not enough to get you past this. We have to do something more. Otherwise we'll end up where we were last night. Or worse." I squeeze her hand firmly. "I really really don't want worse."

Jaye squeezes back, but she also frowns, hesitates before speaking her next words. "You want me to see a therapist, don't you?"

"Yes. It helped me. A lot."

She sighs. "Mom said the same thing. Actually, she said I'd be crazy to lose the two most important things in my life without trying everything, and therapy could help me so I should do it."

Marcia Stokes is going to be a great mother-in-law. "Mother knows best."

Jaye's face brightens, and she smiles, just a little. "Hold me?"

I ease my body down again, snuggling up with the love of my life. I feel hope in the closeness, hope in the soft lips gently kissing my forehead.

"I love you, Rachel," Jaye says, for the first time since August.

A tightness I didn't know I was carrying eases, and the first tendrils of a renewed belief in us begin to grow.

Epilogue

On a crisp December evening, I stand on the balcony of a luxury suite at an MLS stadium, Sporting KC's very nice soccer-only venue. A sellout crowd streams in, gathering to watch the international match between the U.S. Women's National Team and Ireland. The players are on the field doing pregame warmups. Jaye is with them, standing next to the coaches and watching, the end result of a series of events that began with a November phone call.

We were in Denver by then, having moved back to my house in October. Colorado agrees with Jaye; there are only good memories for her here, and over the weeks I have watched pieces of her old self return, bit by bit, rebuilding the whole with each passing day. She is religious about her physical rehab and also about the sessions with her new therapist.

The latter is more difficult than the former. "Rehab is like soccer drills," she tells me. "It's a familiar thing. Talking to a therapist about what happened, how I feel about it, that's tougher."

"A pain in the ass," I say, "but the end result is worth it."

I believe, though, since Jaye's natural disposition is upbeat and positive, she won't need the therapy for very long. She will banish her gorilla permanently. But now, perhaps she will understand mine a little better. When my future dark moments come—and they will—they won't scare her, and I won't have to shut her out.

We've already done enough shutting out. Both Jaye and I are working hard to keep our communication honest and open, including couples therapy, and, in keeping with the trend, getting good results all around.

So our life together is well on the way to "getting back what we had" before Jaye's injury, with a deeper appreciation of each other this time around. We sleep together, and we've resumed making love—carefully—delighted to discover sex between us is still fantastic.

By mid-November we've settled into a nice routine. Jaye does rehab and therapy while I work on a new writing project and prepare for the Christmas release of my latest novel, *Triangle*.

The phone call which shakes us up again comes on one of Jaye's difficult days. She's pulling a double, as it were, doing rehab in the morning and therapy in the afternoon. Apparently neither session goes well. She comes home cranky and frustrated. I take a break from my writing to keep her company as she ices her knee, and fix us both sandwiches and drinks so we can get French bread crumbs all over the sofa while we chat.

"The therapist made me talk about life after soccer today. I didn't want to."

"But you did."

"She made me cry, Rachel. It still hurts, you know, the idea that I might not play again."

"I know."

Jaye frowns. "I was so close to playing for my country, to playing against the absolute best. I still want it."

"How did she make you cry?"

"She's good at getting me to listen to my inner self, you know?"

"Deep down."

A nod. "Deep down told me today there will always be some hurt, there will always be emotional pain, especially if I can't play again." She blinks back tears. "Hard to take."

I put my sandwich down. "Jaye, your inner self is usually wise, but I think it's wrong here. You won't always hurt. Granted, it may take a long time, but you'll get to the point where you'll truly be okay with how things turn out."

"You think?"

"Yes. You know I'll always wonder how many books I didn't write because of my depression. Thirty years is a long time to lose. But, while it haunts me sometimes, I'm okay with it, because of where I've ended up. I may only publish ten books instead of twenty or thirty, but I'll write those ten books. And you may not ever see the National Team, but you've had a good career, and this season was a great one. That's what you'll remember."

"And I met you."

"The most important thing of all," I say solemnly. Then I wink at her and laugh.

A sweet kiss follows. Jaye's touch is still tinged with sadness. But the grief is diminishing, working through her as she faces the loss of her true first love. I sometimes still doubt I'm enough to fill the void, but I firmly believe she and I, together, can find things that will.

Jaye's cell rings. Our lips part, and she picks up the phone resting on the coffee table. She stares at the display, clearly puzzled, then swipes her thumb across the screen and takes the call.

"Hello? Yes, Coach Hatfield, how are you doing?"

I raise my eyebrows. The National Team coach? Whoa.

Jaye has one of those cell phones where you can't hear the caller's side of the conversation, so I sit patiently and glean what I can from Jaye's words, which are not too forthcoming.

"Yes, I know about that . . . no, I'm in Denver now, yes, with my partner . . . the crutches are long gone, but I'm still limping a little . . . the rehab's going well . . . funny, Rachel and I were just now talking about my future, and it's still too early to know . . . yes, ma'am, my schedule's free . . . what?"

Jaye's body goes utterly still. Her mouth is open, jaw locked in place. Several seconds pass before she shakes off her surprise and speaks.

"Yes, ma'am, I'm still here. I—could you repeat that please?"

Jaye grips my arm. Tightly. Hatfield does a lot of talking then, and whatever she's saying has Jaye completely stunned.

"Yes, I think so," Jaye says when it's her turn again. "I'm sorry, this is a little surprising . . . yes, definitely . . . Thank you, Coach . . .yes, any time. Good-bye."

Jaye ends the call and slowly lowers the phone. She stares blankly out in front of her, still stunned.

Gently I loosen her tourniquet hold on my forearm. "Jaye?"

"The National Team's last match of the year is in Kansas City on December tenth." Her voice sounds almost disembodied.

"Against Ireland," I confirm. "I was thinking about us going, actually, if you were up for it."

Now Jaye turns to me, wide-eyed. "I'm going to have to be. She named me to the team."

A lightning bolt, out of a clear blue sky "What?"

"Coach Hatfield named me to the National Team! She said she talked to the players, and to U.S. Soccer, and they all agreed, and I'm even going to start, so I can walk onto the field and be introduced." Jaye takes a deep breath, and from her expression, her brain starts to function again. "She'll have to sub me right out, of course. But I'm on the roster. If I want to be."

Suddenly she glares at me. "Did you have anything to do with this?"

I shake my head. "No," I say honestly. "It never even occurred to me something like this could happen."

We're back to reading each other well again. Jaye knows I'm telling the truth. "Nickory," she mutters. "Must have been Nickory."

"But she's still suspended." And will be through the rest of the year. At least.

"She has clout, though."

"Okay, so?" I get back on point. "What are your thoughts?"

Jaye frowns. "I don't know. What do you think?"

"You *could* see it as a charity thing, I suppose."

"Yeah, because it is. And people will say so."

"But," I pause to emphasize my next words, "you could also see it as an unprecedented act, for someone who is truly deserving. Because you earned it, Jaye. You told me yourself Hatfield was going to put you on the team." I shrug. "It just happened a few months later than originally planned."

The frown is not gone. "But I can't play!"

I nudge her mind a bit further. "What does deep down say?"

"Half an hour ago you thought deep down was wrong."

"Only on that one thing. What does deep down say now?"

Jaye goes still, listening to her inner thoughts, and finally comes forth with a bittersweet smile. "Deep down says to accept it as an honor because I'm never going to get another chance."

So here we are, three weeks later, blessed with a cool, clear evening of perfect soccer weather. The suite whose balcony I occupy for the night belongs to Rick and Becky Kaisershot. Turns out they make a tradition of renting a suite for the last National Team game of the year.

"We like to invite friends and have a big party," Rick admits. Tonight's shindig consists of about twenty people, mostly teammates and assorted family from the KC Blues. They let me invite Toni and Paula, too. Everyone here knows what's up with Jaye's newest honor. Everyone heartily approves.

"It wasn't fair, her getting injured," Kirstie Longstreet says with her killer Georgia twang. "I'm glad Jaye's going to get some recognition."

"Would you have taken it, if it happened to you?" I ask her.

She looks at me like I'm crazy. "In a heartbeat."

Rick comes up and stands beside me after the warmups end. The players have gone back to the locker rooms, but will return shortly, in uniform, to walk onto the pitch and be introduced.

"Are you sure your friend Toni wasn't an air traffic controller?" he asks. "She's kinda scary."

I smile. "Publishers are much fiercer than ATC people. But she's got a heart of gold underneath the evil stare."

"If you say so."

I raise an eyebrow. "How did she scare you?"

"She had Nickory backed into a corner looking for escape. Like a wolf trapped by a badger."

I crack up laughing, and Rick joins in. The warrior queen and I will never be best buddies, but we have made an honest truce now, and even been amiable since October. The détente has been a source of relief to Bree, though we're still trying to bring Jaye around. But, detente or no, I take a not-at-all-guilty pleasure in hearing someone get the better of Ms. Nickerson.

The announcer booms a good evening to the crowd, and we turn our attention to the field. The teams come out of the tunnel and start marching in parallel lines toward midfield. I don't have to hunt for Jaye in the line of players wearing red white and blue. I'd know her gait, the blonde ponytail, and the aura of her happiness anywhere. I watch her walk, and my heart swells up with love, pride, and my own happiness.

Rick casually drops a bomb. "Becky set this up, you know. She asked Coach Hatfield to put Jaye on the team."

Well. This is unexpected. "We thought maybe it was Nickory."

"Nope," Rick says. "Becky all the way. She hated how Jaye's season ended. And she was pissed it cost Kansas City the championship. When Jaye wouldn't see us afterwards—"

"Yeah, sorry about that."

"Not your fault. It happens. But anyway, Becky talked to Allerton and a couple of the team leaders, and they went to bat with the coaches." He grins. "Hit it out of the park, huh?"

Impulsively I turn and give Rick a hug. "A grand slam. Thank you."

The teams reach the center of the pitch and line up facing the flags of each nation. The Irish side is introduced first, and people in the stands clap politely. Then it's the USA's turn, and the claps grow to cheers.

The starters are introduced by number. Each woman steps forward and waves. Jaye, wearing 22, will go last. Her story has been the talk of the soccer news sites, and she's not been forgotten by Kansas City Blues fans. When her name is finally called half the crowd rises up to give her an ovation. I know those fans are the ones who followed her play all summer long, who were there when Jaye took KC to the brink of the

Promised Land, unable to enter it herself. They are the ones who witnessed it all and remembered. She waves, first to one side of the stadium, then the other, with a heartfelt smile and (I'm sure, even if I can't see them) tear-filled eyes.

Someone comes up, joins me and Rick. I glance over and see Toni. Rick casually drifts away.

"Well, Bogart," she says, "It's not exactly what she dreamed, but now you'll always have Paris."

I give a short laugh, thinking about all Jaye has been through and all that's yet to come. Then I stick my tongue out at my dear friend. "I hope so, Sam. I hope so."

After the national anthems, the captains shake hands and exchange banners, and then the game begins with an unusual set piece. Jaye stands over the ball at the very center of the field. The referee blows her whistle, and for a brief but noticeable moment Jaye pauses, as if she's soaking in every sensation as best she can, filing it away in her brain. Then she takes the game's first touch, kicking the ball over to Wendy Allerton, who promptly boots it fifty yards into the stands. The ref blows her whistle again, action stops, and Jaye is subbed out. The cheers rise up as she strides to the sideline, doing her best not to limp. She hugs her replacement, then makes her way to the stands where her parents have front row seats. She hugs both Tom and Marcia and returns to take her place on the USA bench to watch and cheer on her teammates.

A moment. Momentous.

The game turns out more competitive than maybe the U.S. thought it would be. Ireland has a talented goalkeeper, and she keeps the home team scoreless through the first half while her teammates get several chances on goal. The young keeper defending the American net, though, is equally flawless. Nickory will have competition when she comes off her suspension. The teams go to halftime with no score. I watch the match, but glance at Jaye often, over on the bench. I see her interacting with her fellow players, and even from my far viewpoint she's happier than she's been in a long time.

I'm grateful to Hatfield. Jaye and I spent a lot of time talking about the coach's decision to include her on the team. We both know if tonight's opponent had been higher ranked, say, Germany or Japan, Hatfield couldn't have done what she did. The match taking place in Kansas City also helped, as the Blues' fans would appreciate the gesture. And frankly, the American women are so good, and so deep, they could field a team essentially one player short.

They prove it in the second half, scoring twice on Ireland while Evans, the American goalie, records a clean sheet. 2-0 is the final. All in all, it's a perfect night for soccer, and the people who love it.

When the game is over, Becky and Rick invite everyone, even the Irish side, up to the suite for a blow-out after party. The stadium officials make a half-hearted attempt to close things down, but Wendy Allerton talks them into moving the whole shebang to the stadium's largest party area instead, so there's plenty of room for everybody. A good time is had by all.

Especially Jaye. She keeps me by her side while we mingle with everyone. Jaye introduces me to players I've admired for years, so I have a blast, too. When her knee tells her to sit we find a table and let people come to us, and many do, visiting for a minute or two or ten.

When the U.S. Soccer press staff shows up to film a brief interview, I duck out of the way of the cameras. Jaye, though, strays from the clichéd party lines to give me some credit.

"It was hard for me after I got hurt," she says. "It still is. I owe everything to my partner, Rachel Johnston, for helping me to see what a fantastic season I had, right up until August fifth." She pauses, spots me lurking well off-stage, and smiles. "I wouldn't be here without her."

When the cameras turn away to other players, I rejoin Jaye. "Your first cap may not have happened the way you dreamed," I say, "but you have it."

Jaye waves and smiles at someone calling her name, then turns her attention to me. "I'm happy, but it still feels incomplete. Will I always wonder what could have been?"

Before I can reply, Linda Hatfield herself approaches us. "You're a class act, Stokes," she says. "I wish things could have been different."

"I got more than most players do, Coach," Jaye says, living up to Hatfield's words. "Thank you again."

"You'd work well within my system," Hatfield says. "When your knee is healed, and you're ready, let me know. Your name is in the player pool now, and you'll be invited to try out."

Jaye is not expecting this, and in her surprise all she can manage to say is another "Thank you." It's enough. Hatfield claps her on the shoulder and heads off toward Ireland's coach. Jaye watches her go, then turns wide eyes to me.

"Good thing you've been doing rehab so faithfully," I comment.

Jaye lays her head on my shoulder. "I'll have to try, won't I?"

"Of course." I gently stroke her back. "Tired, finally?"

"I don't want to leave, but yeah."

"Let's find the Kaisershots and say good night."

Before we can, though, Kathleen Nickerson heads our way. Jaye sees her coming and frowns.

"What are you doing here?" Jaye asks, maybe more harshly than she has to.

"Rick invited us," Nickory says. "Bree wanted me to keep a low profile with US Soccer around, so we've been hiding out."

I somehow forgot to mention Nickory's presence to Jaye earlier. *Mea culpa.*

Jaye gives her a nod, her expression neutral. The warrior queen still carries herself with a regal bearing, but the power and confidence she used to emanate is considerably diminished. In all likelihood Nickerson will be the National Team's goalkeeper again, but punching an opposing player has made her inclusion no sure thing. The uncertainty has taken a toll.

Nickory gives me her own neutral glance. "Can I talk to Jaye for a minute?"

I press my hand gently between my lover's shoulder blades. "Your call."

Jaye thinks for a second, then shrugs. "Sure."

"I'll get some fresh air," I say. "Hunt me down when you're finished."

I turn away, spot a nearby balcony door, open it, and step into the mild winter night. I'm alone out here, and when I close the door I find blessed quiet. I take a deep breath and walk down past a few rows of seats to the railing, then stand there and gaze out at the empty soccer pitch.

I'm alone, but Jaye is nearby, so I'm exactly where I want to be. Whether she plays again or not, whether I ever write another word or not, my life is okay, and blessed, as long as she is with me.

Living, at long last, feels completely worthwhile.

I put my hands on the railing, a little staggered at the strength of this realization. Looking up, I find a star in the December sky and remember doing the same thing on a clear April night eight months ago. I thought my contentment then was happiness. No. Not even close. True happiness is so much more. I blink back tears, grateful and humbled that the Universe gave me the chance to discover this. Grateful, humble— and lucky.

The door opens behind me, and I feel Jaye's presence. I don't turn around, but listen to her steps as she approaches. I smile as her arms slide around my waist. Gently she pulls me against her.

"Hey, Bogart," Jaye murmurs into my ear, "all peopled out?"

I lean back into her embrace. "Yeah. How did it go with Nickory?"

"It went. We'll talk again."

"Be friends again?"

Jaye loosens her hold and turns me around, puts her hands on my cheeks and kisses me on the lips. "Maybe. I'll tell you about it later."

"You're peopled out, too."

"My knee more than anything."

"We still have to find Rick and Becky, but then I think we've done our duty here."

"Almost."

"Almost?"

Now Jaye steps out of our embrace, though she takes my hand. "When my parents were here, before I got hurt, you told them you wanted to be with me for the rest of your life. Do you still feel that way?"

"Of course," I say immediately, confusion taking root as I watch her free hand reach into her jacket pocket.

With a deft flick, she opens a small velvet box ensconced in her palm and presents it to me. I stare at the gold band within and am utterly speechless. The ring is almost identical to the one from Boston, right down to the Celtic pattern, and it gleams even in the low light coming from the party area.

"Good," she says. "Because I want you around for the rest of my life. Will you marry me, Rachel Johnston?"

I literally cannot talk, I'm so moved. I gaze into Jaye's hopeful face and as usual, get lost in her beautiful gray eyes. How wonderful it is to be in love, I think, to be in love with her.

I take my free hand and close my fingers over her palm and the ring, and finally, finally I manage the one all-important word.

"Yes."

Jaye bursts into tears of happiness. She takes the ring, slides it onto my left ring finger, and kisses me.

"By the way," she says, "gold is good in water. Never tarnishes, never gets rusty. You'll never have to take it off."

I raise my eyebrows. "Never?"

Enough light is reflected for Jaye to see I'm teasing her. "Never," she says, firmly.

I pretend to ponder this. After a moment, I nod. "I'll obey that on one condition."

"What?"

From my pants pocket I pull out a little velvet box of my own. With somewhat less panache than Jaye, I manage to get the lid open, revealing a slimmer gold band, adorned with two white diamonds. "If I wear your gift to me, you wear mine to you."

Jaye's eyes widen. "You were going to propose, too?"

I give a tiny shrug. "I was going to wait 'til we got back to the hotel. But I think it's okay to give this to you now?"

Jaye's face goes radiant, a wonder I haven't seen since summer began to fade. It's my turn to take her left hand, slide the ring on. Before I can kiss her, though, she pulls me into a tight hug.

"I want to have a ceremony," she says. "It doesn't have to be big, but I want it out there for the world to see. I want everyone to know how happy you make me."

"You'll invite us, right?" The question comes from the direction of the door into the suite, and it startles both of us. I'm somewhat disconcerted to see Becky, Rick, Toni and Paula, Kirstie and Shawn, Wendy Allerton and this month's flame, a couple of Irish players, and tonight's match referee crowding outside to join us. Twenty or thirty people stand behind them. Cripes, is everyone still left at the party coming out to the balcony?

The match referee shouts, "She said yes!" The group erupts into cheers.

"I didn't know they were there," Jaye says, suddenly concerned. "Are you okay?"

A year ago (heck, six months ago) I'd have been appalled that this—to me—private moment would have so many witnesses. A year ago I would have wanted to find a closet or a hole in the ground and burrow into it. A year ago I would likely have had a full-bore panic attack. But a year ago was another life.

I look into Jaye's eyes, sharp with worry but full of love, too, and smile. "I guess we'll have to have a big ceremony."

The worry vanishes. Jaye grins. "You think this place will be available?"

"If not, I suppose there's always Coors Field."

Jaye laughs, turns and gives a thumbs-up to the onlookers. "You're invited to the wedding!" she shouts.

The cheers sound again. Jaye wraps me in her arms and kisses me, and the crowd goes wild, their whistles and whoops and laughter echoing out across the stadium and the night. I kiss her back, then put my lips to her ear.

"I love you, Jaye," I say, words for her alone.

Her hold on me tightens. "I love you, Rachel," she whispers back. "Forever and ever."

"Good," I say, and we laugh, then break our hug, join hands, and start up the steps to the happy group of people we know and love, walking side by side toward the rest of our lives.

The End

Acknowledgments

Big, huge, massive, couldn't-have-done-it-without-you thanks to: Lori Lake, publisher and editor supreme (and supremely patient), and Jill Owen, to whom I owe everything.

Big, huge, eternal gratitude to: Riley Adair Garrett, whose encouragement kept me plugging along; Lynda Sandoval, whose comments on an early draft of this novel helped make it much better; and Rachel Spangler, for agreeing to say nice things about the book in public (the name is strictly coincidence, I swear!).

More-than-honorable mentions to: Brian Cox (don't blink or you'll miss your cameo), Jaime Cox, Luca Hart, Lori Lindsey, Michelle Montee, Laura Shipley, and everyone and everything about Provincetown, Massachusetts.

Heartfelt thanks to pretty much everyone else I ever mentioned this book to. You all helped make it happen, and I hope you all enjoy the result.

To all the girls and women who play soccer, you have my undying admiration. (I'm a little jealous, too.) To those who play at the highest levels, be it the NWSL, Europe, Australia, or in international competition, you have both my admiration and my utmost respect. May you be able to keep doing what you do, and may your love of the game never fade. (And may you someday be paid every penny you are worth.)

Jane Cuthbertson
November 2019

About The Author

Jane Cuthbertson was an air traffic controller in Colorado for 23 years. Since her retirement she has spent her time reading, writing, and traveling about the United States and Canada. She was lucky enough to attend several matches of the 2015 Women's World Cup, including the final. Her love of women's soccer will survive her, and its spirit will attend games long after she is gone. She currently lives on an island in the Pacific Northwest.

Jane's Website:
www.JaneCuthbertson.com